Advance Praise for

SAVE *the* DATE

"*Save the Date* deftly examines how various people can experience the same event in wildly different ways. Set over the course of one wedding weekend, it is laugh-out-loud funny, romantic, and heartwarming—a love story, but also a story about family, and the friends who become like family."

—Katharine McGee, *New York Times* bestselling author of *American Royals*

"Brilliantly crafted, *Save the Date* weaves together three stories of love and friendship and sisterhood that take place over the same wedding weekend. Reading this book made me feel like I was watching a favorite, classic romantic comedy, full of twists and turns and hijinks. I laughed, I cried, and loved living inside these pages!"

—Naina Kumar, *USA Today* bestselling author of *Flirting with Disaster*

"A book so bright and full of sparks that it feels like reading fireworks. I absolutely adored it."

—Rachel Griffiths, author of *The Trouble with Anna*

SAVE the DATE

A Novel

MALLORY KASS

ATRIA PAPERBACK

New York Amsterdam/Antwerp London
Toronto Sydney/Melbourne New Delhi

An Imprint of Simon & Schuster, LLC
1230 Avenue of the Americas
New York, NY 10020

This Atria Paperback edition April 2026

ATRIA PAPERBACK and colophon are registered trademarks of Simon & Schuster, LLC

Interior design by Jill Putorti

Manufactured in the United States of America

1 3 5 7 9 10 8 6 4 2

Library of Congress Control Number: 2025949014

ISBN 978-1-6680-9447-1 (pbk)
ISBN 978-1-6680-9448-8 (ebook)

For Benjamin Hart, my happily-ever-after

SAVE

the DATE

Prologue

The ceremony was scheduled to start at five p.m., which meant that at 4:55, people began to drift toward the white folding chairs that clung to the edge of the rocky bluff like sea-foam. The advanced guard was composed of the oldest guests who worried about being late, and the youngest guests who were keen to secure an unobstructed view of the lilac-wreathed altar so their photos would be grid-worthy. The majority remained under the tent until 5:10, knowing full well that these things never started on time and that it'd be foolish to leave the shade—and the open bar—earlier than necessary.

By 5:20, nearly everyone was seated, even the women most worried about sweating off their makeup. The string quartet was on their second movement, and the excited chatter began to give way to muted grumbles. "*So* typical of her," one guest muttered as she fanned herself with the program.

At 5:35, necks were beginning to pinch from the strain of

twisting to scan the bluff for signs of movement. A few minutes later, whispers rippled through the crowd as wide-eyed guests cupped their hands to their dates' ears, or frantically texted friends sitting in other rows. "Holy shit," a man in a seersucker suit said, staring at his phone. "I don't think they're coming." A few paces away, the wedding planner stood in her pink suit, her matching lips frozen in a huge, unnatural grin while she spoke ventriloquist-like into her headset. They'd missed their window. Now the altar would have to be moved six inches to the right in order to frame the setting sun, a process far too messy and laborious to perform in front of guests in their light-colored, dry-clean-only finery.

By 5:45, the whispers had given way to a tense, uneasy silence, and the live music took on a slightly manic, desperate quality. Some of the guests were on Zola.com, reading the refund policy on wedding gifts purchased online. A few of the bride's friends were drafting texts in their Notes app, planning the supportive missives they'd send once the news was confirmed. *Love you, girl. Don't worry—we're all here for you.* Or *You're so brave to listen to your heart!*

The wedding planner's head shot up, eyes widening as she clutched her earpiece. She nodded crisply. "Roger that." She caught the violinist's eye and nodded again. A moment later, the musicians seamlessly transitioned to Pachelbel's Canon, their bows seeming to sigh with relief as they slid across the strings. The guests swiveled and looked around, some faces clearly relieved, others visibly disappointed that the drama was ending.

Or was it?

The couple appeared at the top of the aisle, standing hand in hand as they surveyed their guests with warm smiles. But something was wrong, and the guests squinted for a better look. “Wait,” a woman whispered to her friend. “She’s not . . .”

“Nope,” her friend confirmed. “Definitely not. What the hell is . . .”

She trailed off as the officiant cleared his throat. “Dearly beloved, please rise.”

CHAPTER ONE

Natalie

Just relax, Natalie told herself as she approached the check-in desk of the Sandpiper Inn, her best friend's wedding dress draped over her shoulder. *You have every right to be here. The reservation is literally in your name.* But even after a decade of friendship, Natalie still felt like an impostor in Marigold's world.

Part of the problem was that the goalposts kept shifting. It took years before Natalie could make it through dinner with Marigold's family without making a faux pas like asking for parmesan on her seafood pasta or, horror of horrors, ordering a cappuccino with dessert. ("They'd ban you from Italy for life for that!" Marigold's stepfather, Bill, had said with a smile. When a red-cheeked Natalie had tried to laugh it off, faux-pleading, "Please don't report me; I've always wanted to go to Italy!" an awkward, pitying silence fell over the table as if Natalie had just admitted she'd grown up without indoor plumbing.) Then just as she found her footing in Marigold's Manhattan, she was dropped into places with entirely new social minefields to navigate. Who knew you weren't supposed to wear shoes on a yacht? Or that inquiring what a European did for a living was as uncouth as asking *So, how big is your penis?*

But this weekend would be different. Natalie wasn't Marigold's plus-one at a gala fundraiser where tickets cost more than her yearly salary. She was the *maid of honor*, a veritable VIP in the wedding world. She half expected to hear murmurs of excitement when she entered the inn with Marigold's dress. But no one even looked up as Natalie struggled toward the reception area, dragging her heavy suitcases and the cumbersome garment bag. Not even the suited woman behind the desk.

"Hi there," Natalie said, suppressing a grimace. *Hi there* was one of the phrases that only slipped out during awkward interactions with strangers. The worst was *Have a good one!*, which she'd inexplicably started saying after she'd turned thirty, a change as bewildering and unwelcome as the errant chin hairs she'd begun plucking around the same time.

The suited woman behind the desk looked up. "Hello. How can I help?" She had an unplaceable accent—maybe a Brit who'd moved to the US in high school and studied abroad in Sweden?

"I'd like to check in, please. The reservation is under Natalie Pickard."

"Check-in is at three p.m.," the woman said with a tight smile.

"I know. But I called last week to confirm early check-in? And I also called yesterday to double-check and was told it wouldn't be a problem?"

"Check-in is at three p.m.," the woman repeated. Her tone implied that if Natalie had heard otherwise, it was because she'd hallucinated the conversation or was simply too dense to comprehend the information she'd been given. "You're welcome to leave your luggage here, if you wish, and we'll bring it up when your room is ready. At three p.m."

With a sigh, Natalie hoisted the garment bag onto her shoulder and staggered over to a pair of leather armchairs. The Sandpiper Inn looked like it'd been unchanged since its 1816 founding—all polished mahogany, brass handles, antique silver candlesticks, and oil paintings of distinguished sea captains and wave-tossed whaling ships. Under normal circumstances, Natalie would've been delighted to sit and people-watch, relishing how far she'd come from the Cleveland suburbs where she'd grown up. But not when she had urgent errands to run and a twelve-thousand-dollar dress in her possession. She glanced at her phone—it was almost two p.m. and she had to be back at the ferry dock by three to meet the courier delivering the wedding rings. Natalie didn't mind leaving her suitcases with the bellhop, but she couldn't risk letting Marigold's wedding dress out of her sight. Then again, wasn't it safer to leave it at the inn than to lug them back down to the harbor, where countless dangers lay in wait, from sea spray to motor oil to sugar-mad children brandishing Popsicles?

Olivia never would've ended up in this situation, Natalie thought ruefully. There'd been some awkwardness when Marigold had asked Natalie to be maid of honor instead of her older sister. Marigold and Olivia hadn't always gotten along, but the hypercompetent, intimidatingly organized Olivia would've never found herself marooned in the reception area, clutching a custom-designed Danielle Frankel gown. The suited woman never would've used a patronizing tone with her; one raised eyebrow from Olivia was enough to make anyone cower, from junior associates at her law firm to the power-tripping hostess at Carbone.

Natalie had vowed to be the world's best maid of honor—it was the perfect chance to pay Marigold back for all her generosity and to show everyone that Natalie wasn't a clueless suburban rube. But above all else, it'd assuage the guilt that'd been festering for the past few months. No, *years*. If Natalie helped make Saturday the best day of Marigold's life, then she'd be absolved, it wouldn't matter how many selfish wishes Natalie had whispered in the dark. How many twisted prayers the universe had rightfully seen fit to ignore.

As she fretted about what to do with the dress, she pulled out her phone to check her messages. She'd asked the makeup artist and hairstylist to email her when they'd landed in Portland and found the car Natalie had sent for the two-hour drive up the coast. But when she saw the bolded name in her inbox, her heart lurched, and a familiar mix of hope and dread flooded her chest.

Over the years, she'd developed a ridiculous ritual whenever he emailed her. Instead of opening the message, she'd first fantasize about the contents—sometimes for a minute or two, sometimes longer. She'd allow her mind to flit from one unlikely scenario to another, from the fairly innocuous, like asking if she wanted to meet for drinks, to the laughably improbable—a confession of love. Then once she'd settled on a scenario, she'd write the email in her head, editing the words as carefully as she did her tutoring students' papers, even though it was entirely imaginary. The longer she spent crafting the message, the more crushing her disappointment when she eventually read the actual text.

Crushing disappointment wasn't something Natalie could deal with today, so she forced herself to open the email right away, prepared for a businesslike question about logistics for the weekend. But to her surprise, it had nothing to do with ferry schedules or meal selections. She grinned with pleasure at the opening: *Hey Bumpy.*

She'd first met him in an American Lit seminar in college, and over the course of the semester, as friendly run-ins at the campus coffee shop turned into study sessions and lunch outings, he'd shortened "Natalie" to "Nat," which morphed into "Natty." And then when their professor assigned *The Deerslayer*, "Natty" became "Natty Bumpoo" and eventually "Bumpy," which he'd called her off and on for the last twelve years. She read on:

> Hey Bumpy,
>
> Did you see that *Howl's Moving Castle* is playing at the Metrograph next month? There's still time to redeem yourself. I'll be in Bora Bora, but I expect a full report from you on my return.

It'd been years since they'd last discussed Natalie's childhood obsession with Diana Wynne Jones and her irrational fear that watching the *Howl's Moving Castle* adaptation would taint her love for the book. This was why Natalie had never been able to get over him, hard as she tried. Just when she'd managed to convince herself that they weren't anything more than friends, he'd do or say something like this—a small gesture that reminded her how carefully he listened to her. *He just has a really good memory*, Natalie told herself. *It doesn't mean anything.* But she wasn't sure she truly believed it.

A door opened and the pleasant tang of ocean air wafted into the lobby. Natalie turned and looked longingly at the terrace, where guests were drinking cocktails or having lunch. Surely the dress would be safe with her out there. Feeling a bit like a modern Ms. Havisham, Natalie left her suitcases with the bellhop and carried the garment bag out to the terrace, placing it carefully on the chair across from her. She smiled as she accepted a menu from the waiter, then winced when she scanned the prices. The cheapest entrée was a twenty-eight-dollar club sandwich, fries not included.

With a sigh, she started to log into her banking app to see how much was in her checking account before remembering that she could charge lunch to her room, which Marigold's parents were paying for. They wouldn't bat an eye—they'd *want* to cover her overpriced lunch at the expensive hotel they'd chosen. But there was a difference between accepting an invitation to dinner and billing something to their credit card without permission.

"Would you like to start with anything to drink?" the waiter asked.

"I'm good with water, thanks . . . No, wait, I'll have an iced tea." She glanced at her phone, where her bank balance had finally materialized. "Sorry, water is fine, actually."

"Are you here for the wedding?" the waiter asked, nodding at the garment bag.

"Yep. I'm the maid of honor–slash–dress courier. I've literally taken a plane, trains, and automobiles to get it here. And a boat, of course."

"Sounds like you could use a drink," the waiter said. "How about a mimosa? On the house."

Natalie gratefully accepted and, a few minutes later, felt the stress start to slip away as she sipped the cold, fizzy-sweet cocktail. She loved it up here in Maine, the one part of Marigold's world where she felt truly at home. She loved that you had to take a ferry to reach Sandpiper Island. (Apart from when she had a wedding dress in tow.) She loved that cars weren't allowed and that everyone rode around on rusty, squeaky bikes, or lumbering golf carts. She loved drinking coffee on the porch in the morning, taking deep breaths of pine-scented air while seals splashed in the bay. She'd even accepted Bill and Lulu's invitation to stay at the cottage after Marigold and Jonathan left for their honeymoon. Perhaps she'd finally finish the query letter she'd been rewriting for five months. Part of her was desperate to send her novel off to agents, but the thought of a publishing professional frowning over her manuscript—dismayed that yet another talentless wannabe had wasted their time—made her want to puke.

After mustering the courage to order the club sandwich, which was, after all, a steal compared with the forty-two-dollar lobster roll (fries not included), she opened Instagram and perused the accounts of her fellow bridesmaids, checking for important life updates so she'd be prepared for small talk. Liesl had posted another moody black-and-white photo of her smoking on a fire escape; Bri had gotten one of the new salmon semen facials; Richie shared a selfie of her and Margaret Qualley from their *Harper's Bazaar* photo shoot, and based on her excitement over their "newest addition!" Hannah was either pregnant again, adopting a puppy, or renovating their house.

Natalie placed her phone on the table as the waiter arrived with the sandwich, but then her phone buzzed and without thinking, she rushed to grab it, jostling the mimosa she hadn't realized the waiter had moved to make room. "Sorry, sorry," Natalie said, using her napkin to mop up the droplets with one hand while she grabbed her phone with the other. Her brain raced through a variety of scenarios: the hairdresser was sick, the guy delivering the ring had (literally) missed the boat. Or maybe, just maybe, this was the text she'd been waiting for, the one where he finally admitted that he'd made a terrible mistake . . .

But it was just a text from Mrs. Friedlander, the mother of Natalie's least-favorite student.

"No worries," the waiter said kindly as he cleaned the stem of her champagne flute with a cloth.

Natalie checked to make sure nothing had spilled on the garment bag, then opened the message with a sigh.

natalie r u free today esme needs help with draft of admissions essay due to college advisor monday. can you call her at 4 thx.

Typical. Natalie had told Mrs. Friedlander *three times* that she'd be unavailable this weekend, but it never made a difference with the Upper East Side families who comprised the majority of her tutoring clients. They wanted her to be on twenty-four-hour call, just like the rest of their extensive staff.

Hi Mrs. Friedlander, I'm sorry but as we discussed, I'm taking a few days off for a friend's wedding.

A moment later, Mrs. Friedlander's reply popped up.

r u serious? esme is freaking out this is very unprofessional.

Natalie rolled her eyes. There was no point in reminding Mrs. Friedlander that Natalie had given her and Esme ample warning, let alone trying to explain why this was an essay Esme needed to at least *try* to draft herself. For the past two years, Natalie had sat by Esme's side for hours at a time whenever she had a paper due, guiding her sentence by sentence until they both grew so tired and frustrated that Natalie eventually grabbed the laptop and cranked out the rest for her. Their agreement was that Esme would rewrite it "in her own voice," but of course, that had never happened. Natalie didn't have strong moral qualms about enabling Esme's cheating—everyone at her sixty-thousand-dollar-per-year private school had tutors doing the exact same thing, so the playing field was level. But college applications were a different story. Esme would be competing against all sorts of kids, most of whom didn't have access to this kind of help. Natalie couldn't stomach the thought of giving her lazy, entitled, not particularly bright student a leg up. But if she refused, Mrs. Friedlander would bad-mouth her to every mother north of Fifty-Ninth Street.

God, she really needed to sell her book. Even a moderate advance would be enough to let Natalie quit tutoring for a year, enough time to figure out something that'd allow her to pay her bills without mortgaging her soul.

Okay. I'll see what I can do. I'll get back to you shortly.

what is bella garfield writing about? I know ur helping her too. she did the same summer program as esme so make sure she doesn't write about volunteering in mexico that is esme's topic.

As Natalie did her best to decipher the text—Mrs. Friedlander tended to dictate while she worked out on the Peloton—a voice behind her made her jump. "What are you *doing*?" Natalie whipped around to see Olivia striding toward her. As usual, Marigold's older sister looked like she'd come from a work cocktail party in her navy silk sheath dress and heels, her hair pulled back in a sleek ponytail. "Why is the dress out here?"

"Check-in isn't until three!" Of course Olivia was going to treat this as the screwup of the century. She was constantly in crisis-management mode, even when there was no crisis. "I couldn't take anything up to my room."

"So you decided the best idea was to dump mimosas on it?" She pointed a pinky-beige nail at the single orange droplet that had made its way onto the heavy plastic garment bag. It was so small, Natalie hadn't noticed. "Are you drunk?"

Natalie could feel her cheeks turning as red as the bottoms of Olivia's shoes. "Come on, you think I'd get drunk at *two in the afternoon*?"

"I don't give a shit what you do on your own time. I just don't want anything to happen to Marigold's dress."

Yeah, right, Natalie thought. *You'd* love *it if something happened to the dress. You'd love to prove that Marigold blew it by not choosing you as her maid of honor.*

"Come on," Olivia said with a sigh, hoisting the garment bag over her shoulder.

Natalie jumped to her feet to follow, then glanced back at her untouched sandwich. "Oh, wait. I need to pay for that."

"Charge it to the Harding party," Olivia called to the waiter, ignoring Natalie.

Natalie grabbed her bags and hurried after Olivia, who was moving at an impressive clip given the height of her heels. She followed her back inside and then over to reception, where the same blond woman was still standing behind the desk. Natalie shrank, bracing for another rejection, but as Olivia approached, the woman's demeanor changed. She looked up right away and greeted Olivia with a smile. "Hello. How may I help you?"

"Yes, hi," Olivia said briskly. "We're both checking in. One room under Natalie Pickard, one under Olivia Harding. It's part of the block for the Harding/Stein wedding."

"Of course, welcome," the woman said, fingers tapping on her keyboard. "Just give me one moment . . ."

"She said I couldn't check in until three! I swear!" Natalie whispered to Olivia.

"Here you go," the woman said brightly as she passed each of them an old-fashioned brass key. "Ms. Harding, you're in room twelve. Ms. Pickard, you're in room nineteen. I hope you both have a wonderful weekend. If you leave your bags here, I'll have them sent up right away."

"Why aren't you staying with your parents?" Natalie grumbled as she followed Olivia up the wide, gleaming wooden staircase lined with candle sconces and more oil paintings.

"Cell reception is too spotty on that side of the island. I need to be reachable in case a client calls me."

"You're *working* this weekend?"

"I'm always working." Olivia paused on the first landing. "This is me. I think you're on the next floor. Do you want me to take the dress?"

"No, I'll take it," Natalie said, snatching the bag off Olivia's shoulder. "I brought it all the way from New York. I think I can handle a flight of stairs." It came out a little pricklier than she'd intended, so she forced a little laugh. "I'll see you at the welcome drinks."

Natalie continued up the stairs, turned into the next hallway, and found room nineteen near the end of the corridor. She fumbled with the key for a moment before managing to turn the heavy lock. The door swung open, and Natalie staggered inside with the heavy garment bag, which she carefully draped over the back of a brocaded armchair before collapsing onto the four-poster brass bed. She needed to close her eyes for a minute before she could muster the energy to head back down to the dock for the ring delivery.

"Jesus Christ!" a male voice said.

Natalie shot up into a seated position and stared wide-eyed

at the man who'd apparently just walked out of the bathroom. His dark curls were damp from the shower, making him seem younger and even more boyish than usual, just like it did back in their dorm all those years ago. But for once, Natalie didn't have to imagine what was under the towel, as this time, he was completely naked.

When their eyes met, the shock on his face faded, replaced by a much more familiar expression—the amused smirk that had been making her heart race for the last twelve years. The one that had kept her awake at night back in college; the one that had lured her to New York years later, causing her to abandon her plans to attend grad school in Scotland.

The one that made her feel like the shittiest maid of honor in the history of weddings.

"Hey, Bumpy," Jonathan said. "What are you doing in my room?"

CHAPTER TWO

Marigold

Marigold frowned into the small, warped mirror above her dresser. It felt wrong to be wearing makeup on Sandpiper Island, something she hadn't done since age sixteen, when she spent the summer trying to seduce Paul, the college student her parents had hired to redo the garden. Well, not the whole summer, exactly. Poor Paul had done his best to avoid looking at Marigold while she sunbathed in increasingly tiny bikinis, but his resolve had crumbled by the end of June.

She hadn't applied *much* makeup—just mascara and lipstick—but even that was enough to make her feel like she was in costume, playing the role of the bride. "Mare? Are you almost ready?" her mother called up the stairs. "Olivia's bringing Jonathan's family over from the inn."

"One sec!" She stepped back to view her whole outfit, but the mirror was too small. There wasn't a full-length mirror anywhere in the cottage, something Marigold had grown to appreciate. She spent so much time looking at the photos of herself brands paid her to post that it was refreshing to go weeks without seeing her full reflection.

Marigold looked around her bedroom, scanning the cluttered surfaces for some sign of the gift she'd bought for Jonathan. She hadn't planned on giving him a wedding present, but when she'd stumbled across a first edition of his favorite book, *Of Human Bondage*, in the antiquarian bookstore on Madison, she'd known she had to buy it for him. She'd even read the summary on Wikipedia so they could discuss it on their honeymoon, but had been secretly disappointed to discover it had nothing to do with S&M. Not that she thought her sweet, slightly nerdy fiancé would've spoken so highly of *Fifty Shades of Grey*–esque erotica; she'd assumed it was one of those sexy classics that were banned for making people too horny in the 1950s. But it turned out that *Of Human Bondage* was actually about an unhappy doctor who spends his whole life wishing he'd made it as an artist, a slightly worrying reveal given Jonathan's profession.

She could picture the navy-and-gold-striped paper she'd selected, but didn't see it anywhere among the wedding detritus. A tiny prick of worry twinged in her stomach. It felt weirdly important to give the book to Jonathan before the wedding. Had she left it behind in New York? No, Natalie had scoured Marigold and Jonathan's apartment to make sure they hadn't forgotten anything. It had to be in the cottage somewhere.

She ran down the stairs, reaching up to touch the antlers mounted above the landing. When she was little, she'd pet the antlers as a form of apology to the poor deer who'd been murdered for wall décor. Now it was mostly just habit. Marigold paused at the bottom of the stairs to survey the scene, scanning for any early guests who might use the opportunity to corner her. The coast seemed clear, so she headed into the living room, where her mother was arranging flowers in an asymmetrical ceramic vase she'd made herself.

When she heard Marigold approach, Lulu looked up and beamed. "Oh, that looks fabulous on you."

Her mother had lent her a spectacular white Halston jumpsuit that Lulu had worn to Studio 54 as a teenager. Marigold shimmied and did the disco-fingers dance move. "Are you sure you don't mind? What if I spill something on it?"

"Who cares? It was meant to be lived in, to be *danced* in. It's a crime to leave it in a closet for decades."

Lulu looked radiant in a vintage black silk slip dress that'd always been a favorite of Marigold's. It wasn't a conventional choice for the mother of the bride, but that was to be expected. Growing up, Marigold had taken pride in how different Lulu seemed from the other Upper East Side moms with their identical blond highlights, identical SUVs they were all too nervous to drive in the city, and identical opinions. Lulu was an artist—she painted, sculpted, wrote poetry, and played the guitar. She'd also been the muse to a famous painter back in the late '70s, and there were nude portraits of her at MoMA and the Guggenheim, a fact that had never embarrassed Marigold, even during field trips with her classmates.

That's why Marigold had been surprised when Lulu insisted on throwing her and Jonathan a lavish wedding instead of letting them run down to city hall and then jump on a plane to Bora Bora as they'd been planning. But Marigold wasn't going to stand in the way of anything Lulu wanted. Not now, anyway.

Stop it, Marigold told herself. Her mother was going to be fine. She was about to start a new drug, one that'd performed miracles in trials. Eager for a distraction, she asked, "What can I help with?"

"Can you devise an excuse to bring Bill inside?" Lulu gestured at the back door. "He's doing that thing again."

Marigold turned toward the garden, where her stepfather was overseeing the caterers building a pit for the lobster bake. Bill had worked on a lobster boat for one summer as a teenager and then spent the next forty years in finance. But the fact that he hadn't worked with his hands since the Reagan administration never stopped him from offering "advice" whenever a tradesperson entered his home. The impulse seemed to stem partially from a desire to connect with blue-collar workers so Bill could feel like a man of the people, and partially from that quality so common among men of his ilk, the belief that because they'd made a shit ton of money doing one thing well, they were capable of doing *anything* well, practice or expertise be damned. But Bill was a good man at heart, and generally only needed a gentle reminder to let people do their jobs without interference.

"I'm on it," Marigold said. "Have you seen my gift for Jonathan? I can't find it."

"I don't think so. Does Natalie have it?"

"Yeah, probably. I'll text her." She patted the jumpsuit pockets. "Have you seen my phone anywhere?"

Lulu gave her an affectionate, exasperated smile. "This is why I'm so glad you're marrying Jonathan. He'll look after you."

"I don't need looking after!" Marigold insisted, a bit petulantly. Sure, the old Marigold might've lost her phone from time to time. And her keys. And yes, she'd been known to miss the occasional appointment, like that time she blew off jury duty and flew to Copenhagen because a reservation had opened up at Noma. But those days were behind her. She'd made the grown-up choice to get married. To a doctor! And while she would've fallen for Jonathan no matter what, she did appreciate how his respectability seemed to have rubbed off on her. People no longer implied that her two hundred thousand followers and multiple brand partnerships were the result of nepotism and dumb luck rather than creativity and business acumen. Jonathan's love served as an endorsement; if a rising star oncologist at Columbia deemed Marigold a worthy partner, then she couldn't be *that* shallow.

"I'll go get Bill," Marigold said, bounding off.

Her stepfather was standing with his hands behind his back, peering down at the coals the caterers were laying in the fire pit. "Is that the best way to maximize heat distribution?" Bill asked.

"Yup," a tan, blond kid said with an affable smile, clearly accustomed to this type of client.

Bill looked skeptical. "Wouldn't it be more efficient to do a pile instead of a single layer? That way, the heat will spread—"

"Bill! I need you!" Marigold called.

He whipped around. "What's up?"

"I can't find Jonathan's present. Can you come help me look?"

Bill glanced from Marigold to the pit and back, torn between his primal urge to master fire and his inability to see his cherished stepdaughter in distress.

"Please? I'm so worried about it." Marigold pouted—a cheap trick, but it never failed.

"Of course. Don't worry, we'll find it. Where have you looked so far?"

"Everywhere! It's just vanished."

"Okay, I'll look inside. You go check the boat." Since cars weren't allowed on the island, they left theirs on the mainland and took all their belongings over in a small motorboat.

Marigold started down the hill that led to the dock but didn't make it more than a few yards before someone called her name. "Ahoy there, Marigold!"

With a sigh, she turned and forced a bright smile. "Ahoy, Paulson family!"

Skip and Lindy Paulson ambled across the lawn, their teenage children, Milly and Cooper, trailing behind.

"We came early to see if your mom needed help," Lindy said. She had deeply tanned skin that contrasted too dramatically with her light blond hair, and she never seemed to find Lilly Pulitzer dresses small enough to fit her small, wiry frame.

"That's so sweet of you," Marigold said, knowing full well that the Paulsons had only arrived early to avail themselves of free booze. God forbid they had to wait until six p.m. to start drinking, or, horror upon horrors, open a bottle of wine they'd paid for themselves.

"I have to grab something from the boat. I'll see you in a bit!" Marigold said, breaking into a jog. She ran down the dock and made a half-hearted attempt to look for the missing gift. She knew it wasn't on the boat, but she wasn't in any particular rush to return to the house.

Her head shot up at the familiar rumble of their old golf cart. Without thinking, she slunk down into the boat, eager for just a few more minutes of solitude. But then she saw Jonathan looking for her, turning from the house to the dock and back again, and something tugged at her heart.

She stepped back onto the dock, ran up the splintery wooden

steps, and jogged up the hill. Jonathan's face lit up when he spotted her. Lulu was right; he loved her so much.

"Hi." She leaned in for a kiss. "You look so handsome, I can almost imagine myself marrying you."

And he did. His thick, dark curls gave him a boyish air, but the stylish glasses she'd selected for him gave him a hot professor vibe. Except that Jonathan was a hot *doctor*, which was even sexier. As good as he looked in his gray trousers and light purple check button-down, it was nothing compared to the dashing figure he cut in his white coat at work. Hospitals freaked Marigold out, but seeing Jonathan in doctor mode made it worth meeting him for lunch in the cafeteria. She loved seeing him in his element; the nurses respected him, and his patients trusted him. At work, he projected a mixture of quiet authority and kindness that more than once had inspired Marigold to forget about lunch and pull Jonathan into his office . . .

"Hi, sweetie." Jonathan's mother, Carol, gave Marigold a tight hug, then stepped back to survey her. "You look stunning—what a fabulous outfit." Carol turned to face her sister, Jonathan's Aunt Debbie. "Isn't she gorgeous?"

"Lovely," Debbie said admiringly. When Jonathan had first introduced Marigold to his family, she'd felt like an exotic creature who'd strayed from its natural habitat. His parents had always been warm and welcoming, but couldn't quite hide their surprise at how different she was from Jonathan's studious, serious ex-girlfriends. Carol seemed at a loss for how to talk to Marigold, and spent an uncomfortable amount of time exclaiming over her beauty. And whenever Marigold mentioned a TV show she liked, or new restaurant she'd been to, Carol would say, "I'll have to look it up!" in the same tone the old Marigold used whenever someone recommended a book that wasn't on *People*'s list of hottest beach reads.

But now that people were interested in her opinions about things other than luxury bedding and Botox, Marigold had leaned into the opportunity to rebrand, dropping tidbits about Jonathan's research in conversation, and forcing herself to read the buzziest novels, even if she did sometimes rely on Natalie to give her the right talking points.

"Debbie, what did you think of the new Sally Rooney?" Marigold asked. "I gather Carol wasn't a fan."

Debbie sniffed. "Overrated, navel-gazing solipsism. But you know who makes her look like a genius? That man who wrote that *awful* book set at Smith. He can't write an authentic female voice to save his life."

"Marigold's reading that one," Jonathan said, turning to her. "What do you think so far?"

Oh, shit. The book had been on her nightstand for weeks, but she'd gotten bored and abandoned it after a few pages. Yet she'd kept moving her bookmark farther along so Jonathan would think she was making progress. "I agree," she said smoothly. "The female voices are completely inauthentic."

"And what did you think of that ridiculous twist in the middle?" Debbie asked. "It's insulting to the reader, isn't it?"

"Totally." Marigold nodded.

"What's the twist?" Jonathan asked.

"Oh, I couldn't spoil it for you," Marigold said.

"It's okay. I'm never going to read it."

"Well . . ." Marigold stalled for time, cursing herself for bingeing the new season of *Love Is Blind* when she should've been reading. "I suppose it's up to interpretation, but I guess—"

"Mare!" Someone grabbed her hand. It was Natalie, thank god. "Sorry, I need to steal you. Urgent wedding business," Natalie said, nearly dragging Marigold away from Carol and Debbie. Natalie lowered her voice. "Don't worry, everything's fine. You just looked like you needed an out."

"Thank you," Marigold said, grateful but not surprised. Natalie had been coming to her rescue since their single-girl days back in Brooklyn, teaching her how to do laundry in the grimy, damp basement of their apartment building, or disposing of the horrifyingly effective mousetraps laid by the gruff superintendent. Of course, after eight months of this, Marigold had grown tired of trying to make it on her own and had allowed Bill to buy her a two-bedroom in a prewar doorman building in the West Village. But she and Natalie had stayed friends, becoming even closer as the years went on. She'd given Natalie a key so she could sleep over whenever a bad date left her too weary to trek back to Bushwick, and so they could spend the next morning giggling over bagels and mimosas as Natalie recounted the previous night's horrors.

"You have to give me something smart to say about that book set at Smith." Marigold paused to wave at another group of far-too-early arrivals. "Jonathan thinks I've read it."

"No way. You know I hate that guy—he was in my creative writing class in college. The one who spent all year transcribing *Infinite Jest* by hand so he could 'understand what genius felt like.'"

"Oh my god, yes, didn't we run into him at a bar once? And he was wearing a black armband?"

Natalie nodded. "He was mourning the death of Philip Roth. According to Instagram, he wore it for a whole year. I'm not reading that douchebag's book."

"Okay, *fine*. I'll find a summary online."

"Come on, Mare. You don't need to try this hard. Jonathan loves you."

"I'm not trying hard!" Marigold insisted. "It's a *good* thing that Jonathan makes me want to expand my horizons."

Natalie pursed her lips and fixed her with Marigold's least-favorite look, the one that basically amounted to, *I have so many things to say, I don't even know where to begin, so I'm just going to stay silent.*

Eager to change the subject, Marigold asked, "How was your trip? Everything okay at the inn?"

"Great!" Natalie said a bit too enthusiastically.

"What's wrong?"

"Nothing, nothing . . ." She looked around, then lowered her voice. "I just had a little . . . run-in with Olivia, and now I'm pretty sure she thinks I'm an even bigger idiot than before."

"Olivia thinks *everyone* is an idiot. You know that."

"No, I know, it's just that there was a little mix-up at check-in and then—"

"There she is! The gorgeous bride!" Someone Marigold couldn't see pulled her into a hug. Probably her uncle Barry, given the distinctive scent of his hair growth serum. Natalie disappeared behind the throng of guests that seemed to have appeared out of nowhere, swarming her like well-meaning locusts.

As soon as she freed herself from one conversation, she was pulled into another; she couldn't take more than three steps without having someone call her name, grab her arm, or pull her into a hug. Two of her bridesmaids, her childhood friends Liesl and Bri, managed to extricate her from Bill's cousins, but then immediately asked to be introduced to Richie. "I mean, of course we've *met*," Liesl said. "But not as fellow bridesmaids." As if that were all it'd take to make the recent Best Supporting Actress nominee take an interest in Liesl. Not that Marigold had any special appeal herself—it was pure chance that she and Richie had the same dermatologist and the same psychic, and kept running into each other in the waiting rooms.

"She's coming tomorrow. You'll meet her then."

"Re-meet her," Bri clarified.

"Of course. I'll be right back, okay? I need to find Jonathan."

But instead of heading back into the crowd, Marigold snuck into the cottage through the side door. Contrary to what everyone thought, she wasn't a natural extrovert, and needed time to recharge. She secretly worried that Jonathan sometimes felt a bit cheated, resenting the fact that the rest of the world got the glamorous life of the party while he got the makeup-free couch potato.

"There you are!" Lulu emerged from the kitchen, beaming. "Did you see Paula? She's been looking for you. I can't believe she and Karen came all this way. You know how hard it is for them to travel."

"Not yet. I just needed a little break. I'll find her in a sec."

Lulu looked out at the lawn, teeming with friends, family, and neighbors. "I'm sorry if this is all . . . a bit much for you. I think we might've gone overboard with the guest list. It was just such a wonderful opportunity to bring everyone together. But this weekend is supposed to be about you and Jonathan, and I'm so sorry if it's not the wedding you wanted."

"Mom, stop! This is *exactly* what I wanted, okay? I promise." It was true, in a way. After everything she'd been through, her mother deserved one perfect weekend. "I'm going upstairs to look for Jonathan's present. If anyone's looking for me, tell them I'll be right back."

"Do you want me to help you look?"

"I'm fine. You go have fun."

Marigold headed back upstairs, as Natalie's words echoed in her head. *You don't need to try this hard.*

But that was ridiculous—as Bill liked to say, "Nothing that comes easy is worth having." (Unless he was imitating one of his insufferable business partners when he said that? All of Bill's impressions sounded the same, so it was sometimes hard to tell.) She'd struck gold when she'd found Jonathan, and he made her want to become the best version of herself. Was that so terrible? Wasn't it a small price to pay to build the perfect life with the man of her dreams?

CHAPTER THREE

Olivia

As she made her way to the bar, Olivia smoothed her sleek bob, more out of habit than necessity. She'd convinced Philippe to open the salon early so she could squeeze in an appointment before her flight, and his handiwork could withstand even the most egregious summer humidity. That's why she shelled out over two hundred dollars per blowout, more than she could really afford even on a corporate lawyer's salary. In order to justify triweekly visits, she'd have to switch from soul-crushing work to something that required the *absence* of a soul, like defending billionaire drug lords or members of the royal family accused of sex trafficking.

But at the moment, she didn't feel an ounce of guilt; it was essential that she look her very best tonight. Yes, her prettier, *younger* sister was getting married before her, but no one would dare look at Olivia with pity tonight. Not in this dress. Not with this hair. Not with her name in bold on *New York* magazine's list of the most powerful lawyers under thirty-five. Yet that wasn't the real reason Olivia had invested nearly five thousand dollars in outfits for this weekend. That reason was standing by the bar in an impeccably tailored navy suit, accepting a glass of scotch from the bartender.

Olivia had harbored a secret crush on Andrew, Bill's younger colleague and protégé, for years but had never made a move. She wasn't afraid of going after what she wanted, or being seen as too aggressive, but Andrew was a handsome Harvard MBA who dated people like that Swedish princess who produced Oscar-winning documentaries. Olivia was no slouch, but Andrew was out of her league. At least, that's what she'd thought until the Met Apollo Circle gala two weeks earlier. Andrew had been there solo—the first time she'd seen him at an event without a date—and he'd ignored the bevy of beautiful socialites circling him like fruit flies and spent all night talking to Olivia. At first, she'd assumed he was just being nice to his boss's stepdaughter, but after three drinks and a conspicuous amount of knee touching, she'd stopped tamping down the excitement fizzing up from her stomach. He'd even walked her home and lingered by the door. The tension had been both agonizing and delicious, and just when Olivia felt positive that Andrew was going to kiss her, his phone had buzzed. "Sorry," he'd said with a sigh. "I have to take this. But maybe we can pick up where we left off in Maine?"

Olivia had nodded. Or maybe she'd said sure. All she could really remember was the electric feel of his fingers as he'd touched her arm in farewell. She'd spent the next few days in a daze, succumbing to the kind of daydreams she hadn't indulged in since she'd been a teenager. Slow dancing with Andrew at the wedding. Watching him smile with pride during her witty, heartfelt toast. Seeing the look on her mother's face when Lulu realized that this wasn't just a weekend fling—that something real was brewing, and that she just might get to see Olivia happy and settled after all.

And now the moment was finally upon her. She'd even spent an hour in Central Park last week practicing walking on grass in her new heels to ensure that she didn't stumble when she made her approach. The cottage had never looked more beautiful. Strings of fairy lights hung from the trees, twinkling like fireflies, while hurricane candles glowed on the dozens of tables that'd been set up on the lawn for the dinner. A jazz trio played off to the side, filling the night air with music that seemed to keep time with the sound of the waves lapping against the rocks. She was going to remember this evening for the rest of her life.

Andrew turned and caught her eye at just the right moment, when she was close enough to greet with a knowing, secret smile, but still too far away to say anything. He handed her a glass of champagne that he'd seemingly conjured out of thin air, then stepped back to survey her. "Wow," he said, breaking into a grin. "You look amazing."

"You don't look too shabby either." She tugged on the sleeve of his suit. "How'd you resist the siren call of baby-blue seersucker?"

"There's so much about me that's insufferable already. I can't add seersucker to the mix."

"That's true. You already tell people you went to school 'outside of Boston.'"

"That's slander! I'd *never* say that."

"I've heard you!"

"You must've imagined it."

"At Bill's birthday this spring. We were talking to Jimmy's wife and you said that you had a 'fondness' for the Red Sox because you went to school outside of Boston."

"That doesn't count *at all.* It's only douchey when someone asks, 'So, where'd you go to school?' And instead of just saying Harvard, you go, 'Outside of Boston.' This was a completely different context."

"I'm not sure your reasoning would hold up in court," Olivia teased.

"Hold on. Let me consult with my counsel." Andrew reached over to tap the tanned, slender arm of the women standing to his right. She turned and flashed a blindingly white smile. A smile Olivia knew from somewhere . . .

"Emerson, this is Olivia. Olivia, Emerson."

Emerson. Emerson Wyle. The supermodel-turned–#MeToo activist who'd abandoned fashion for law school and was now a prominent human rights lawyer. Her recent speech at the UN women's conference had gone viral. "It's nice to meet you," Olivia said, using every ounce of self-control to keep her voice from shaking. To keep her whole *body* from shaking.

"I know it's bad guest etiquette, but Marigold said it was fine to add a plus-one at the last minute," Andrew explained. "Emerson wasn't sure she'd be back from Indonesia in time, but here she is!"

"Here you are," Olivia echoed weakly. "I'm so glad you could make it."

"Thanks!" Emerson said with a warm smile. "It's really great to meet you. Andrew said that you and Marigold have felt like sisters to him ever since he started working with Bill."

"*For* Bill," Olivia corrected before she could stop herself.

"Will you excuse me? I need to look over my notes for my toast. Have fun tonight!"

She hurried off, praying that she'd slipped out of sight before either Andrew or Emerson noticed her burning cheeks. He'd brought a date? What the hell had happened to picking things up where we'd left off in Maine?! That'd been *two weeks* ago! Had Andrew had a girlfriend the whole time? Then why on earth had he been flirting with Olivia?

It's not complicated, a weary voice sighed inside her head. *It's because he was bored and you were there. You only convinced yourself it was more than that because you wanted it so badly.* But that wasn't true, was it? That's not who Olivia was. That wasn't how she operated. She didn't let her imagination run away with her. Andrew had been about to kiss her when he got that call.

She just needed a moment to collect herself, to straighten the knot of thoughts sparking like tangled wires in her head.

Oliva drifted toward an empty table on the edge of the lawn. She knew she was expected to sit with her family, but right now, she needed to mope. And drink.

She slumped into a chair and sipped the champagne Andrew had handed her, trying to pace herself so she wouldn't be too hungover to run in the morning. She was already itching to sprint down her favorite trail, letting the fire in her lungs incinerate all memory of tonight.

A server appeared at her shoulder and began to refill her glass. "Actually, I'm fine, thanks." Olivia said, pulling her glass away so quickly, champagne spilled onto the table.

"You just spilled a hundred bucks on that tablecloth." She looked up to see someone walking by, his plate piled comically high with seafood. It was Jonathan's insufferable best man, Zack.

Olivia ignored him, just like she always did whenever Zack chimed in with his shallow critiques of the 1 percent. When he'd first moved to New York after college, Zack had started an anonymous blog about class politics in the city. Despite its hyperbole and reductive, familiar arguments, it had developed something of a cult following to the point that *Gawker* had launched an "investigation" to discover the author. He now taught at CUNY despite offers from Columbia and NYU, a decision that made him some kind of saint in Jonathan's and Marigold's eyes, and a fool in Olivia's.

The irony was that Zack had never experienced anything close to poverty, not like Olivia had. And of course, Marigold wouldn't have told him what their life had been like before Lulu married Bill. Marigold had only been five—three years younger than Olivia. A lifetime at that age. She knew that Lulu had struggled as a single mom to two young girls, but only because she'd been told about it. Marigold didn't remember moving every six months to stay ahead of the eviction notices. She had no memory of birthdays without presents, of weeks spent eating instant ramen in poorly heated apartments. But Olivia did. She knew what life was like without money, and she sure as hell wasn't going back.

Bill was supremely generous and had set up trust funds for Olivia and Marigold as large as he would've given to any biological children. But Olivia knew how quickly money could vanish, which is why she'd fought so hard for a career that would allow her to support herself, no matter what happened. Markets crashed. Bequests got tied up in legal battles. But no one else had any claim to her salary. She'd be able to take care of herself—and her family—if necessary. Because, let's face it, Marigold had never held a real job in her life. She made decent money as a brand ambassador, leveraging her It Girl status, but it was just a matter of time before a new crop of ingenues arrived on the scene. And what would Marigold do then? Why did she just assume that life would always work out for her?

Because it always has, Olivia thought, looking around the party. A gathering of happy, beautiful people eager to celebrate her happy, beautiful sister who'd never known heartbreak. Who'd never obsessed about a man after an almost-kiss. Who'd never been rejected by anyone, for anything.

Before Olivia realized what she was doing, she'd downed another glass of champagne, one that'd been filled when she hadn't been paying attention.

I should get some water, she thought. But before she could make her way to the bar, she spotted Andrew and Emerson making their way toward her. From a distance, Emerson looked even bonier than she had up close, as if she'd just stepped off the runway. "We just wanted to say good night," Andrew said, clapping a hand on Olivia's shoulder. "Emerson's still on Western Indonesian time, so we're going to have to miss the speeches, unfortunately."

"I told you to stay!" Emerson smiled, even as her eyes darted uncomfortably from Andrew to Olivia.

"It's okay. I want to swing by that whiskey-tasting thing on Ed Growler's yacht, anyway. There's an investor I need to butter up."

"Of course," Olivia said. "Thank you so much for coming. I'll see you tomorrow." She imagined Marigold rolling her eyes at what she called Olivia's "suggested response" voice. "You sound like those prompts at the bottom of an email." But there was nothing wrong with being polite, even if she did occasionally veer toward formality. Those stock phrases were a weapon—

words untainted by emotion. Because she'd rather die than betray the slightest hint of the hurt and shame that would've made her cheeks flush red back before she started using Botox.

Andrew and Emerson said good night and headed toward the golf carts shuttling guests back and forth to the inn, and Olivia refilled her glass with a bottle the server had left on the table. Would it kill them to replace the water carafe as well? She *really* needed to start hydrating.

Olivia stood up and stumbled slightly, grabbing on to the table for balance. The bar suddenly seemed very far away, and the fairy lights looked weirdly blurry. Across the dance floor, Lulu rose from her table. The chatter and laughter died down as she clinked her champagne flute with a knife. "Thank you all so much for coming," Lulu said, eyes shining as she surveyed the crowd. "It means a great deal to me, Bill, and to Jonathan's wonderful parents, Carol and Robert. And most of all, I know it means the world to Marigold and Jonathan to have you all here to celebrate the start of their joyous life together. I believe some of you have been asked to say a few words, so I'm going to pass the proverbial mic—or the actual mic," Lulu said with a laugh as the party planner handed her a microphone, "to my lovely daughter, Marigold's sister, Olivia."

"Oh, shit," Olivia muttered as she fumbled for her phone. She'd saved her notes in her email. But now they seemed to have disappeared? She frantically tried to type *toast* into the search bar, but her fingers wouldn't cooperate. *It's fine,* she told herself. *I remember enough of it. No big deal.* She grabbed another glass of champagne from a passing caterer, downed half of it in one gulp, then made her way toward Lulu, trying not to sway. She couldn't recall the last time she'd had this much to drink.

"Hi . . . hello," she said, leaning too close to the mic. The speakers screeched, and a few people yelped and covered their ears. "Sorry." She lowered the mic and tried again. "Is this better? Okay, good. Well, as you know, I'm Olivia, Marigold's sister. Though some of Marigold's newer friends might not have known she *has* a sister, since I've never made it onto her Instagram grid. I guess I'm not right for the 'aesthetic,'" she said, using her free hand to make air quotes.

Laughter bubbled up from the guests, and Olivia felt herself relax slightly. "I couldn't be happier that she and Jonathan have found each other. Because now, it's someone else's job to make sure Marigold gets home safely. I don't think she's ever made it through an entire night out without losing her phone, or her keys . . . or her underwear." There was more laughter, though not quite as much as before. *Shit*, Olivia thought. *Why did I say that?* That hadn't been in her script. Out of the corner of her gaze, she saw her mother raise her eyebrows.

"I'm joking . . . joking!" Olivia raised her glass to punctuate her point, and champagne sloshed over the rim. "My sister has never actually *lost* her underwear . . . though, okay, that's probably because she doesn't always wear underwear. She doesn't like panty lines, and says that thongs are unhygienic." She heard a few guffaws, but for the most part, the crowd had gone silent. Out of the corner of her eye, she saw two of the bridesmaids, Liesl and Bri, exchange faux-horrified smiles.

"Jeez, everyone, relax," Olivia said, turning to survey the guests. "It's how my sister makes money. Would you trust a beauty ambassador with visible panty lines? Um, no. It's called *branding*, people."

Bill had stood up and was walking toward Olivia with a huge, fake smile. "Okay, let's hear it for Olivia, ladies and gentlemen!" he said loudly as he reached for the mic.

Olivia twisted away. "I'm not done!" She couldn't end like this. She needed to get things back on track. "But of course, we all know that Jonathan is the lucky one here," she continued. "Marigold has a heart of gold. She's kinder and more creative than anyone as beautiful as her has any right to be. She loves deeply, and Jonathan will have the fiercest champion in his corner at all times. They make an amazing team, and the world is going to be a better place with this kind of love in it."

There, she thought. *That was sweet, wasn't it? More than enough to make up for the misstep.* But when she braved a glance at her sister, her heart sank. Marigold was staring at her with a fake, frozen smile that was far worse than a scowl, or even tears. Her defenses were up; she'd retreated into her cheerful, public persona, hiding behind a shield, where no one could hurt her.

I guess she was right not to make me the maid of honor.

"So please join me in raising a glass to Marigold and Jonathan," she said quickly, rushing off the dance floor and toward the house before anyone could stop her.

CHAPTER FOUR

Marigold

Marigold woke up but resisted opening her eyes. Today was her last full day as a single woman, and she wanted to savor every second. The moment her eyelids fluttered open, the countdown would begin.

Don't be ridiculous, she chided herself. She wasn't on death row. She didn't even have cold feet. She *wanted* to marry Jonathan. He was the best man she'd ever met. Marigold rolled over and buried her face in her pillow, conjuring her favorite images from the previous night: Lulu beaming with pride and love as she watched the festivities; Jonathan snapping into doctor mode when Bill's aunt Jessie fainted during dessert. Was it weird to be turned on by the sight of her fiancé tending to an eighty-four-year-old woman with low blood pressure? Whatever. She'd deserved a little pick-me-up after Olivia's "tribute." Marigold knew that the toast reflected much worse on her sister than it did on her, but it still hadn't felt great to sit there while seventy-five people tried not to think about her missing undergarments.

She got out of bed, pulled on the pajama shorts she'd wriggled out of in the night, and padded downstairs barefoot. Everyone else in her family wore slippers or flip-flops, depending on the season, to protect their feet from the ancient floorboards. But Marigold never worried about splinters, one of her many so-called quirks that drove Olivia crazy.

She poured herself a cup of coffee, then went to join her mother on the porch where Lulu was drawing with watercolor pencils, a sketch pad balanced on her lap. Marigold lowered herself into a creaky wicker rocking chair, then leaned over for a better look. Lulu had drawn a variety of birds, all incredibly realistic, save for their human accessories. The blue jay wore a top hat; the robin clutched an ornate walking stick; and a large swan smoothed the skirt of her high-necked Victorian wedding dress.

"Oh, wow," Marigold said. "They're gorgeous. I wish they were coming to the wedding instead of Jonathan's cousins." It made her happy to see her mother drawing again—the chemo generally made her too sick to do more than listen to audiobooks and nap. The wedding festivities were clearly a source of artistic inspiration.

A sound grabbed her attention, and she looked up to see Olivia crunching up the gravel drive, red-faced from her run.

"Morning, hon!" Lulu called. "Everything okay at the inn?" Olivia had apologized to them both at the end of the night—and then sent about a dozen more apology texts to the family group chat—but it still irked Marigold to hear their mother greet her so warmly.

Olivia came to a stop and held up a *one second* finger as she leaned over to catch her breath. Marigold rolled her eyes. Her sister regularly ran half marathons. There was no way three miles would've left her winded. Olivia couldn't resist playing the martyr; she seemed happiest when showing off her capacity for pain, whether bringing a stack of legal documents to the beach, ordering a plain chicken breast at a restaurant famous for pasta, or getting up before dawn to run.

Olivia's phone must've buzzed, because she pulled it out and said, "Hello?" in a normal voice, miraculously no longer gasping for breath. "Yes, she's right here . . . No, I have no idea why she never answers her phone . . . Bruce, stop, you're not supposed to share privileged attorney/client information . . . I know she's my sister, but it's still not professional . . . Okay, hold on . . ." Olivia trudged up the porch steps and shoved her phone at Marigold. "It's Bruce."

Bruce was their family's Maine lawyer, the one they used for things like boat permits and work visas for their summer staff. Why would he be calling today?

"Hi, Bruce," Marigold said. "How are you? How's Lucy?" Bruce and his wife bred dairy goats; Lucy was their current cherished prizewinner and there were no fewer than three framed photos of her in Bruce's office.

"We're all fine," he said in his Down-Easter accent. "Listen, I'm calling about your marriage license."

Marigold frowned. It was highly unusual for Bruce to skip the small talk. "Jonathan and I are picking it up from the registrar today."

"She doesn't have her marriage license yet?!" Olivia hissed to Lulu, correctly interpreting Marigold's side of the conversation. "This is ridiculous, even for her."

Seriously? Marigold mouthed, then made a *you're still on thin ice* face.

"There's been a slight setback," Bruce continued. "My paralegal was preparing your paperwork and discovered that, well . . ." He lowered his voice. "It appears that you're already married."

Marigold jerked the phone from her ear as if scalded. "That's not possible," she said in the most relaxed, cheerful voice she could muster despite the panic mounting in her chest. She headed into the house, aware of Lulu's and Olivia's eyes on her.

"Jessica performed a standard search using your social security number and found a certificate of marriage between you and a gentleman named . . . hold on a sec . . . Hugo Berlanger?"

The name knocked the air from her chest, and she grabbed on to the back of an armchair for balance. "Hugo Berlanger," she repeated in a daze.

"Does it . . . ring a bell?" Bruce asked.

Hugo Berlanger. The name didn't sound right coming from Bruce—it felt like he was quoting from Marigold's own dreams. She'd barely heard anyone say Hugo's full name aloud before; they'd cut themselves off from the world for those few stolen weeks, creating a reality that belonged to them alone. She'd almost managed to convince herself that she'd imagined the whole thing.

"That was . . . a long time ago." Marigold's voice sounded hoarse. "We got a divorce. I can't imagine why that'd be a problem now."

"And everything was finalized? Do you have copy of the paperwork?"

"I'll . . . I'll need to check with my New York lawyers. I'm sure it's all in order." It had to be, right? She *knew* Hugo had signed the papers—her lawyer had confirmed receipt. Marigold had been at a restaurant opening in Brooklyn, and she'd slipped out the back door to take the call. "We've received Mr. Berlanger's signed papers, so all you need to do is return yours," the lawyer had said cheerfully. Marigold remembered slumping against a pile of empty produce crates, unsure if the sudden weakness was the result of relief or shock that it was really all over. And then, of course, she'd mailed her signed copy. Or dropped them off at the office. She must have, right? Who forgets to finalize their own divorce?

"Do you want me to call?" Bruce asked. He often coordinated with their family's New York lawyers.

"Sure . . . yeah." Marigold stumbled through the kitchen and out into the backyard, where she'd be out of earshot. "If, for whatever reason, they never got my signed document, what happens then? My wedding is tomorrow, and I can't . . . I mean, I need to . . ." How could she tell Jonathan they needed to postpone? How could she tell *her mother*? There was no way. She had to figure this out.

"Given how much time has passed, you'll need to sign new copies. If you and Mr. Berlanger sign and get them notarized today, we should be able to get everything in order by tomorrow."

"Okay . . . okay," Marigold said, more to herself than to Bruce. "I'll find a notary, get the signatures, and send them over."

"The town clerk would normally insist on hard copies, but if you send a scan by tomorrow morning, it'll be fine. Mary owes me a favor. She was in a bit of a jam a few years back. Turns out her son had opened a credit card in her name and then flown to Russia to meet a woman he met on the internet, but the woman—"

"That's probably not something you should tell me, Bruce,"

Marigold said, a bit more shrilly than she'd intended. "But thank you for the call. I'm on it. You'll have the paperwork in time. Talk to you soon." She pressed "end" and started to scroll through her contacts before remembering that she was holding Olivia's phone, not her own.

"Can I have that back, please?"

Marigold flinched, then spun around to see her sister glaring at her from the back door.

"Just gimme a sec," Marigold said, taking a few steps backward as she planned what to do next. First, she had to grab her phone. She still had Hugo's number buried in her contacts, but what would she do if he didn't pick up? It was too risky just to forward the paperwork and hope for the best. It needed to be signed and notarized *today*. Which meant that if Hugo didn't check his texts or look at his email, someone would need to hand deliver the documents. And as far as Marigold knew, Hugo was still living in Canada.

"No, now. I have to check my email. Immediately."

Marigold tossed the phone to Olivia. "God forbid you make anyone wait thirty seconds for a response."

"It's my job to be available and responsive. To be someone people can count on."

"And you're saying I'm not?"

"You're getting married tomorrow and you don't have a marriage license. Classic Marigold."

"It's not my fault," Marigold said faintly. "There was a mix-up with the paperwork."

"Nothing's ever your fault, is it?"

"I appreciate your support, Olivia. It's *super* helpful."

Olivia sighed. "Fine, I'm sorry. What do you need?"

"Nothing. I'm just going to grab my phone and head to the ferry. I need to get my . . . birth certificate. From my apartment. I didn't realize I needed it for the license."

"You're going to *New York*? That doesn't make any sense. We know a hundred people flying up today. Just ask someone to bring it for you. Your doorman can let them in."

"It's in a safe with all my jewelry, so I don't think I should risk it. Or it might be in a safe-deposit box at the bank. I'm not one hundred percent sure. It's just easier if I go. I'll be back in time for the rehearsal dinner."

Olivia gave her an odd look. "Are you okay? Whatever it is, we'll figure it out."

For just a moment, Marigold felt an urge to tell her sister everything. Olivia would be horrified, but she'd fix Marigold's mess, just like she always did. But she'd never, ever let Marigold forget it. She'd bring it up, regularly, for the rest of their lives. And could she really trust Olivia not to tell anyone about Hugo? No, her little performance last night had made it clear—she wasn't afraid to humiliate Marigold when the opportunity arose. Jonathan could never hear about this. Neither could Lulu and Bill. "There's nothing to figure out. I just need my birth certificate. It's fine. I'm on it."

"Will you be okay doing all this by yourself? Do you want me to come with you?"

"I'm good. I'd rather you stay here, hold down the fort. I'll just go grab my stuff." Thankfully, the one thing she *really* needed was up in her room—her passport.

She wasn't going to New York; she was heading to Canada. She had eight hours to find Hugo Berlanger and fix the biggest mess she'd ever made.

CHAPTER FIVE

Natalie

Flying back to NY to get birth certificate. Need it for marriage license. Back tonight. Xoxo.

Natalie stared down at Marigold's text in dismay. How could this have happened? Marigold had a wedding planner *and* a lawyer in Maine. Why had they waited so long to get the license? Wouldn't Jonathan have checked in at some point?

She knew it would all work out in the end, though. This was how Marigold rolled. Natalie couldn't count the number of times she had left her passport at home, or arrived forty-five minutes before a flight only to realize she was flying out of Newark, not JFK. And yet she always managed to salvage the situation. Or, at least, called someone who salvaged it for her, like when Bill sent a helicopter to take her to the correct airport.

The more immediate issue was that they were supposed to take bridesmaid photos in an hour, and Natalie had spent a ridiculous amount of time coordinating with the photographer's "team"—his booking agent, his admin assistant, his production coordinator. Jean-Luc Duchant famously never shot weddings, but he'd made a special exception for his friend Marigold. However, even his affection for his muse wasn't enough to overcome his powerful disdain for traditional bridal party photos, so the plan had been for a "day before" photo shoot in the black vintage cocktail dresses they'd found for the occasion. Or, more accurately, that *Natalie* had found for the occasion . . .

Needless to say, Natalie wasn't particularly keen to let everyone know that the shoot was off. As she considered what to tell Jean-Luc, she perused the inn's breakfast menu, torn between lobster benedict and wild Maine blueberry pancakes. That was one of the many small indignities of singlehood no one ever talked about—without someone to share with, you had to make the impossible choice between savory and sweet that always left you feeling cheated.

As Natalie dithered over the menu, Liesl sauntered over. She had an exaggerated, almost choreographed way of moving, swinging her hips far more than necessary. And if you called her name, she'd turn her head and raise a questioning eyebrow before responding, as if she were always auditioning for the femme fatale role in some unknown film. "We're taking photos soon, yes?" she said in her usual affected manner that often morphed into a vaguely European accent despite the fact that she'd grown up in Connecticut.

"Marigold actually had to fly back to New York to grab her birth certificate." Natalie kept her voice breezy, as if this were a normal errand for the bride to complete the day before her wedding. "Turns out she needs it for the marriage paperwork."

Liesl raised an eyebrow. *"Do you think she practices that move in the mirror?"* Natalie once whispered to Jonathan during a cocktail party at Marigold's apartment, causing him to splutter into his beer. "No one else could bring it?"

Natalie shrugged. "Guess she figured it was easier this way."

A server in a white button-down and a sleek bun approached the table. "Can I get you anything for breakfast?" she asked cheerfully.

Natalie glanced back down at the menu. "I'll have the pancakes, please."

"You're *so* lucky," Liesl said as the server bustled off. "I wish I could eat gluten and sugar, but my body just can't process it."

"That's so weird." Startled, Natalie turned to see Jonathan smiling at them from the table behind her. "The pizza we had delivered last night wasn't gluten-free. Were you sick after?"

"I only had a few bites."

"If you had celiac disease, that'd be more than enough to trigger a flare. So great news! You're not gluten intolerant!"

Liesl smiled tightly. "Jonathan, I'm sure this isn't your intent, but you've been conditioned by the medical establishment to dismiss female pain. I know my body, and I'm not going to let you gaslight me into ignoring my symptoms. You might want to take some time to explore your bias."

"Noted," Jonathan said gravely. "I'll work on that."

As Liesl strode off, Jonathan raised one eyebrow at Natalie, who covered her mouth to stifle her laughter.

"Poor Liesl," she said. "Her whole personality is built around her made-up food restrictions."

"I know, that was a dick move. I wouldn't have said anything if she hadn't tried to pancake-shame you."

"My knight in shining white coat armor. How can I ever repay you?"

"Actually, I could use your help with something. Do you mind taking a look at my vows at some point? I've been fiddling with them on my own, but they need your writerly eye."

"Of course," Natalie said, ignoring the twinge in her gut at the thought of helping Jonathan write the words that would bond him to Marigold for the rest of her life. That was a problem for later today, or better yet, tomorrow morning. "I just heard from Marigold. I assume she told you about her errand?"

"Yeah." Jonathan laughed and shook his head. "Typical Marigold. I knew something like this would happen. But it seems more like the lawyer's fault for not filing all the paperwork earlier. She should be back in time for the rehearsal, though."

"Definitely. You know Marigold always figures it out somehow, no matter the chaos beforehand."

"Just more material for my vows. So do you want to meet up this afternoon? Maybe around three?" He flashed her a mischievous smile. "I believe you know how to find my room."

By the time her pancakes arrived, Natalie had lost interest in eating. The prospect of hanging out one-on-one with Jonathan always made her too anxious and excited to focus on anything else. She knew he was in love with Marigold. That was never going to change, and she'd already pulled back on their friendship. She hadn't hung out with him alone in more than a year. But surely there'd be no harm in helping him with his vows.

She headed back into the reception area and was just waffling about calling off the photo shoot when an elegant older woman caught her eye. "Do you work at Horatio Street Press?" she asked, gesturing at Natalie's tote bag.

"Oh no." Natalie blushed, feeling like a tourist in a Harvard sweatshirt. "I interned there one summer, a long time ago." It'd been one of the best things that'd ever happened to her. She'd loved everything about Horatio Street Press—the nerdy-glam editors who'd made Natalie feel so welcome; the quirky, literary books they published; the beautiful West Village town house that served as their office. They'd even offered to bring her on full-time, and for weeks, an elated Natalie was walking on air . . . until she realized that it was mathematically impossible for her to live in New York on an editorial assistant salary, not when the company didn't offer health insurance. And so she'd turned down her dream job, moved back home to Arizona after college, and spent five years in the communications department of a hospital until she'd managed to claw her way back to New York, this time to ghostwrite college essays for the 1 percent.

"I wonder if we overlapped." The woman had short silver hair, thick red glasses, and wore a loose, slightly asymmetrical black dress that probably came from one of those oddly sterile boutiques that never had more than four items on display, none of which cost less than eight hundred dollars. "I worked there for decades before moving over to a bigger house a few years ago."

"Oh!" Natalie said, recognition dawning. "Are you Susan Denver?" Susan had been a legendary editor at Horatio Street Press. It'd caused quite a stir when she'd left to run her own imprint at a big-five competitor. Natalie made a point to stay on top of the publishing news, even though it seemed unlikely she'd ever be a part of that world again. She doubted she'd ever get an agent for her manuscript, let alone an actual book deal.

"That's me," she said. "Are you here for the wedding? I think I saw you at the welcome drinks last night."

"I am. I'm the maid of honor."

"How wonderful! I've been friends with Lulu and Bill for ages, and I've known Marigold since she was a little girl. I didn't realize she had any close friends in publishing."

"Oh, I'm not in the book world anymore, unfortunately. I work as a private tutor, mostly on the Upper East Side."

Susan raised a knowing eyebrow. "I've heard some wild stories about working with those children. Did you read that *New York* magazine article about the family who paid for the tutor to join them on safari in Botswana?"

"Yes! I was so jealous. I shouldn't complain, though—one family brought me down to Florida for a few days." Natalie paused for dramatic effect. "Though I did need to fly with the horse."

"I'm sorry, what? With the *horse*?"

"Yup. The family was already down there, but they needed to transport the daughter's horse for an equestrian competition. I guess they figured since they were already chartering a plane, I might as well tag along. But it wasn't exactly the private plane experience I'd imagined. It was just the pilot, a groom, the horse, and me. I sat in a tiny jump seat next to a pile of hay."

"You poor thing," Susan said with a laugh. "That's quite an image. It'd make a great scene in a novel. I've always wanted to read a book set in that world—sort of a *Nanny Diaries* for private tutors."

Natalie's heart lurched. That was *exactly* how she'd been describing her novel, a fictionalized account of her tutoring misadventures.

Tell her! an urgent voice shouted inside her head. *This is your big chance!*

But wasn't it bad form to pitch an editor on her personal time—when she was on vacation, no less? And what if Susan thought Natalie had manufactured this run-in like some kind of stalker? Worse still, what if she agreed to read the manuscript as a favor only to decide that Natalie was a delusional hack? The thought of someone like Susan Denver laughing at Natalie's writing was enough to make her physically ill.

"I'd better get a move on," Susan said. "They stop serving breakfast in five minutes. It was nice to meet you."

"You too." It was only when the older woman walked off that Natalie realized she'd never even told Susan her name. *Typical*, she thought. She was the queen of missed opportunities; it was the story of her life.

CHAPTER SIX

Olivia

Olivia usually sprinted for the final quarter mile of her shorter runs, but today she slowed to a walk as she emerged from the woods and turned onto the path that led into town. She could normally power through a hangover, but her brain felt heavier than her limbs. Nothing threw Olivia off-kilter like plans falling apart. She'd spent so long imagining this perfect weekend: Lulu, blissful and beaming, surrounded by loved ones, secure in the knowledge that her younger daughter was happy and settled. Olivia, cradled in Andrew's arms on the dance floor, feeling almost like a bride herself: Beautiful. Loved. *Chosen.*

How had everything gone pear-shaped so quickly, with Andrew producing a date seemingly out of thin air, and Marigold *flying back to New York* the day of her rehearsal dinner. Olivia wasn't sure which of these scenarios seemed stranger. At least the second conundrum was something she could investigate—she'd already asked her paralegal to look into the logistics. But she couldn't exactly text Andrew and ask, *Did I really just imagine our chemistry the other night? What the hell did you mean when you said "maybe we can pick up where we left off in Maine"?*

Instead of heading back to the inn, she made her way onto the small public beach down the hill, one of the only sandy stretches on the otherwise rocky island. Olivia's family usually avoided it—they came to Maine to escape the crowds—but Olivia often stopped here to stretch after a run. She liked watching fearless little kids play in the frigid surf—tiny, hearty New Englanders who didn't care that the water was rarely warmer than fifty-eight degrees.

Olivia placed her heel on a bench, pulled out her phone, then let out a small gasp that had nothing to do with her protesting hamstring.

Correct, her paralegal, Carly, had texted. You do not need a birth certificate to get married in the state of Maine.

Olivia knew something about the situation smelled fishy. Either wedding planning had broken Marigold's brain, or she was hiding something.

Of course, erratic behavior was part of her sister's brand—whether that meant wandering around the Met barefoot because her painful shoes "distracted her from the art," trying to liberate a sad-looking snake from a pet store, or jumping into a hotel pool while wearing a borrowed designer gown. Actions that would signal mental instability in everyone but pretty, rich white women. But this was something else.

Did Marigold have cold feet? The idea of settling down with one person, forever, would be daunting to anyone, but especially to someone like Marigold. Committing to a *nail polish shade* could be overwhelming for her. Was she really ready to commit to one person for the rest of her life?

But running off like this—this wasn't just nerves. Something was wrong.

Olivia pictured what came next: the worried whispers spreading through the guests. Jonathan retreating into his cool, detached doctor persona—the mode he always adopted in a crisis—but unable to disguise the panic in his eyes. And Lulu, who'd been looking forward to the magical weekend that might now end in heartbreak instead.

If Marigold wanted to call off the wedding, that was one thing. (Well, not ideal, but better than making a mistake.) But Olivia couldn't just let her sister disappear like this. She had to find her. Help her. Fix this—somehow.

Olivia clicked on her favorites and called Marigold. Naturally, it went to voicemail. She couldn't remember the last time her sister had actually picked up. Call me, Olivia texted, then followed that up with, Whatever's going on, I can help you.

The next time she looked at her phone, Marigold's status had been set to "do not disturb."

"Oh, for the love of god," Olivia grumbled. Why couldn't *she* be the one getting married? Why couldn't she be the one whose wedding gave their mother the gift of one perfect weekend? One last chance to be surrounded by friends and family before . . .

You don't need your birth certificate!! Olivia's fingers pounded on the screen, leaving sweaty smudges behind. Then she pressed "notify anyway." Fine. If Marigold was ignoring her, then Olivia would just need to outsmart her. Even if she *was* running away, she'd likely still be headed for the airport. Marigold didn't like to drive, and it was nearly impossible to book a same-day rental car during the high season. So all Olivia needed to do was intercept

Marigold before she got into a taxi on the mainland. With a weary sigh, she shoved her phone into her pocket and broke into a run. If she went straight to her family's boat, she should be able to catch up with the ferry.

She sped up, ignoring the protest from the muscles she'd already exhausted earlier that morning, and headed to the nearby marina, where she'd left the boat yesterday after dropping some of the guests at the inn. She ran down the pier, her sneakers slapping against the wooden boards in a rhythm she knew well from the countless miles she'd clocked jogging around the island. She skirted around a group of cotton-candy-eating tweens, squeaked to a stop at the end of the pier, and began to untie the knot securing the boat to the mooring.

"Where's the fire?"

She whipped around to Jonathan's best man, Zack, smiling at her from a weathered gray bench, a dog-eared paperback copy of *The House of Mirth* open in his lap.

Olivia groaned. She *really* didn't have time for this right now. "Don't worry about it," she said, unwrapping the damp, prickly rope and then hopping into the boat before it could drift too far from the dock. "As you were." She pulled her keys from the pocket of her jogging shorts, found the spare boat key, and started the motor.

"Everything okay?" Zack asked, rising from the bench.

"Fine! You can go back to pretending to read your book now."

He didn't take the bait. "Where are you going?"

"I need to run an errand. Time sensitive. I'll see you later."

He tucked the book under his arm. "I'll come with you. I like boats."

"Sorry, next time. Gotta go," Olivia said. Even if she didn't find Zack insufferable, she couldn't risk anyone else learning that Marigold had gone AWOL.

"Oh, come on. Let me come. It's the least you can do, given how much time I'm devoting to the longest wedding in history."

"Um, *I* didn't ask you to be the best man. And anyway, I'm sure you'll use this whole weekend as clickbait for your little blog. I can see the headline now: 'Why Rich People Are Even Worse Than You Think.'"

"I don't have any time for the blog these days," Zack said with the trademark grin that made Olivia like him less each time she met him. "I'm working on a book. But don't worry—I won't use any of your real names in my chapter on conspicuous consumption and liberal hypocrisy."

Olivia snorted. "You didn't seem that bothered when you helped yourself to two hundred dollars' worth of seafood last night."

"Better than letting it go to waste. Now come on, let me come with you. It'll be faster. I can drop you off so you don't have to worry about docking."

Olivia thought for a moment. If she didn't beat the ferry to the mainland, then she might have to make a run for it to reach Marigold before she got into a taxi. Every second would count.

"Fine," she said with a sigh. "Come on."

Despite the fact that the boat had already drifted a few feet from the pier, Zack managed to hop in with impressive ease.

"Hold on," she said, putting the boat into gear. She turned sharply away from the dock and then accelerated as quickly as she dared. Unlike Marigold, Olivia couldn't afford to have a reckless driving ticket on her record.

Zack settled into the seat next to her. "Don't you have one of those floaty key chain things?" he asked, gesturing at the ignition. "What if it falls in the water?"

"We have one for the main set of keys. Marigold lost those last week. This is just the backup key, for emergencies.

"And what's the 'emergency'?"

"Just some wedding stuff."

"So you're not sneaking off to see a client or something?"

Actually, that wasn't a terrible cover story. Perhaps she should let Zack believe she was frantic about work rather than intercepting a runaway bride. As they passed the buoys that marked the no-wake zone, Olivia pulled back on the gearshift and the boat leaped forward. Despite everything, she smiled—the rush never got old.

"Something I promised my mother I'd handle." It was true, in a sense. Olivia was the only person besides Bill who knew the truth—a secret she'd never wanted to carry to begin with, but that she now would fight to protect, no matter the cost.

It had been a sunny day six months ago, at her parents' apartment in the city.

"No," Olivia said emphatically. "Absolutely not."

Lulu and Bill exchanged *I told you so* looks, although Olivia wasn't sure who was blaming whom. They were perched on the uncomfortable kitchen stools the interior designer had bought when they'd redone their penthouse a few years earlier. Everyone hated them, but there was an unspoken rule against complaining, though Olivia was unsure whether this was to protect the reputation of the designer or Bill's ego since he'd been the one who'd insisted on redecorating in the first place. That seemed to be their family's modus operandi these days—unspoken rules, unarticulated feelings. Sometimes Olivia found herself thinking wistfully about the old days, back in their one-bedroom apartment, where there was no space for secrets. Where she could glean her mother's mood from the way Lulu closed the front door, whether she hung up her coat on the hook or tossed it over the back of the couch.

But now Lulu and Bill were trying to change the rules. They wanted to bring Olivia into their inner circle for the express purpose of excluding Marigold.

"We'll tell her after the wedding," Lulu said. "We don't want to ruin this special time."

"Don't you think she'll notice that you're not going to chemo?" Olivia asked.

Lulu cocked her head and gave Olivia a knowing smile. They were all deeply familiar with Marigold's ability to ignore anything she didn't want to deal with, from a pile of dirty clothes on her bedroom floor to the sudden cessation in her mother's bimonthly trips to Sloan Kettering and the days of illness that always followed.

"Fine," Olivia conceded. "Maybe she won't notice right away. But she'll never forgive you when she finds out. She deserves to know the truth."

"She's not as strong as you are, Olly-pop," Bill said, using his special nickname for Olivia.

But what if I'm not stronger than her? Olivia thought. *What if I've only been pretending because I didn't have any other choice*? What else could Olivia have done—not taken care of her little sister? Not acted like everything was going to be okay when she was as scared as Marigold was? Just because Olivia had been forced to grow up quickly didn't mean that she had superhuman powers.

It didn't mean that this news wasn't going to eat away at her heart bit by bit.

"Are you sure?" Olivia asked, unable to keep her voice from breaking. "What about that trial Jonathan mentioned? The one in Sweden?"

Lulu smiled sadly. "I'm not eligible for that now that it's spread to my brain. It's time to stop fighting and just enjoy the time I have left."

Olivia had spent the past five years preparing herself for this moment. She'd imagined this conversation countless times so she'd be ready. Pre-grieving, her therapist had called it. But Dr. Hardy had been right—you couldn't train your body to withstand pain like this.

"It's okay, hon," Lulu said, reaching across the cold marble counter to squeeze Olivia's arm. "I'm fine, I promise. I've had enough adventures and seen enough beauty to fill ten lifetimes. This is a small price to pay for all the miracles I've experienced. Miracles like you and Marigold."

Bill passed Olivia a tissue. She hadn't realized she was crying.

"How long?" Olivia asked quietly.

"They don't know. It could be a year. It could be less. But without all the chemo, I'm going to have a wonderful summer. I'll be able to enjoy the wedding. And we'll tell Marigold as soon as she gets back from her honeymoon—I promise."

"She'll never forgive me," Olivia said, more to herself than to Lulu and Bill.

"Yes, she will," Bill said firmly. "We'll make it clear that this was all our idea, and that we made you promise to stay quiet. This isn't on you."

Olivia turned to Lulu. "But what if she doesn't forgive *you*?"

"It's a risk I'm willing to take. She deserves the chance to be a happy, carefree bride."

There it was—the heart of the matter. They'd tie themselves in knots to protect Marigold and leave Olivia to carry the burden. It was habit at this point. She'd never said anything, never complained, so of course they'd assume she could handle it.

"I'm sorry, Livy," Lulu said, as if reading her mind. "I know it's not fair. But you're different people. I knew you'd *want* to know, hard as it is."

"No, you're right," Olivia said, meaning it. "I do want to know." She could handle the slow-growing rot festering in her stomach.

All that mattered was making this the best summer of her mother's unfairly abridged life, whatever it took.

CHAPTER SEVEN

Marigold

Flying commercial wasn't an option given the end-of-day deadline for the signed papers, so en route to the private airfield in Brunswick, Marigold called NetJets and booked a plane using Bill's account. Miraculously, they'd had a late cancellation and she'd been able to confirm her flight to Nova Scotia. Bill had given them all access to his membership for emergencies, and while this wasn't a matter of life or death, Marigold had a feeling he wouldn't argue with her once the whole story came out later. After the wedding. Way after, ideally. She'd have to tell Jonathan the truth at some point as well. She'd called him from the boat and he'd immediately shifted into problem-solving mode: Did she want him to go to New York for her? Wasn't there someone in the city who could bring it up? Why had the lawyer waited so long to file the paperwork? Did she want Jonathan to call Bruce? Marigold had felt terrible lying to him, but why upset him now, when it was all so close to being fixed? She'd tell him the whole story eventually, when the timing was better.

As the jet made its way up the Maine coast, Marigold stared out the window, thinking about her first and only other trip to the Canadian Maritimes.

She'd been on a yachting trip with her then-boyfriend, Jack Pemberton, and a bunch of his finance buddies. She hadn't wanted to go in the first place; after eight months of dating, she'd had her fill of banker bro posturing. Jack was sweet on his own, but she couldn't stand the way he acted around his friends, and the last thing she'd wanted was to spend a week sitting around while they got wasted and went spearfishing. Chances were high they'd end up accidentally impaling one another instead of the fish.

But Lulu and Bill had strongly encouraged her to go. Lulu had recently been diagnosed, and after weeks of sitting with her mother at chemo and running around the city on the hunt for whatever specialty food items Lulu thought she might be able to keep down, it'd been clear that Marigold needed a break. A distraction.

She'd been fond enough of Jack. He was attractive, if in a generic, conventional way, and she appreciated that they took each other at face value. He was handsome and rich enough to feel good about his place in the world and didn't see Marigold as a trophy. He was happy just to have a good time with her. But on his yacht with his buddies, he lost his charm. At dinner the third night, the conversation turned to "the weight cutoff for fuckability." Jack's creepiest friend, Mikey, claimed that he'd never slept with a woman who weighed over 110 pounds, prompting Marigold to ask if he carried a scale around with him.

"I have an eye for it," Mikey said, leering at Marigold. "I can guess any woman's weight within five pounds. I've never been wrong."

She snorted. "You're full of shit. What kind of woman would let you *weigh* her?"

"It's true," the sycophantic hanger-on Ryan had said, never one to miss a chance to ingratiate himself with the more powerful members of the crew. "I've seen him do it."

"Bet I can do you," Mikey said, eyeing Marigold up and down. "Let's see . . . I probably need to account for the boob job. Silicone weighs more than you think. But you don't really have an ass, so . . ."

With her skin crawling under Mikey's hungry, lecherous gaze, Marigold turned to Jack. "I want him off the boat. *Now.*"

"Come on, relax. He's just joking," Jack said, shifting uncomfortably.

"Fine. Then I'll leave."

"Yeah, sure." Mikey snickered. "Like you'd leave before you finished filming all your little videos for the week."

Marigold stood up and walked over to the railing. They'd dropped anchor close to shore, although it was hard to judge the distance in the dark. But it couldn't be more than a quarter of a mile, and the night was unseasonably warm. Without a word, she climbed over the railing and balanced on the edge of the yacht. It was only two floors. She'd jumped from higher before.

"Marigold, come on!" Jack shouted. "Don't be stupid."

"She's just doing it for attention," Ryan said.

Marigold smiled into the darkness, took a deep breath, and leaped into the air.

The water was freezing, but she'd been prepared for that, and after breaking up through the surface, she began to swim, muscle memory kicking in as she sliced through the water with even, powerful strokes. After a few minutes, the voices on the yacht were swallowed by the night.

After about ten minutes, she reached the shore, took a few awkward, lurching steps, and collapsed on the sand to catch her breath. Perhaps this hadn't been the smartest plan. She was freezing. She had no dry clothes to change into, no phone, no wallet. Jack would realize this and come fetch her in the tender eventually. The best thing was to stay put until he came for her. But the thought of returning to the boat made her queasy, and it was too cold not to keep moving. So with a groan, she'd risen to her feet and begun trudging down the beach until a warm orange glow caught her eye, beckoning to her from the darkness. It was a bonfire—a beach party, probably. She could hear music in the distance, barely audible over the crash of the waves. Surely they wouldn't mind letting her warm up for a bit while she waited for Jack. As she approached, she recognized the chorus of her favorite Father John Misty song, except it sounded slightly different than usual—a live version maybe. Then she realized that the music wasn't coming from a speaker. A man with a guitar sat on the sand, singing as he played.

Marigold stopped, hesitant to emerge from the shadows. This wasn't a party, just a guy playing music on his own. What kind of weirdo did that? Probably the type of weirdo she didn't want to encounter alone in the dark. Barefoot and sopping wet, with no way to call for help. *Turn around*, said the voice in her head. It sounded like Natalie. The smart part of her brain always sounded like Natalie. Except that it was hard to believe that this gravelly, soulful baritone could belong to someone dangerous. Murderers didn't listen to Father John Misty. *Famous last words*, she thought, then laughed to herself. At least, she *thought* it was to herself.

The music stopped suddenly. "Is someone there?" the man called.

"Yeah, hi," Marigold said as she stepped into the glow of the fire. "I'm sorry to intrude. I'll keep moving."

The man stared at her, seemingly dumbfounded by the unexpected sight before him, a drenched woman in what was most likely a transparent white dress. "Are you okay?" He rose to his feet. "Where'd you come from?"

"Out there." She inclined her head. He raised his eyebrows, and she realized that the yacht probably wasn't visible in the darkness. "My friend's boat. I went for a swim and ended up here."

"But you're okay? You're not hurt?"

"I'm fine . . . Oh, thanks," she said as he handed her a sweatshirt. "Are you sure? I don't want to get it all wet."

"Don't worry about it," he said, surveying her. "This is some right Little Mermaid shit."

"*You* were the one singing. Maybe you're the mermaid."

"And you're the sea witch here to take my voice."

"I don't have anything to offer you in return." She patted her skirt. "No pockets."

"It's okay. My voice isn't worth much."

"I beg to differ. It's beautiful."

"I think that might be the hypothermia talking. Do you want to go warm up somewhere while you wait for your friends? My house is just there." He inclined his head toward the narrow dirt road that ran parallel to the beach. She hesitated, and he added quickly, "Or I can bring you some dry clothes and a blanket if you're more comfortable staying out here."

Marigold waited for the voice in her head to sound the alarm, but it never came. "I guess I'll wait inside, if you're sure you don't mind." He picked up his guitar and motioned for her to follow him. "So, what were you doing out here?"

"I don't like to play in the house. My neighbors have a new baby, and I don't want to disturb them."

"But you're so good! I swear, I thought someone was playing Father John Misty, like out of a speaker."

He shook his head. "I still think I might be hallucinating this."

"Why?"

"That's the only way to explain how a girl emerged from the sea to compliment my singing. So what's your name, mystery lady?"

"Marigold," she said, extending her hand.

"Marigold," he repeated, as if trying it out. It'd been a long time since she'd met a man who hadn't already known of her. *The famous Marigold*, they'd say. Or they'd pretend not to know who she was as some sort of power play, and then she'd sneak off to check her Instagram and discover that they followed her. They had opinions about her before they'd even exchanged a word. It was kind of refreshing to have a blank slate. To just be the girl from the sea. "I'm Hugo."

Hugo had been true to his word. His house was just on the other side of the road, a small gray cottage. He apologized for the mess, and Marigold couldn't argue with him there. It *was* a mess—old pizza boxes in the corner, empty beer bottles on windowsills, stacks of unopened mail. But it was also surprisingly cozy, especially once Hugo lit a fire in the fireplace and gave her an oversized flannel shirt to put on.

She accepted the whiskey he offered her, and they sat down on the threadbare couch. A minute later, Hugo's gray pit bull–Lab mix, Humphrey, leaped up and sprawled across them. It should've felt awkward. It should've felt *dangerous*. She was in the home of a stranger she'd met on the beach, and not a soul knew where she was. But there was something about him that felt comfortable, safe. Not like she'd known him forever, because she was certain she'd never met anyone like him before—a Canadian college dropout who worked at a marina, refueling boats. It was more like stepping into a house she'd never been to but that felt like home, like it'd been waiting for her.

She didn't go back to the yacht that night. As the fire died down and the first signs of dawn streaked across the sky, Marigold used Hugo's computer to email Jack and instructed him to leave her wallet at the marina when he refueled for the trip home. She didn't bother asking for her luggage.

The next two weeks were the most magical of Marigold's life. Her friends, family, manager, and booking agent all assumed she was off the grid at sea, so she didn't have to worry about getting back to anyone. There were no Instagram comments to respond to in order to boost engagement. No parties where she'd be cornered by vague acquaintances asking for photos or favors, who'd inevitably slink off and call her a bitch behind her back when she kindly explained why she couldn't get them an invite to the Met Gala or fast-track their application to Zero Bond. Hugo was the first person she'd met since Natalie who didn't want anything from Marigold apart from her company.

Hugo took Marigold out in the small sailboat he'd refurbished, and they spent a blissful day island-hopping with a cooler full of beer and ham-and-cheese sandwiches. Most of the beaches were deserted, allowing Marigold to play out the *Blue Lagoon* fantasies that'd been living rent-free in her head since she'd watched it at a middle school sleepover. But whenever they caught sight of other people, she and Hugo would quickly devise some ridiculous roles to act out. They spent nearly an hour pretending to be lost German tourists until Marigold dissolved into hysterical laughter and had to run back to the boat. Tears were still streaming down her cheeks as they sailed back into the harbor, recounting Hugo's feigned confusion at being informed they were on Wagmatcook Island. His eyes had widened as he said in a terrible German accent, "Wagmatcook? That has not been legal in Germany since the war!"

"I think this was the best day of my life," Marigold said as they climbed into the dinghy to row back to the dock.

"It's not over yet," Hugo said with a smile.

"Good. I wish I could do this with you forever. I never want to go back to real life." She hadn't told Hugo much about her life in New York, but he knew she wasn't happy in the "media relations" job she'd alluded to.

"So don't," Hugo said. "Stay here with me." He reached into a tackle box, twisted a piece of fishing wire into a ring, and knelt down. "Marry me, Marigold."

She couldn't remember if she'd said yes aloud or if she'd just kissed him. They'd gone straight from the harbor to the small courthouse in town and spent the rest of the night celebrating, first at the local bar with all of Hugo's friends, then on the beach, where they downed two bottles of champagne before stripping down and having sex on the shore as the tide rolled in.

It was the happiest Marigold had ever felt.

But the next day, she woke up with a skull-shattering headache, a terrible sunburn, a rash from rolling around in the sand, and a stomach full of bile and regret. This was insane, even for her. It turned out that everyone who'd ever called her flighty, careless, and irresponsible had been right. She'd married a man she'd known for *two weeks*! A man who'd spent his whole life in a small Canadian fishing village and said he'd never move to New York. Marigold winced as she imagined the look on Olivia's face when she told her family the news—the mix of disappointment and resignation, as if she'd always expected something like this to happen. No, she couldn't go through with this; it'd just confirm everyone's worst fears about her. It was time to be an adult for once, to do the right thing, no matter how much it hurt.

After throwing up in the bathroom, she staggered into the living room and scribbled out a shaky note; her head was spinning so badly, it was hard to write. She told Hugo that he was a wonderful man but that this was a fantasy, not real life, and that he had to forget all about her. *P.S.*, she'd written, *Tell your mom I'm sorry and that I hope she doesn't hate me.*

Then she'd kissed the sleeping Hugo on the cheek, scratched Humphrey behind the ears, and tiptoed out of the house.

Six weeks later, after Hugo's confused, worried messages to her eventually tapered off, Natalie had asked Marigold if she wanted to meet up for drinks with a friend of hers—a "really hot doctor." He hadn't sounded like Marigold's normal type, but maybe that was for the best. It was time to grow up and date a man in the real world, not in fantasyland.

And so she did her best to push Hugo from her thoughts and agreed to go meet Jonathan.

Marigold stepped out of the taxi outside Hugo's house—the one Bruce had confirmed he still lived in, according to tax records. It'd taken a private jet, a boat, and a car for her to get here. The gray shingled house looked exactly as Marigold remembered—the same gravel path lined with white seashells, the same weathered blue door, the same battered pickup truck in the drive. No wait, *something* was different. Marigold took a step back and surveyed the house. Those window boxes hadn't been there before; she would've remembered the cheerful pansies and zinnias, especially since Hugo had told her that he'd never been able to keep plants alive. Maybe he had a girlfriend? Marigold paused on the path; she hadn't considered that possibility. It wasn't fair to spring this on some innocent girl who might not have any idea that her boyfriend was technically married to a woman he'd spent two crazy weeks with four years ago and hadn't seen since. But what other option did she have? She needed those papers—*today*. She had just a few hours to clean up the mess she'd created.

She'd tried calling Hugo's old number on the way here, but he didn't answer. She DMed him on Instagram, but he never read the message.

Only Hugo's truck was in the driveway, so there was a good chance he was home alone. Though if Hugo *did* have a girlfriend, she was probably some free-spirited, earthy type who rode a vintage bike to her job at the vegan bakery. Whatever. If the phantom girlfriend was home, Hugo could explain everything to her after Marigold left, signed divorce papers in hand. Steeling herself, she marched up the front steps and rapped on the door. A dog barked, and a second later, she heard the sound of nails scratching. When no footsteps followed, she knocked again, louder this time.

"Coming!" a familiar voice called, and Marigold felt her stomach lurch.

The door opened, and then there he was, exactly as she remembered. Tall and leanly muscular, dirty-blond hair pulled back into a wavy man bun that emphasized his sharp jaw.

"Holy shit," he said, eyes widening. She'd forgotten how intensely green they were, how people always asked if he was wearing colored contacts. "It's you."

Hugo stared at her agape, like Scooby-Doo facing a ghost. It would've been comical if Marigold hadn't just left her wedding festivities, chartered a private plane, and flown to Canada to fix the worst mess of her life.

"It's me," she said.

CHAPTER EIGHT

Natalie

Natalie tried to clear her head as she headed up the inn's stairs toward Jonathan's room, but the anxiety that'd been building throughout the day had begun to reach a fever pitch. Marigold didn't have a wedding license and was flying to New York for her birth certificate. Olivia had gone AWOL, and the other bridesmaids were asking a million questions Natalie couldn't answer. And on top of that, she'd completely blown her chances with Susan Denver. She'd probably see her again before the end of the wedding festivities, but Natalie couldn't see a way to bring up her book—*Remember when you said you've always wanted this kind of novel? Well, I have it!*—without sounding unhinged.

She nodded vaguely at a blond woman coming down the stairs in jeans and a fleece. "Natalie!" The woman reached out for a hug.

"Hannah, hi!" Natalie said. "Sorry, I was in my own world."

"I get it. Westleigh is also a dreamer. Maybe she'll be writer like you!" Westleigh was Hannah's five-year-old daughter and, in Natalie's recollection, screamed bloody murder if forced to part with her ever-present iPad. "We were supposed to stay with my folks, but my mom *refuses* to buy new kitchenware, and I can't be around all those microplastics in my . . . present condition."

"Of course." So her "new addition" *was* a baby and not a home renovation. "Congrats!"

Hannah beamed. "Thank you. I hope our news doesn't distract too much from Marigold's big day. This weekend is all about her, of course! I haven't seen Marigold yet. Is she saying here or at the cottage?"

"At the cottage, but she actually had to fly back to New York to get something. She'll be back tonight."

"Oh no! There wasn't anyone who could go for her?" Hannah gave Natalie a pointed look.

"She wanted to take care of it," Natalie said as brightly as possible. "Sorry, I gotta run. I'll see you at the rehearsal later!"

When she reached Jonathan's room, she paused and took a deep, steadying breath. She'd already mortified herself enough for one weekend; she needed at least one social interaction to go smoothly or else she'd turn around and walk straight into the sea. She knocked loudly.

"Come in!" Jonathan's voice called.

"You sure? Are you decent?"

"Only one way to find out!"

Natalie opened the door and stepped in, blushing with residual embarrassment from yesterday's mishap, and found a fully dressed Jonathan standing next to an old-fashioned writing desk, fiddling with his laptop. He wore the same thick-framed glasses that'd always made Natalie's heart flutter in college, the ones Marigold kept calling outdated.

"I'm sorry again about yesterday," Natalie said. "I still can't believe they gave me the wrong room key."

"It's fine," Jonathan said with a grin. "Consider it your consolation prize."

The air hissed out of Natalie's lungs like a leaky air mattress. "Sorry, what?"

"You know, because the stripper fell through? At the bachelorette party?"

"Oh, right," Natalie said, trying to hide her relief.

He picked his laptop off the desk and flopped onto the bed just like he'd done hundreds of times in college, back when Natalie wouldn't have hesitated to flop down next to him. But that was a lifetime ago. Now they were fully fledged adults and Jonathan was less than thirty-six hours away from marrying Natalie's best friend.

But didn't that make things safer, in a way? There was no more ambiguity. No more what-ifs. Everyone had made their choices. There was nothing Natalie could do to change things. Perhaps there'd been a point years ago when she could've pulled a Hail Mary and gone for it, but now Natalie couldn't confess her feelings without looking like the most delusional sociopath on the planet.

Jonathan opened his laptop. "So I have a draft of my vows, but I want to make sure they aren't too cheesy. You know how much Marigold hates that stuff."

"Definitely," Natalie said, still standing. "Do you want to email it to me?"

"Sure . . . or you could just read it on my computer? I promise

I've showered since I was last in the hospital. Although I guess you know that already. Hey, is that why you walked in on me? Did you need firsthand proof that I'd washed off the hospital germs before you got too close?"

Twin waves of embarrassment crashed over her—the reminder of yesterday's mortifying mishap and the reference to her notorious germophobia. Back when Jonathan was in med school, he'd sometimes swing by her apartment after work, and even Natalie's all-consuming crush hadn't been enough to allow him to sit on her couch in his scrubs.

She rolled her eyes and sat on the bed next to Jonathan. "I only freaked out when there was that outbreak of antibiotic-resistant bacteria, which even you have to admit isn't unreasonable."

"And the so-called Ebola outbreak?"

"There were cases in New York!"

"Not at my hospital!"

"You don't know that. They could've had asymptomatic Ebola."

"That's not a thing."

"You know, I think Liesl might be onto something. You *are* one of those know-it-all doctors."

"If I were, would I be asking you for help?"

"Touche." She purposely mispronounced the word it so it rhymed with *douche*, a family joke of Natalie's that Jonathan had adopted.

She took the laptop from him and steeled herself for the inevitable stabs of pain. She'd accepted that Jonathan was marrying her best friend, that he'd chosen Marigold over her. But she wasn't super keen to read Jonathan's justification for *why*. Not that it was all that difficult to understand: Marigold was model-pretty, funny, and supremely sweet to boot. She had her clueless, callous moments—as did most beautiful, rich people who led charmed lives—but at her core, Marigold was kind and caring. Natalie didn't begrudge Jonathan for his choice, but she didn't have a burning desire to see it all through his eyes.

Yet to her surprise, Jonathan's vows were a tad generic. He praised the same qualities everyone saw in Marigold; it was a speech that could've been written by anyone close to her. Or even just someone who knew and liked her.

Don't read into this, Natalie told herself. *He's not a professional writer.* Except that Natalie had worked with students long enough to know the difference between style and content. She'd tutored gifted writers whose elegant prose revealed nothing, and kids with no grasp of grammar, diction, or rhythm but whose clunky sentences still communicated intelligence or humor or passion.

"Is it okay?" He sounded nervous. "Don't hold back. I want your notes."

"It's . . . lovely. I just wonder if there might be room to make it a bit more . . . specific to you and Marigold."

"Oh." Jonathan frowned. "Yeah, no, I can see that."

"Maybe something about when you knew she was the one?" Natalie asked, unsure whether this was the impulse of a skilled editor or just a masochist.

Jonathan's face lit up. "Oh, that's easy. She gave me the most incredible card for my birthday. We'd been dating for a few months, and I was pretty smitten, but then she gave me this card—*twenty-nine reasons why I love Jonathan*—for my twenty-ninth birthday. It was thoughtful and creative, it made me a little teary. I have a photo of it." Jonathan reached for his phone and began to scroll. "Listen to this: number seventeen, 'I love how you scoop ants out of the shower before you turn on the water.' Or number twenty, 'I love how your forehead wrinkles when you cut vegetables.'" He ran his hand through his dark curls, embarrassed. "I know it's stupid, but I was like: this woman gets me. That's when I knew I was all in."

Natalie stared at him, a frozen smile on her face as she tried to process what she'd just heard. Surely Jonathan was oversimplifying things for the sake of his vows. That *couldn't* have been the moment everything changed between him and Marigold. That's not how things worked in real life. You didn't decide to propose just because someone gave you a nice birthday card! But as she watched Jonathan smile at his phone, reading it for the umpteenth time, Natalie couldn't ignore the coil of regret that had been tightening inside her for the past four years.

Jonathan was about to marry the wrong woman, and it was all her fault. A woman she'd practically thrown into his arms because Natalie had been too cowardly to confess her real feelings.

Jonathan glanced up from his phone and frowned again. "You okay, Bumpy? You look a little pale."

"I'm fine." Natalie jumped off the bed lest he place a hand on her forehead to feel for fever. She felt so hollow and fragile, she was sure she'd shatter under his touch and lose any semblance of self-control.

"So what do you think? Do I mention the card in my vows? Because it's true—that's the night I realized: I could spend the rest of my life with this woman."

"I don't know," Natalie said weakly. "It might not work for the vows. Maybe add some humor? Some promises, not minding that she always falls asleep during movies?"

"Are you sure you're okay?" Jonathan placed the laptop on the bed and rose to his feet. "Do you need some water?"

I need a time machine, Natalie thought. Marigold hadn't done anything wrong. Natalie was the one who'd screwed up time and again. She could've made a move anytime during the first ten years of their friendship, but she'd let her insecurities get in the way. Jonathan loved Marigold. And only a truly terrible person would try to sabotage what they had. The day before the wedding. When the bride's mother was fighting cancer.

"I need to go. Lots to do before the rehearsal dinner tonight. Good luck with the vows. I know they'll be great," she said, then hurried out of the room before he could respond.

It was their five-year college reunion, and Natalie had stayed for the annual campus dance—a party for students and their families, alums, and faculty outside on the main quad. Between the fairy lights glowing in the trees, the jazz band, and the surprising number of older alumni in tuxes, Natalie felt like she'd been transported back to the 1920s. It would've been supremely romantic, except for the fact that she was the only one of her friends who was currently single or hadn't found someone to hook up with that weekend.

"Why don't you ask Jonathan to be your date?" her old roommate Chloe had asked when they'd arrived on campus a few days earlier. "Didn't he just break up with that girl from med school?"

"That's exactly why I *can't* ask him out. It's too soon and it'll make me look aggressive and desperate, like I was just waiting for the right moment to pounce."

Chloe had sighed heavily, looking pained. "You always have

some excuse. He either has a girlfriend, or just broke up with a girlfriend, or seems too stressed about exams. Why can't you admit that you're just too afraid of rejection?"

"Because it's the most painful, humiliating outcome I can imagine? And why are you acting like it's entirely in my control? He's had more than half a decade to ask me out. He's clearly not interested."

"That's because you give off *stay away from me* vibes. No, don't shake your head, I've seen it! Anytime things get mildly flirty, you make up some excuse to leave. Or you ask about some girl you assume he has a crush on. The man's not psychic, Natalie. He can't read your mind."

"I'm not his type *at all.* You've seen the girls he's dated. Remember Kelsey? The freaking pageant queen who got a full scholarship to Harvard Med School?"

"Give me a break. She was Ms. Teen Delaware. That's the second-smallest state in the country. How stiff could the competition have been? I know you think Jonathan's some kind of god, but I promise you: he's just a nerdy guy with good hair. Don't give me any of this 'out of your league' shit."

They hadn't spoken about it again, and Natalie had gone to the dance solo, resigned to being a third wheel with Chloe and her girlfriend, Luna. But once she'd arrived, she struggled to find them in the crowd. Feeling supremely awkward, she snuck around the back of Wilson Hall and sat on a bench while she decided between toughing it out and heading back to the dorm. It'd gotten a bit chilly. Even after many New England winters, she still shivered whenever the temperature fell below seventy.

"Hey, Bumpy," a voice called from the shadows. She looked

up to see Jonathan standing in front of her, more handsome than ever in his gray suit. "What are you doing back here?"

Natalie racked her brain for an explanation that wouldn't make her seem pathetic. "Just soaking it all in. It's nice to be back, isn't it?" She'd underestimated how hard it'd be to settle back into life in the Cleveland suburbs after four years amid ivy-covered clock towers, coffee shops and bookstores tucked into decommissioned eighteenth-century churches, and apartments with working fireplaces. Every time she pulled into a strip mall, attended a high school friend's baby shower in a newly built tract home with wall-to-wall carpeting, or dropped by a coworker's birthday party at the Cheesecake Factory, a little piece of her soul died. She was ashamed of her newfound snobbery, but she knew she just didn't belong there anymore.

"Sure is. Okay if I join you?"

She'd been about to protest and say something like, *I'm fine! You should go have fun!*, but then remembered what Chloe had told her. So instead, she'd said, "Of course."

Jonathan settled down next to her. "Remind me, when do you leave for Scotland?"

Against all odds, Natalie had somehow won an obscure but well-funded scholarship to do an MFA at the University of Edinburgh. It covered tuition, housing, and even included a travel stipend. Natalie hadn't been able to afford to study abroad junior year—she'd never been out of the country at that point—and was more excited than she'd ever been in her life.

"Not until September. Their academic year starts late."

"I'm jealous. My orientation begins in July."

"Are you *really* going to complain about that? After getting into your top-ranked residency?"

"This is why you need to move to New York. Who else is going to call me on my bullshit?"

"In a city of eight million people? I'm sure you'll find *someone*." A breeze swept through the back quad, rustling the dark leaves as Natalie shivered. Without saying a word, Jonathan slipped off his jacket and draped it over her shoulders. "Thank you."

"You should go to grad school in Hawaii; you're always so cold." Jonathan wrapped his arm around her, and every nerve ending in Natalie's body crackled to life. It wasn't the first time he'd done this—he was naturally physically affectionate—but his arm was lower this time, snug around her waist.

"Wait, isn't Hawaii next to Alaska?" she asked with feigned confusion. First semester of freshman year, Jonathan had told her about a girl from high school who'd been befuddled by the map in their classroom.

"It's been tough hanging out with people who don't get any of my inside jokes." He sighed and pulled her slightly closer to him. "I wish you were moving to New York."

She stiffened and braced for the inevitable joke that would undercut the statement, but Jonathan was uncharacteristically still and silent. "That would be fun," she said, careful not to meet his eye.

"It'd be the best."

The moment passed, and a few minutes later, they drifted apart—Jonathan to find his friends, Natalie to finish packing for her early flight. But Jonathan's words echoed through her head for the rest of the night. For the rest of the week. For the rest of the summer.

In July, she emailed the University of Edinburgh admissions

office, explaining that due to "unforeseen circumstances" she'd have to decline the scholarship and withdraw from the MFA program.

Two weeks after that, she was sleeping on her family friend's couch in New York as she desperately hunted for a job. She didn't tell Jonathan right away. She needed a watertight explanation, something he wouldn't see through. Because if he had even the smallest inkling that she'd given up Scotland to follow him to New York, it'd be all over.

But then she'd gotten the tutoring job, and a few days later, she worked up the courage to send him an email. She told him how she'd decided that her heart was in publishing and so she'd deferred her acceptance to Edinburgh (a lie) in order to pursue her dream job (another lie—an editorial assistant gig was still out of the question, given the sixty thousand dollars she still owed in college loans, but Horatio Street Press had agreed to let her read submissions for them on weekends).

Jonathan had been surprised but thrilled, and for a while, they'd met up for dinner or drinks once a week. She'd even spent the holidays with him and his family in Philadelphia when she hadn't been able to fly home for Christmas. Natalie felt a bit icky about misleading Jonathan, letting him believe that she only tutored on the side, that her publishing job was full-time, but it felt minor in the grand scheme of things.

They were closer than ever, and Natalie was convinced it was just a matter of time before he finally made a real move. But then one night, about a year after moving to New York, she'd gotten too drunk at dinner and slipped up, using the word *reader* for the first time to describe her role at Horatio Street Press.

"Wait, what?" Jonathan's brow furrowed. "I thought you were an editorial assistant. Isn't that why you deferred grad school? Because you landed a full-time job?"

Fear coursed through her, and instead of calmly telling Jonathan he'd misunderstood, she began to babble, just like she always did when she was terrified. She had to cover her tracks. She couldn't let him think for one millisecond that she'd made it all up to move to New York for him.

"Yeah, no, that's what I thought, but it turns out they didn't have a budget for an editorial assistant, so they hired me as a part-time reader instead. I should've told you, but I was too embarrassed. And then I guess I forgot. When I get embarrassed, I forget things. Does that ever happen to you? Maybe it's a medical condition? Let me know when you get to that unit!" She forced a laugh, but Jonathan didn't smile in return. The expression on his face was unreadable. Natalie's panic surged into an even higher gear. She had to throw him off the scent somehow. "Speaking of things I forgot to mention, did I tell you about my neighbor Marigold? I think you'd *really* like her. Maybe she can meet us for a drink later?"

And that was that. Marigold happened to be free and met them at a bar in the West Village. Jonathan got her number that night, and they started dating shortly after. And when Marigold couldn't figure out what to do for Jonathan's birthday, Natalie had offered to help her write a sweet card, listing all the things she loved about him. Then when Marigold struggled to come up with more than a few, Natalie had been happy to nudge her in the right direction, supplying a few examples. Twenty-nine of them, to be exact.

After all, that's what friends were for.

CHAPTER NINE

Olivia

"That was quick," Zack said as Olivia stepped back into the boat with a sigh. They'd beaten the ferry to the marina, but Marigold hadn't been on it. According to Albert in the ticket office, Marigold had arrived forty-five minutes earlier in a private boat and then gotten into a taxi. She was gone. "So what now?"

"Just . . . hold on." Olivia tried calling Marigold for the umpteenth time.

"Everything okay?"

"Just give me a second!" Olivia snapped. "I . . . I need to get in touch with a client before we lose reception on the water."

"You didn't take off for your own sister's wedding?" he asked incredulously.

"Of course I did. I'm here, aren't I? But that doesn't mean I can just check out. Not all of us get summers off."

"And not all of us have been tricked into believing moving

money from one corporation's account to another is a matter of life and death."

"Do you have *any* original ideas?" Olivia asked as she opened Find My Friends and searched in vain for Marigold. "I feel like I'm arguing with ChatGPT."

"Not really," Zack said affably. "But I'm excellent at putting a new spin on old arguments. At least, that's what my editor tells me. Now do yourself a favor and tell your boss you're going to be unavailable for the rest of the weekend."

"Do you have any idea how patronizing you sound? You barely know me. And you literally know nothing about my job."

He had the decency to look somewhat abashed. "Okay, fair point. You're right—I don't know you that well. But I do know you're super smart and it seems like a waste for you to spend your life at the mercy of greedy corporate clients who won't even let you take the weekend off for your sister's wedding. But I get it—there's comfort in feeling needed, in the status that comes from working at that kind of firm."

"I'm not sure taking one psych class at Vassar qualifies you to analyze me. If you need people to fawn over your 'intelligence,' stick with your college students, okay? They're too young to know that you're full of shit."

For the first time, it seemed like her words managed to pierce his armor of smug self-satisfaction.

Olivia looked away, trying to ignore the twinge of guilt. Then she turned the key, shifted into gear, and sped away from the dock. The sky had turned a threatening gray, and she was eager to get back before the rain started. The water was already choppy, and the boat pitched back and forth in the swell. As the mainland faded behind them, Olivia tried to stay calm and focus on her next steps. She needed to find a way to reach Marigold, to assure her that whatever she was feeling was normal, but that running away wasn't the answer.

"Oh, hey—look at that!" Zack's voice jolted Olivia from her thoughts. She followed his gaze and saw a number of dark shadows in the water, about thirty yards ahead. A moment later, the top of an enormous humpback whale broke through the surface. A second followed shortly after, then a third and a fourth.

"Oh, wow!" Zack said, leaning over for a better look. "That's incredible."

"For the love of god," Olivia grumbled, and yanked the wheel to the side, throwing Zack off-balance.

"What are you doing?"

"We have to go around. It's illegal to get too close."

"Just wait a second. This is amazing. I've never seen whales in the wild before."

"I'll buy you a ticket to a whale-watching tour later. I don't have time for this right now."

"Oh, come on, nothing's better than the healing power of nature!" As if on cue, one of the whales breached, spraying them with water as its magnificent body flew through the air with the grace of a dancer and the power of a missile.

Thanks for that, buddy.

Before she could stop him, Zack turned off the engine and removed the key. The engine sputtered and they jerked to a stop. "Give that back," Olivia snapped, reaching for the key, but he held it over his head, out of reach.

"Just look at the whales for sixty seconds. Then you can have it back. It'll be good for you. Take a few deep breaths and—"

"Give me the fucking key!" She jumped and managed to

knock it out of Zack's hand, watching in horror as it bounced off the side of the boat and into the water. "Shit!" she screamed.

Zack leaned over and frantically pawed at the water. "I'm sorry, I'm sorry," he said, then sat up and gave her a sheepish smile. "I guess even the backup keys should have the floaty thing, huh?"

"So this is all a joke to you?" Olivia tried to temper her fury. She wanted nothing more than to shove Zack over the side of the boat, but even half-mad with rage, she knew that a manslaughter charge would lead to more trouble than Zack was worth. Still, she was well and truly fucked.

"Oh, come on. This is going to be an epic story. It's, like, *biblical*."

"Okay, Jonah. While I'm delighted that you'll be able to update the 'two truths and a lie' section of your Hinge profile, this is actually kind of a disaster for me."

"It'll be okay, I promise. You'll reach your client. Just relax."

That was it. There was no holding back now. Those were the two most loathsome words in the English language. Her whole body pulsed with anger as she thought about every patronizing douchebag who'd ever told her to *just relax*—the boys she'd yelled at for mocking a janitor's accent in high school, the college dean who'd refused to correct a huge error on her transcript two days before law school applications were due, the third-year associates at her firm laughing over leaked nude photos of their client. She'd spent her whole life being told that she was "too intense," that she "couldn't take a joke." She wasn't going to let this condescending pseudo-intellectual nobody tell her to *relax*.

Olivia opened her mouth to unleash the tirade of insults sharpening on her tongue, but to her surprise, she began to cry instead. *Stop it*, she told herself. She was Olivia Harding. She didn't *cry*. Let alone in front of other people. She took a breath to steady herself, but when she exhaled, it released a sob instead.

"Oh god, I'm sorry," Zack said, face falling. "You're right. I don't have any idea what I'm talking about. I can tell you're under a lot of stress with the wedding and work and I shouldn't have been so dismissive."

"I'm not crying about the work."

"Okay—whatever. It's none of my business. I'm sorry."

"It's Marigold," Olivia said, unable to hold it in any longer. "I don't think she went to New York for her birth certificate. You don't even *need* your birth certificate to get a marriage license in Maine."

Zack's eyes widened, but he didn't say anything.

"I think she might be freaked out," Olivia continued. "And when she's freaked out, she runs. Always has. That's why I need to find her—I need to talk some sense into her before she does something she'll regret forever. I can't believe I'm telling you all this. You have to *swear* not to tell anyone, especially not Jonathan. I know that's breaking bro code, but . . ."

"I won't," Zack said gently. "But is this really your responsibility?"

Marigold's always *been my responsibility*, Olivia wanted to say. It was hard for people to understand, given the privilege Olivia and Marigold had now. They had no idea what their lives were like before Lulu married Bill, when an eight-year-old Olivia had taken care of a five-year-old Marigold because their mom worked nights. And then even after that—even when Olivia was no longer in charge of making dinner or scaring off the mice that pranced around their apartment every evening—she'd still been the responsible one, the straight-A student, the rule follower who covered for Marigold when she failed a test, scratched the car, or got busted for using a fake ID.

"What I'm saying is, can you really stop her?" Zack continued.

"No, I mean, I'm not going to drag her to the altar. But she can't just *vanish* like this. It'll kill our parents." Olivia knew how much this wedding meant to Lulu. Not just the party, but the peace she got from knowing that Marigold was settled, safe. It'd be so different if Olivia were the one getting married. If her own love life hadn't been such a disaster, if her younger sister hadn't gotten engaged first, all the pieces would've fallen into place so perfectly. This weekend would've given Lulu the kind of peace she was looking for, that she deserved.

The tears returned, and Olivia searched her pockets in vain for a tissue. Zack reached into his shirt pocket and produced a white handkerchief with blue stitching. "Here, take this."

Olivia examined it. "It has your initials on it," she said between sniffles. "I don't want to get snot all over it."

"Isn't that part of the appeal?"

She half laughed, half sobbed, then blew her nose. "Who carries monogrammed handkerchiefs?"

"It's goofy, I know. But my grandma makes them for me, and I feel guilty when I let them pile up at home. And they're better for the environment than tissues."

"Too bad the whale didn't know that. He would've dived down and fetched the key for us."

"I know, right?" Zack leaned over the side of the boat and cleared his throat. "PLEASE HELP US, MR. WHALE. I'M A VEGETARIAN AND I VOTE FOR THE GREEN PARTY."

He sat up and turned back to Olivia. "That should do it. Just give him a second."

Despite herself, Olivia smiled. "Don't hold your breath. He's probably pissed you threw away your vote." She pulled her phone out and sighed. "No service. You?"

"I left my phone at the hotel."

"Of course you did." She opened the storage container under the back seats, pulled out an oar, perched on the stern, and began to paddle—a few strokes on the port side, a few on the starboard, repeat.

"Need any help?" Zack asked.

"Nope."

"So where are we heading?"

"Land."

Zack bit his lip. "Okay, I really don't want to accidentally mansplain here . . . but aren't we going the wrong way?"

"We're too far from the mainland, and the current is pushing us away from Sandpiper Island. There's a smaller island over there. There are a few cottages on it—we'll find someone with a landline."

"Got it," Zack said, sounding impressed. "I didn't realize I was out here with Captain Nemo."

For a second, Olivia allowed herself to imagine what it would've been like to have Andrew on this expedition with her. Would he have been similarly impressed by her nautical skills? Would it have made him look at Olivia in a new light? Then again, none of this would've happened had Andrew been with her—he would've never dropped the key in the water. Or if he had, he would've dived in after it. According to Instagram, he'd spent two weeks last year at an intensive free-diving workshop in Morocco.

They fell silent for a few minutes as Olivia found her paddling rhythm. The current was more or less pushing them in the right direction, so she kept the paddle mostly on the port side. The air grew misty as the sky darkened, and even the effort of rowing wasn't enough to stave off the chill. In the distance, thunder rumbled ominously.

"I'm sorry," Zack said again, even more contrite than before. "I fully acknowledge that this is mostly my fault."

"'Mostly'?"

"Eighty percent, at least."

"Any reasonable person would know that dangling a key over the water could lead to said key being lost. The outcome was foreseeable."

"Great, I forgot that Captain Nemo also went to law school."

"You didn't forget. You bring up my 'soul-sucking' job every five minutes."

"I'm sorry, I was being a dick. I just have a thing about smart, driven people devoting so much time and energy to making rich people richer. You're a badass—think about what a force you'd be as a public defender or working for the ACLU."

"And I just *have a thing* about lecturing people you barely know. Do you realize how naïve and shortsighted you sound? Sure, I could be a public defender with two hundred cases at once, rolling up in court without any time to review the evidence, let alone craft a strategic plan, and eat instant ramen for dinner every night just in case I can't get my loans forgiven. Or I could work for a big firm, do tons of pro bono work, and make significant donations to causes I care about . . . which, for your information, includes the ACLU. Now sit down. We're almost there."

Zack did as he was told, looking slightly chastened. "How can you tell?" The fog had grown so dense, they couldn't see more than a few yards ahead of them.

"I can feel the bottom when I paddle. The water's getting shallow. We'll probably hit ground in about—" The boat lurched to the side as a scraping sound filled the air. "Oh, shit."

"What just happened?"

"We hit a rock. It's not safe to paddle any closer. We'll have to tow in."

"Tow in? With what?"

In answer, Olivia unlaced her sneakers, loosened the rope attached to the side of the boat, and slid down into the water. It was only about waist-high at this point, but cold enough to make her grimace.

"Hold on," Zack called. "This doesn't seem safe. Can't we just stay in the boat and call for help? If we're this close to the shore, won't someone hear us?"

Olivia took a few careful steps, tugging the boat behind her. "There are only a few houses on the island, and they're all on the other side. No one will hear us."

"No one can hear you scream," Zack muttered. "Cool, cool."

Olivia kept one arm stretched out in front of her, feeling for rocks, and managed to keep walking until the pebbly mud beneath her feet turned to damp sand. Up ahead, she could just see a narrow beach obscured by wisps of fog. They were almost there. Eager to get out of the water, she sped up, then yelped as a jolt of pain shot up through her foot.

"Are you okay?" Zack shouted. "What happened?"

"Nothing, I'm fine. I just stepped on something sharp."

"Get back into the boat. I'll tug us in."

"I said I'm *fine.*" Olivia took another step forward and winced. She looked down to see blood swirling in the murky shallows. "Okay, maybe I'm not."

Zack slid into the water and waded toward her. Then, without a word, he placed his hands on her waist and hoisted her onto the side of the boat. "Let's take a look," he said, splashing her injured foot to clear away the mud. "Oh boy . . ."

Olivia crossed her leg and placed her foot in her lap, smearing blood on her shorts. The cut wasn't wide, but it looked weirdly deep, and the amount of blood pouring out made her head spin.

"Don't worry," Zack said. "You're going to be fine. Is there a first aid kit?"

"In the cabinet under the bench."

Zack pulled out the white metal box, fished around for antiseptic and bandages, then came to help Olivia hop onto one of the seats. "Keep your foot elevated up here," he said, rapping on the side of the boat. "I'm just going to clean the cut and then we'll get it wrapped up."

"I can do it," Olivia said wearily.

"I have a better angle. Just relax; it's all under control."

Olivia watched as Zack expertly disinfected the cut—holding her ankle gently but firmly as she involuntarily jerked away from the sting—then wrapped it in a water-resistant bandage. "Not your first rodeo, huh?"

"I spent many summers as a camp counselor. You become an expert very quickly. Kids are walking medical emergencies." He snapped the kit closed and placed it on the seat next to her. "Do you want to rest here a bit and I can go to shore to find help?"

Olivia shook her head. "We can't leave the boat here. There's nothing to use as a mooring—it'll drift away."

"Okay, no prob." He turned in the direction of the beach. "It's not that far. I can carry you."

"Absolutely not."

"Are you doubting my strength?"

Olivia looked him up and down. She'd initially objected because it felt awkward and overly dramatic. But now that he'd mentioned it, yes, it seemed unlikely that a skinny guy about his height would be able to carry her easily. "The bandage is waterproof. I'll be fine."

"Water *resistant*. It's not a good idea to mess with it before the bleeding stops."

"Thanks for the TED Talk." She winced slightly at her tone. "Okay, fine. Carry me to the shore."

Zack helped her hop back to the side of the boat, where she perched while he lowered himself back into the water. Then he wrapped one arm under her legs, placed the other behind her shoulders, and lifted her up with surprising ease. "I'll come back for the boat," he said as he trudged through the water. They reached the sand, and he lowered her carefully to the ground before running back into the water to tug the boat up onto the sand as well.

"Thank you," Olivia said, examining her dry, injured foot.

"No problem. So now what?"

"Well, my phone still doesn't have any reception, so I guess we have to head to the other side of the island."

"You wait here. I'll go."

"I'm not sure that'll work. There are only a few houses, and they're kind of hidden in the woods. You'll never find them when it's this foggy."

"Then I guess you're getting another ride on the Zack Express."

"Absolutely not. We'll just find a stick for me to use as a crutch. I'll be fine."

With a sigh, Zack jogged over to the pile of mangled, wet wood and returned with a tall, jagged slab. Olivia took it gingerly from him and immediately felt at least three splinters pierce her skin.

"It's fine," she said, throwing it onto the sand. She hooked her arm through Zack's and began to half limp, half hop down the beach. "See? No problem."

He raised his eyebrows but said nothing.

That's when the first raindrops began to fall.

They hopped along in silence, thunder rolling in the distance. Olivia's hip was starting to ache from the awkward movement, but she gritted her teeth and kept moving. There was no other option here, at least not one she would entertain.

"There should be a little footpath up ahead on the right. Turn there."

A moment later, Zack veered to the right and began to trudge up a steep slope. She could feel him breathing heavily, but he never seemed to falter. "I think I can see a house," he panted. "Do you know the people who live here?" he asked, pointing at the gray-shingled cottage nestled among the trees.

"Kind of. The family's called the Varicks. I think they're distant cousins of Bill's." She took Zack's arm and resumed her hopping, bolstered by the knowledge that this would soon be all over. The rain was coming down hard, and the temperature seemed to have dropped fifteen degrees within minutes. She didn't care about asking near-strangers for a favor at this point; all that mattered was finding somewhere dry and warm to rest.

"Wait here. You don't need to bother with those stairs yet."

Zack bounded up the wooden steps that led to the front door and rapped a few times. He waited, then knocked again, and Olivia felt her heart sink. "It doesn't seem like anyone's home. Should we find somewhere to take shelter and wait for them to come back?"

"They're not coming back," Olivia said weakly. She felt like she might cry again. It'd be some kind of record for her.

"How do you know?"

"There's no generator running. It's too quiet." She hadn't noticed it at first with all the rain and wind, but now she was certain.

"What are you talking about?"

"There's no electricity on this island. It's all run on generators. They buzz all summer—at least, once people open their houses, which the Varicks clearly haven't."

"So what now?" Zack asked, sounding truly weary for the first time.

"I'd say we're stuck here."

CHAPTER TEN

Marigold

"I can't believe you're here," Hugo said, still staring agape from the doorway of his cottage. "I didn't think I'd ever see you again."

"Neither did I. But it turns out we're still married." The words flew out before Marigold could stop them. So much for easing into this conversation.

"What are you talking about?"

"Our divorce was never finalized," she said, heat rising to her cheeks. "I forgot to return the signed documents."

He stared at her, waiting for her to continue, then said, "And you came up here because . . ."

"Because I'm getting married and need to sort out the paperwork again."

"You're getting married," he repeated, sounding slightly dazed. "When?"

"Tomorrow."

"Tomorrow?"

"My lawyer said we have to sign the new set of divorce papers he emailed me and have them notarized so I can get my marriage license in time for my wedding tomorrow. I just flew from Maine."

"Oh, wow . . ." Hugo leaned against the doorframe and sighed. "Are you serious?"

"Yeah, I'm sorry. I know it's really shitty for me to show up like this. I did try calling, though. I wasn't trying to blindside you."

"I didn't have any missed calls from you."

"I called! Multiple times! I swear!" Marigold opened her call log. "Look!"

Hugo peered at her screen, then pulled out his own phone. "Oh . . . I thought that was a spam call."

"You erased my number?"

Hugo straightened up and looked her in the eye. "Yep, about six months after you ghosted. After you ignored every call and every text."

"I'm sorry, I—*oof!*" Something large and gray barreled into her, nearly knocking her over as it licked her face, whimpering with excitement. "Hi there . . . Hi . . ." Marigold said, scratching the enormous dog's side as she tried to regain her balance.

"I guess he remembers you," Hugo said in a voice she couldn't quite read.

"Humphrey?!" she exclaimed. The sound of his name sent the dog into a frenzy as he tried to lick her cheek, wag his long tail, and roll on the ground all at the same time, his ecstasies too great to be expressed through one movement alone. "Hi, buddy!" Marigold crouched down to scratch the dog's proffered belly. "So good to see you, boy. Aren't you the best boy? Aren't you, Humphrey?"

"I don't think he expected to see you again either."

Marigold winced as she rose to her feet. "I know . . . I handled that badly. It just seemed best to make a clean break, you know? Once I realized what a mistake we'd made."

Something flashed in Hugo's eyes before his face went blank. He opened the door wider and nudged Humphrey back into the house. "Okay, come in and we'll figure this out."

Marigold followed him inside, eyes widening as she took in the scene. The mess and clutter were all gone—everything was homey and pristine, from the folded blanket draped over the couch to the tidy bookshelves to the fresh flowers on the dining table. "Whoa . . . Did you get a housekeeper?"

"A housekeeper?" Hugo snorted. "That's not really how she goes around here."

Marigold fell silent as she looked around the room, struck by the uncanny strangeness of it all. Returning to a place she'd been certain she'd never see again. A place that'd once felt like home. "Have a seat," he said, then shook his head slightly as if struck by the strangeness of treating her like a guest.

"Thanks." Marigold sat on the couch—the same saggy floral one she remembered, except the cushions had been washed and she no longer had to wedge herself in between the piles of laundry that had seemed to be a permanent fixture of the room. Humphrey sprang up next to her, still wriggling and whimpering with excitement. He was too big to fit onto her lap, so he contented himself with placing his enormous paws on her thighs while his tail thumped madly.

"Hi, buddy. I missed you. Did you know that? Did you know how much I missed you?" She scratched his head and he began to lick her cheek. "Okay . . . okay," Marigold said, laughing. "I know, you missed me too. How ya doing, friend? Whatcha been up to?" She wished she spoke dog so Humphrey could tell her everything she'd missed, what had precipitated all these changes. The most obvious explanation was a girlfriend, or maybe even a wife. Surely Hugo wouldn't have bought flowers, let alone a vase. And who had cleaned the ship-in-a-bottle on the mantel? It'd been Marigold's favorite piece in the whole house, but it'd been almost too dusty to view properly during her brief tenure.

"So," Hugo said, still standing. "You're really getting married *tomorrow*?"

"That's the plan."

"Christ." He scratched his head. "Okay, I know the notary in town. He can print the forms for us and then witness us sign."

"Great. Then I'll send them to my lawyer, and we should be all set."

Hugo grabbed his keys off a peg by the door. "Ready?"

"Yeah . . . sure." Marigold stood, unsure whether she was relieved or disappointed to be leaving so soon.

She followed Hugo out to the truck and without thinking, she walked over to the driver-side door and was about to climb in when Hugo called out, "Both doors work now."

"Oh . . . gotcha." For some reason, Marigold felt herself blush as she went back around and hoisted herself into the passenger seat.

"Seat belt works too," she said. "You've been busy."

Hugo started the engine, which, thankfully, was still loud enough to preclude conversation. A zillion questions bounced on the tip of her tongue, none of which felt appropriate to ask ten minutes after arriving out of the blue, four years after walking out without a word. *Are you seeing someone? Are you happy? Did I ruin your life? Is your mom still mad at me? Are* you *still mad at me?*

They rumbled down the drive and bounced along the narrow, pitted dirt road that led past the harbor and into town. Marigold rolled down the window and took a deep breath, relishing the familiar mix of ocean and motor oil. For the first portion of the drive, they sat in silence. That was something that'd struck Marigold about Hugo right away: he was comfortable with quiet. He didn't need to vocalize every thought that flitted into his head, and he didn't expect her to do so either.

However, even Hugo wasn't comfortable with *this* kind of quiet, the awkward silence of reuniting with the person who'd once known your body and your secrets better than anyone in the world, but who now felt like a stranger.

"Why'd you wait so long to get the marriage license?" he asked finally. "Are you guys eloping or something?"

"No, there's a wedding. A big wedding, actually. And I guess I just got caught up in all the other details and forgot about the most important part."

"It's not just your responsibility, is it? What about your . . . fiancé?" Hugo stumbled over the word, as if saying it aloud for the first time. It wasn't impossible given that their own engagement had been about ninety minutes.

"I told him I'd take care of it. His work schedule is nuts—he's a doctor, a pediatric oncologist." Marigold thought she saw Hugo wince, but perhaps she just imagined it. She hadn't mentioned Jonathan's job to brag; she just wanted Hugo to know that a respected, contributing member of society wanted to marry her. That Marigold was more than the flighty, callous girl who'd treated him so badly.

"A pediatric oncologist, huh? Not sure I've ever met one of those."

"Yeah, it sounds fake. Like marine biologist." Marigold waited for Hugo to respond, then continued, "You know, something kids talk about but no one actually pursues."

"I know a few marine biologists." Hugo gestured out the window at the ocean. "Lots of them around . . . the ocean."

"Yeah, right, of course," Marigold said. "Listen, I'm really sorry for showing up out of the blue like this. I know it's—"

"It's fine," Hugo cut her off. "All in the past. Don't worry about it."

As they entered the town, Marigold marveled at how many memories came rushing back to her given how little time she'd spent there. They passed the seafood shack where the server had razzed Hugo for splitting a bottle of Chablis with Marigold instead of his usual beer. ("Want me to bring a beret for you?") They drove by the only store that sold clothing—mostly hunting and fishing gear—where Marigold had tried to cobble together a makeshift wardrobe after leaving her clothes behind on the yacht. She smiled as they passed the library/community center where they'd seen Hugo's twelve-year-old niece Maddie star in *Annie*. The show had been as terrible and adorable as Marigold had expected, but nothing could've prepared her for the tenderness she'd felt watching Hugo's eyes well up while Maddie sang "Maybe."

Hugo pulled up in front of the coffee shop. "I'm sorry your petition to change the name didn't work," he deadpanned.

Marigold groaned when she glanced up at the familiar sign that read Mocha-Latte-Tude. "It doesn't make any sense! Is it a pun on *attitude* or *latitude*? And what do either of them have to do with mochas?"

"I *know*," Hugo said with an exasperated smile. "You've made your displeasure clear."

"It's just such a branding fail."

"Yeah, well, when you're the only coffee shop in town, you have some leeway. Let's go."

"Um, can we get coffee *after* we go to the notary?" Marigold asked as she slid out of the truck and followed Hugo toward the café. "I don't want to be difficult, but we don't have a ton of time."

"This *is* the notary. The owner, Bob, runs a few businesses in town."

Inside, the café was just as cozy and low-key as Marigold remembered. There were two people on laptops and zero on Zoom calls; everyone else was reading or chatting. Hugo walked straight up to the counter, where a portly, gray-haired man was ringing up a customer with one hand while frothing milk with the other. "Hey, Bob," Hugo said.

Bob handed the customer her change, then held up his now-free hand. "Sorry, Hugo, no coffee for you until that ulcer clears up. And don't lie to me because Dr. Lee will be here in twelve minutes for her afternoon matcha latte."

"I actually need something notarized."

"Ah." Bob stood up a bit straighter, untied his apron, and called out to a young woman washing dishes at the sink. "Kyla, I need you up front for a bit." He stepped out from behind the counter and motioned for Hugo to follow him. When Marigold came up to join them, Bob's eyes widened. "Oh, it's you!"

Marigold smiled. "You remember me!"

"How could I forget? I'd never heard anyone ask for coconut milk before." Bob turned to Hugo. "Where did you end up finding it again?"

"I'm not sure." Hugo looked away.

"You went all the way to that health-food store on the mainland, didn't you?"

"I was going anyway," Hugh muttered.

"Sorry, what'd I miss?" Marigold asked.

"This young man drove almost a hundred miles round trip so we'd have coconut milk for you."

"Wait, what?" Marigold didn't remember Hugo taking a trip to the mainland during her stay on the island.

"Bob, do you mind printing the forms for us? Marigold will email them to you."

When they reached Bob's miniscule but tidy office on the second floor, he wrote an email address on a Post-it and handed it to Marigold. "Printer up here's out of ink, so I'll run downstairs for it."

As he left, Marigold forwarded the forms, then turned to Hugo. "What was he talking about? With the coconut milk?"

"It's stupid."

"Come on, tell me!"

"Fine." Hugo sighed. "When you left, I was sure you'd be back, that you'd just gotten freaked out and needed time to clear your head. And I wanted . . ." Hugo shook his head ruefully. "I wanted everything to be perfect for you when you returned, so you'd know you'd made the right decision. I kept the house clean . . . bought coconut milk for the café to have on hand . . . pretty mortifying to think about now."

"That was really sweet," Marigold said quietly.

"I think *naïve* would be a better word. Or maybe *deluded*."

They sat in silence until Bob returned with the papers, and for a man who'd had no qualms about shouting about Hugo's health concerns a few minutes earlier, he was surprisingly discreet when it came to passing them each a copy of the divorce forms. Perhaps Bob the notary was more professional than Bob the barista. He motioned for Hugo and Marigold to sit at the tiny table, asked to see both of their IDs, then handed each of them a pen and took a few respectful steps back.

As Marigold examined the signature line Bob had flagged with a sticky note, her hand felt suddenly heavy, as if she were holding a dumbbell instead of a pen. Her whirlwind engagement and marriage to Hugo had been the most exhilarating, romantic moment of her life. And now it was ending in the office of a coffee shop called Mocha-Latte-Tude. Of course, it'd been over for years—these papers were just a formality at this point. But was there a reason she'd never signed the original documents? Was it really just her usual flakiness? Wouldn't her therapist ask her to dig a bit deeper? And why did it feel so hard now?

Because you're saying goodbye to the old Marigold, the one who went on adventures and made terrible choices. Marrying Jonathan was the right decision—the adult decision. Signing these papers meant she was finally growing up.

When she looked up, Hugo had already handed his documents to Bob. Apparently, he hadn't hesitated before getting down to business. Marigold scribbled her signature and did the same.

Bob stamped the papers, scanned them, and then emailed copies to both Marigold and Hugo. Then Marigold forwarded the scans to her lawyers and the town clerk. It was done. They were officially divorced.

As they followed Bob downstairs to pay (he needed to ring them up in the café), Marigold thanked Hugo for all his help, then added, "I hate to ask one more favor, but can you drive me to the airport? Unless there's Uber on the island now?" Before Hugo could answer, her phone rang. It was her mother.

"Hi, Mom!" Marigold said with forced cheer. "Yep . . . I'm heading to the airport now. No, traffic's not too bad . . . No, don't order a helicopter, an Uber is fine . . . Okay, see you soon, love you."

"Traffic? Helicopter?" Hugo said incredulously. "Where does she think you are?"

"New York," Marigold said in a small voice.

"Christ, Mare," Hugo said, laughing for the first time since she'd arrived. "I guess some things never change."

Something in her chest twinged at the sound of her nickname. Only her family and Natalie called her Mare. Jonathan had tried for a bit, but it'd never sounded natural, and he'd quickly reverted to Marigold. ("Sorry," he'd said sheepishly. "I just keep imagining a horse when I say it. And *Marigold* is such a beautiful name.")

"I didn't want to freak anyone out! So do you mind driving me to the airport? I don't want to miss my flight." She'd called in a huge favor to take a private jet up here, but there was no way she could play that card again.

"Yeah, no problem," he said without hesitating.

"Do you . . . do you need to let anyone know that you'll be home late?"

"Humphrey doesn't have his own phone yet. Maybe when he turns seven."

Marigold blushed. "You know what I mean."

Hugo raised an eyebrow. "Do I?"

"Sorry, none of my business. I get that I can't just show up here out of the blue and demand to know everything about your life."

"Showing up out of the blue seems to be your MO. Come on, let's get going and get you married."

CHAPTER ELEVEN

Olivia

"Well, this is fairly inconvenient!" Zack shouted to make himself heard over the howling wind. But although he was standing right next to her, his voice sounded faint. If Olivia hadn't been so cold and exhausted, she might've howled with it. They were pressed up against the Varicks' front door, sheltering under the tiny overhang. "Should we try to find a way inside? Maybe there's a spare key hidden somewhere."

"What? No! I'm not breaking into a stranger's house. The rest of us still believe in private property."

"This isn't a political statement. This is an emergency. I'm sure they'll understand. Didn't you say you know them?"

"I've *met* them, I don't *know* them. And this absolutely does not constitute an emergency."

"You're injured and shivering, and if this storm gets any closer, we'll be in real danger of being struck by lightning. It might not be an emergency, but it certainly justifies poking around for a spare key. We're not going to climb into their beds like Goldilocks; we're going to use their landline and maybe borrow some towels to dry off. That's it. But sure, if this violates some Maine etiquette I'm too low-class to understand, I can go see if anyone else on the island is home."

Olivia started into the dense thicket of trees; there were no other houses in eyeshot, and for some reason, the thought of Zack disappearing into the woods made her feel even colder. "No, you're right." She sighed—those were not words she'd ever imagined herself saying to Zack. "Let's try to get inside. I'll leave them a note. And maybe send a bottle of wine later."

"Okay, great." Zack stooped down and lifted the doormat. "No key here. Do you see any pots? Or decorative garden gnomes?"

"Look, there's a keypad." Olivia pointed at the panel above the door handle.

"Ah, all right." Zack made a show of cracking his knuckles. "Let's see . . . would you call the Varicks creative, original people?"

Olivia thought about her brief interaction with the couple at Bill's birthday party a few years back. Mr. Varick had said he'd voted for Trump because it'd be nice to have a "businessman in the White House," and Mrs. Varick had gushed about a group tour they'd taken to Europe, and how convenient it was not to have to deal with those "surly Polish folks" who seem to run all the hotels these days. "No," Olivia said. "I would not."

"One-one-one-one it is," Zack said, pressing the keypad. It buzzed and flashed red.

"Maybe nine-nine-nine-nine?" Another buzz. "Okay, okay . . . let's think. Is that the Maine flag on that flagpole? What year was Maine founded?"

“How the hell am I supposed to know? I’m not a third-grade geography champ.”

“Hold on.” Zack closed his eyes. “Maine joined the union as part of the Missouri Compromise. So 1820.” He punched the numbers into the keypad. It buzzed and flashed red again. “Shit.”

“Try 1701,” Olivia said wearily.

Zack pressed 1-7-0-1. A light flashed green, and they heard the lock turn. “What? How’d you know that?!”

“Bill and Mr. Varick met at Yale, founded 1701.”

“Figures,” Zack said, then swung the door open. “After you, Goldilocks.”

They took off their sodden shoes, then fumbled around for light switches before Olivia reminded them that there wouldn’t be any power anyway. Luckily, sunset was still hours away, and even though the sky was thick with storm clouds, the large windows let in just enough light for them to begin their hunt for a landline. “You take the living room. I’ll check the kitchen,” Olivia said, leaving Zack to explore the wood-paneled room. One wall was decorated with old oars and paddles; on another, hunting trophies and plaques surrounded a forlorn-looking moose head. The house felt like a collaboration between L.L.Bean and Tim Burton, but in an organic, unplanned way—the natural evolution of a house used by generation after generation, one that Mrs. Varick couldn’t redecorate to suit her generic taste, as she shared it with her siblings and cousins.

It didn’t take Olivia long to locate the landline mounted on the wall of the kitchen. She picked it up eagerly, but there was no dial tone—only dead silence. She hung up and tried again. Still nothing. “Shit,” she muttered, and then limped back into the living room, where Zack was still scouring the surfaces for a phone. "The landline's dead. Probably because of the storm."

"Great." Zack sank onto a couch with a heavy sigh, then realized he was dripping water and stood back up again. "I don't suppose their internet works, does it? Want to see if you can connect to the Wi-Fi? I bet we can guess their password."

Olivia checked her phone—no bars, no available Wi-Fi networks. "Nothing." Gingerly, she lowered herself onto the hooked rug next to the fireplace.

"So what do you want to do now?" Zack asked, coming to sit next to her on the floor.

"I don't know," she said in a hollow voice she barely recognized as her own. She *always* had a plan. She was the person you could count on in any situation. Hell, two of her college friends still had Olivia listed as their emergency contacts even though they were both married! But her brain felt as heavy and waterlogged as the rest of her. It was all too much—Lulu's deteriorating health and the secret she was keeping from Marigold, the secret Marigold was clearly keeping from Olivia, the multiple humiliations she'd endured last night, and worst of all, the pain she'd have to inflict on Lulu by telling her that there might not be a wedding at all.

She shivered and pulled her knees up to her chest. "You need to dry off," Zack said, rising to his feet. "I'll find some towels."

Olivia opened her mouth to object, but let out a heavy sigh instead. What did it matter at this point? Her reputation was already ruined; she'd gone from being Marigold Harding's less pretty, less charming sister to the unhinged, drunk sister who'd ruined her welcome drinks. What did it matter if she added "towel thief" to the mix? She heard Zack rummaging around on the second floor, and a minute or two later, he bounded down the stairs, holding two towels above his head like an ecstatic soccer fan waving his country's flag. Olivia was pleasantly surprised—the task of locating a linen closet in a strange house would prove too challenging for most men. She'd once asked an ex-boyfriend to grab the purse she'd left on her bed, only for him to return empty-handed, claiming it wasn't there. (She checked. It was.)

Zack approached her with the towel, hesitated a moment, then draped it over her shoulders. "Thanks," she said. She pulled it around her more tightly and shivered again, suddenly freezing.

"I hate to be that guy, but do you, uh, want to get out of those wet clothes?" Zack asked.

Olivia snorted.

"I can find something for you to change into," he added quickly.

She shook her head. Borrowing towels was one thing. Wrapping her naked body in Mrs. Varick's bathrobe was quite another.

"Fine, but at least let me build a fire."

Olivia surveyed the fireplace, which still contained ashes from last summer's final use. "Not a good idea," she said. "Even my stepfather can't afford to pay for damages if we burn down their house." Zack raised his eyebrows. "Okay, fine, he can. But that's no reason to take that risk. It probably hasn't been used in a year, and the chimney probably needs to be cleaned. It's too much of a fire risk."

"Can you stop thinking like a lawyer for five minutes?" Zack bent over and transferred a few logs from a nearby basket into the hearth, then he stuck his head into the fireplace and craned his head to look up. "Flue's open. Should be fine." Without waiting for Olivia to respond, he took a few pieces of newspaper from a stack against the wall, crumpled them into balls, stuck them under the logs, then took a match from the mantel and lit it with practiced dexterity that alleviated some of her anxiety. She watched the paper catch fire then slowly spread to the bark above. A few minutes later, the logs were burning properly.

Olivia scooted closer to the fire, relishing the heat of the crackling flames. "Thank you," she said quietly, without looking at Zack, who was still standing, admiring his handiwork.

"Anytime." He started to lower himself back to the floor, then changed his mind and sat on the couch instead.

"Don't worry, I won't hold you hostage forever. As soon as the rain starts to let up, we can head to one of the other houses. We'll find someone with a phone eventually."

"You're not holding me hostage," Zack said with a smile. "We're having an adventure."

"Right. I'm sure you're thrilled to spend a chunk of your best friend's wedding weekend stranded on a random island instead of getting drunk with the other groomsmen."

"Have you met Jonathan's cousins? I'm good here. I've got everything I need." He pulled his waterlogged paperback out of his pocket.

Olivia rolled her eyes. "Give it a rest. There's no one for you to show off for here. You don't have to pretend to like Edith Wharton."

"But I do like Edith Wharton."

"Uh-huh, sure. You're definitely not carrying that around to impress the women you wanted to meet this weekend. Not that it matters. Marigold's friends might pose with books on Instagram, but they don't actually read them."

"For your information, I had a great conversation about books last night."

"Oh yeah? With who?"

"Your finance bro pal's girlfriend. Emerson? We talked about the new Zadie Smith in line for the raw bar."

"You mean she didn't want to discuss *Walden*?"

"That's Thoreau, not Emerson. And it's not exactly her fault her parents gave her a pretentious name, is it?"

"Are you kidding me? Her name's *Emily*. She changed it to Emerson when she started modeling."

"Are you sure?"

"Yup." Olivia had done a deep dive on Google last night, a binge that left her feeling worse than the four glasses of champagne she'd accidentally consumed. Despite her obnoxious name, Emerson was undeniably impressive: she'd recently argued at the Hague in support of new protections for women in war zones, and published an article in the *Atlantic* about the link between sex trafficking and the fashion world. "Did she . . . did she use the word *girlfriend*? I thought she was just his date." The question slipped out before she had a chance to stop herself, as if the rain had washed away her final shred of dignity.

Zack smirked. "Ohhhh . . . so *that's* why you seemed so angry last night," he continued. "And why you got so trashed."

"Thanks for the reminder," Olivia said dryly.

The amusement on Zack's face faded, and he slid down off the couch to join her on the floor. "Sorry," he said. "I know things are tough right now."

"Things aren't tough. I'm *fine*."

"I just meant . . . the stuff with your mom. It can't be easy."

Olivia braced for the inevitable follow-up: the meaningless *it's going to be okay* platitudes, or the clumsy attempts at empathy—*I know what you're going through. When my great-aunt had cancer . . .* or, worst of all, *When my dog got sick last year . . .* But to her relief, Zack didn't continue talking. He just placed another log on the fire, then sat back and waited for her speak.

"No, it's not," Olivia said finally.

"And then on top of that, the guy you liked showed up with another woman?"

"Yeah . . . we'd been flirting for a few weeks, and I thought we'd finally get together this weekend." She buried her head in her hands. "God, I sound like a teenager."

"You sound like a human. It's kind of refreshing, actually."

Her head snapped up. "It's refreshing to see me rejected for a supermodel who'll probably win a Nobel Peace Prize someday? Thanks so much."

"No, I mean it's refreshing to see you express real human emotion. You always seem so . . . buttoned up."

She shot him a withering look. "We've been in the same room, like, five times."

"I'm a keen observer of human behavior."

"Well, then you've surely noticed that there's plenty of emotion in my family already. Someone has to handle their shit."

"Isn't that what family's for, though? You take turns supporting one another."

"Did you read that on a mug in Target?"

"Would that fit on a mug? Probably better suited for one of those wooden boards." He took the poker and adjusted the logs, releasing a small shower of sparks. "For what it's worth, you're right—I think she's just his date."

"How do you know?"

Zack shrugged. "Just a vibe I got."

"Because you're such a *keen observer of human behavior*," she said, feeling suddenly lighter.

"You know, just because he brought a date, it doesn't mean he's not into you. That's not really how it works with most men. They just get distracted by whatever shiny thing's right in front of them at the moment."

"Please don't refer to women as *things*."

"Come on, you know what I mean. I'm sure he was looking forward to trying to bang you at the wedding, and then just got momentarily distracted. You just need to catch his attention again."

Olivia narrowed her eyes. "Every time I'm close to admitting that you might actually have a brain, you say something like 'bang you at the wedding.'"

"You know what you need?" Zack continued, ignoring her. "You've got to make him jealous. Is there anyone else you want to hook up with?"

"No."

"Then why don't *we* pretend to be a couple?"

"I'm sorry, what?"

"Once he realizes he missed his chance, he won't be able to stop thinking about you."

"That's the best you can come up with?"

"The male mind is simple and predictable. Trust me—seeing you with another man will make him regret putting you on the back burner."

"This is ridiculous. There's no way we could pull that off." But even as she dismissed the idea, a series of images took shape in her head: Andrew's face falling as he spotted Olivia and Zack canoodling. Lulu smiling and turning to whisper happily to Bill. The surprise of the guests, who'd probably spent most of last night thinking, *See,* this *is why she's still single*. "Why would you do that for me? You don't want to ruin your chances of actually hooking up with someone this weekend. Not after you've carried *The House of Mirth* all this way."

"Okay, first of all, I'm reading *The House of Mirth* because it's a powerful example of how capitalistic and misogynistic forces destroy female agency. And second, it's the least I can do after causing such a massive clusterfuck with the boat key." Was he actually blushing? "I'm really sorry about that."

Olivia let his words sink in. She couldn't remember the last time she'd heard a man sincerely apologize. Her male colleagues never admitted fault, something they seemed to equate with showing weakness. That made sense when you were facing down opposing council, but would it kill them to say *I'm sorry* when they gave bad info to a paralegal that resulted in days of lost work? None of her ex-boyfriends ever apologized for anything. Even Bill, the kindest man she knew, hated acknowledging a mistake. "Thank you. But it's okay. You definitely don't need to pretend we're in a relationship. It'd never work, anyway."

"Are you implying no one would believe you'd actually date *me*?" he asked with a smile. "Because I'll have you know, I tend to punch well above my weight. Forget about Emerson. I once dated a neurosurgeon-slash–bikini model named . . . Coleridge. She's also the president of Scotland. And she's going to be the next Bond girl."

Olivia laughed. "Scotland has a first minister, not a president."

"So what do you say? Should we give it a shot?"

A loud hum filled the room, sending Olivia scrambling to her feet.

"What's that noise?" Zack asked.

"Someone turned on the generator. I think that means—"

The front door opened and the lights came on, illuminating the shocked faces of Mr. and Mrs. Varick. They looked tired and bedraggled from their long journey to the island and were apparently arriving for the first time this summer. Mrs. Varick held a massive package of toilet paper, while Mr. Varick carried a case of wine. "Who the hell are you?" Mr. Varick bellowed.

His wife dropped the toilet paper and clutched her husband's arm. "Grab your gun, Gary."

"I'm so sorry!" Olivia held up her hands, unsure if it was a gesture of apology, or a plea not to shoot. "Mr. and Mrs. Varick, it's me, Olivia Harding. Bill and Lulu's daughter. I'm really sorry, it was awful of us to do this, but we had boat issues and couldn't make it back to Sandpiper. And then the storm came in and we didn't have any cell service, so we came looking for a landline, but the lines are down. It was an emergency, or else we *never* would've trespassed like this, I swear."

Mrs. Varick seemed to relax slightly. "Olivia . . . right." But Mr. Varick looked unconvinced. He was probably one of those gun owners who secretly fantasized about finding an intruder. He turned to Zack with narrow eyes, as if searching for *someone* it'd be acceptable to shoot.

"This is my friend Zack," Olivia continued. "We borrowed some towels and lit a fire to dry off. That's all we touched, I swear. I'll replace the towels and pay for any cleaning costs."

"Don't worry about it, hon," Mrs. Varick said, finally stepping over the threshold. "I'm glad you were able to get inside. That storm was awful." She paused. "How *did* you get inside?"

"The door was unlocked," Zack lied smoothly. "You might want to get it checked out."

"Goodness! We could've found something much worse than a few wet neighbors. Now, what do you want to do about your boat? The generator's running, so you can use the Wi-Fi to text someone."

Olivia checked her watch. Everyone would be gathering at the yacht club for the rehearsal on the far side of the island. It would take ages for anyone to get to the harbor, let alone motor over to this island. "I have to think. They're all at the club for the wedding rehearsal."

"Of course, that's right. This is the big wedding weekend. I'd completely forgotten!" Mrs. Varick said in a tone that suggested she hadn't forgotten at all. "It sounds like the quite the to-do. Of course, Gary and I completely understand why were weren't invited. We're such distant relations, after all. I explained that to all our friends. You know, the ones who assumed we'd be there and wanted to hear all the details. It's the wedding of the season, after all!" She glanced at her husband. "Normally, we'd be happy to run you over to Sandpiper, but we had such a long drive, and it's rather late."

"Right," Olivia said slowly, feeling her brain click over into corporate negotiator mode. "Yes, I know Marigold was *devastated* when she had to cut some family members from the list. She had no idea the capacity at the club was so small, and she feels awful about it. She particularly wanted you two to be there." Next to her, she heard Zack snort, but she ignored him and continued. "We've had some cancellations because of the weather.

Would you . . ." She paused. "Would you consider coming? You could take us back to Sandpiper and then stay over at the inn. Then you'll be there for all the activities tomorrow."

"Oh no, we wouldn't want to impose."

"Not at all! Marigold would be so happy and relieved. She feels awful." Olivia wasn't sure her sister remembered that the Varicks existed, but she'd deal with that later. Thankfully, there'd been a few last-minute cancellations, which freed up space at the inn.

"Well . . ." Mrs. Varick exchanged another look with her husband, who looked slightly less grumpy. Perhaps the status boost he'd get from attending the wedding outweighed the disappointment of not getting to stand his ground. "That *is* a lovely offer."

"Great!" Olivia said brightly. "So should we get going?"

CHAPTER TWELVE

Marigold

"Did your lawyer get back to you?" Hugo asked as he steered the truck away from town and headed toward the airport.

Marigold glanced down at the phone in her lap. "Um . . . I'm not sure. My phone's dead. Do you have a charger I can use quickly?"

"I don't have an iPhone charger. Android user, sorry."

"Typical."

"What's that supposed to mean?"

"I mean you have 'green texts' written all over you."

"I have no idea what that means."

"You sweet summer Canadian child." She knew he'd never get the reference. When she'd met Hugo, he hadn't had cable or fast enough internet to support streaming. And the few times they'd tried to watch a movie on his semifunctioning DVD player, he'd fallen asleep shortly after the opening credits. Working in the boatyard had left him bone-tired in a way she wasn't used to.

No one she knew worked the hours Hugo did except for Olivia, who Marigold barely saw during the week anyway. And even Jonathan's hours had become slightly more reasonable since he'd become an attending physician.

"I don't know what that means either." He glanced at the clock on the dashboard. "We have loads of time before your flight. Why don't we stop at the shipyard for a few minutes and you can charge your phone there?"

Since the harbor was so close to Hugo's house, they stopped to pick up a rapturous Humphrey, and then drove the short distance to the shipyard. There wasn't much activity at the moment; the sky had turned gray, and even from a distance, Marigold could tell the water was growing choppy. Hugo parked by the large building where boats were stored and repaired, and Marigold followed him inside.

"Oh, wow," Marigold said as she turned from side to side. Instead of the jumble of motorboats she remembered, about a half dozen sailboats in various stages of completion rested on wooden frames. A few were barely more than skeletons, but the one closest to them was nearly finished. She ran her hand along the gleaming wooden hull, marveling at the elegant lines. "My stepfather would kill for a boat like this. There aren't many wooden ones this size on the market."

"I know. That's why I started designing them."

Marigold whirled around to face Hugo. "*You* designed this boat?" She knew it'd always been a dream of Hugo's to design boats—he had dozens of notebooks full of sketches. But he'd always told Marigold it was an impossible field to break into and that he was better off sticking to repairs.

"This one . . . and those. All of them."

"Holy shit, Hugo. They're *beautiful.*"

"They're all right. The hardest part is saying goodbye. They take so long to build, you get attached."

"Are they all commissions?"

"Not anymore. Once business picked up, I decided I didn't want to design them for rich assholes. I make them the way I want, and then I wait for the right buyer."

"So how do they find you?

He looked away, almost as if he was embarrassed. "I guess you could say I took a page out of your book."

Marigold waited a beat to see if he'd say more. "Yeah, sorry, I have no idea what you're talking about."

"You told me not to contact you in your letter, but I was worried, so I started looking for you on social media, just to make sure you'd made it back to New York okay."

"Oh, right . . ."

"You never told me about all that stuff. That you were, like, this big-deal influencer."

"I was happy to get away from it for a few weeks. And, I don't know, I didn't want you to think I was some shallow . . ." She trailed off.

"Are you kidding? You know that campaign you did? For the sports cars?"

"Yeah?" She'd made a windfall creating content for a company that specialized in refurbishing vintage sports cars. The videos had been her idea, which was rare. Usually, clients had a whole ad agency working for them, calling the shots.

"I thought it was genius how you wrote a dating profile for each car, like 'seeking someone who can operate a stick around dangerous curves.'"

Marigold covered her face. "Oh god, please don't quote me. I'll *die*."

"So I . . . I might've borrowed the idea. I did something similar for the boats."

"You made *videos*?" The Hugo she remembered hadn't owned a smartphone, let alone a camera and editing equipment.

"No, but I wrote descriptions from the point of view of the boat, listing the type of captain they were looking for. I gave each one a personality, a voice, I guess. And it worked. I owe you, big-time."

"You don't owe me anything. I'm happy for you. And *proud.* Is that weird to say? I don't know if I'm still allowed to be proud of you."

He smiled, and the laugh lines around his green eyes crinkled. "I grant you permission to be proud of me." He led her out through a side door, along a short breezeway, and then into the refurbished fisherman's cabin that served as his office.

"Um, is this a joke?" Marigold asked, looking around the room. With its reclaimed wooden floor, hodgepodge of vintage furniture, and paintings of boats, it made the Sandpiper Island Yacht Club's attempt at "nautical chic" look cheap and gaudy. "When did you become an interior decorator?"

"I rented it furnished," Hugo said. He walked over to a file cabinet and, after some digging, found a cord that would work for her phone.

Marigold walked over to look at some sketches on a large wooden desk. "So this is where the magic happens?"

"Sometimes. I do most of my design work on the computer, but clients seem to like the hand-drawn sketches. It makes the whole thing more 'authentic.'" He walked over to a cabinet with an electric kettle and a coffee maker on it. "Want anything?" He opened the cabinet doors, revealing a half dozen liquor bottles. "Pick your poison."

"Bartender's choice.

Hugo glanced at the window, now speckled with raindrops. "How about a hot toddy?"

Humphrey settled onto a plaid dog bed, curled up with his head on his paws, then caught sight of Marigold and ran over to sniff her excitedly, as if he couldn't quite believe she was still here. Marigold gave Humphrey a pat and excused herself to use the bathroom, grateful that her purse always contained spare mascara and lip stain, if not a phone charger.

When she returned, she found Hugh sitting with a mug, staring out the window at the rain like some handsome, melancholy sea captain of yore. Albeit one with a man bun. She tried to imagine Jonathan sitting there like that and found that she couldn't. He'd either be catching up on email, reading the news, or falling down some Reddit rabbit hole about obscure 1970s bass players or the latest theory about life on Saturn's moons. She loved his curiosity and the fact that his brain never turned off, but sometimes it felt like it needed a constant stream of stimulation to feed it. Jonathan couldn't sit in contemplative silence—he needed to be talking, reading, or processing. Whenever Marigold got lost in her own thoughts, Jonathan tried to pull her back, wanting to know what she was thinking. Like her mind was a book he could read cover to cover. And Marigold always felt pressure to make sure it was a book Jonathan would *want* to read, which was why she was always pestering Natalie for smart little tidbits she could stash away.

"Yours is there," Hugo said, pointing to a mug on the side table next to a cracked leather armchair.

"Thank you," she said, taking a seat. "I'm sorry—I've totally hijacked your day."

"That seems to be what you do," he said with a laugh, but there was less bitterness in it than there'd been before. "Hurricane Marigold."

"I guess I deserve that, being compared to a destructive natural disaster."

Hugo took a sip. "Destructive . . . and exciting . . . and cleansing. Depends how you look at it."

She waited for him to continue, desperate for some assurance that he was okay. That she hadn't destroyed his life, or made it impossible for him to trust women. But did she really want him to mention a girlfriend? How would it feel to see him light up talking about the cycling vegan baker Marigold had pictured? Would that provide the closure she was looking for?

"I bet your fiancé is one of those thrill-seeking-doctor types," Hugo said. "You know, the ones who go heli-skiing on their days off."

"*Jonathan*? I could barely get him off the bunny slope the one time we went skiing."

"You provide all the excitement, then?"

"I'm actually trying to be less exciting these days. Turned over a new leaf."

"Why?"

Marigold shrugged. "It seemed like it was time to grow up." She waited for Hugo to make some sign of understanding of approval, especially since he'd witnessed the destructive power of her immaturity. But instead he simply surveyed her with a look she couldn't quite decipher.

Her phone buzzed, and she crossed the room to look.

Humphrey jumped to his feet and skittered over to her, circling her legs as if trying to keep her from going too far. Her stomach clenched as she went to check her texts; Olivia was clearly suspicious, and would never stop poking holes in Marigold's cover story. What if she'd said something to Jonathan? Or Lulu? But the message waiting for Marigold was even worse than another offer of "help" from Olivia. It was an airline alert—her flight had been delayed until tomorrow morning.

"Oh, fuuuuuck," Marigold breathed, leaning against the desk for balance. Humphrey sat on his haunches and pawed at her leg, whining with concern.

Hugo rose from his chair. "What's wrong?"

"My flight was delayed. I need to call the airline."

She paced back and forth while she waited on hold, Humphrey trotting behind her. When she finally got through to an agent, she explained the situation as calmly as possible, having learned the hard way that hysterical tears didn't help in customer service situations. "Can you book me on another flight to Montreal? Or Toronto? Anywhere I can catch a flight to Portland—or even Boston?" Her heart sank as the agent explained that the storm had caused massive delays through the entire system as it moved north from New England. There were no flights leaving the island until tomorrow.

Marigold confirmed that she was booked on the first flight to Portland, now via Halifax, then hung up in a daze.

She was going to miss her own rehearsal dinner.

"There aren't any flights until the morning," she told Hugo.

He sighed. "I'm sorry, Mare. What are you going to tell everyone?"

"I don't know." Marigold resumed pacing around the room,

as if the movement might shake her scattered thoughts into some semblance of order. "I mean, the truth, I guess? That my flight was delayed because of the storm. They don't need to know what city I'm in."

"Or what country."

"Okay, if I were in New York, what would I do . . ." Marigold muttered to herself as she paced. "Even the private planes would be grounded, so I wouldn't be able to charter a flight." She'd learned that the hard way the time she missed her SATs. "I guess I'd drive. People drive in bad weather all the time."

"But you'd still miss your dinner thing anyway, wouldn't you?"

"You mean my *rehearsal* dinner? Is that not a thing in Canada?"

"It's not a thing around here. What do you rehearse, exactly? Cutting your food? Putting your napkin in your lap?"

"I don't have time for this. I need to call Jonathan."

Hugo stood. "I'll wait in the workshop. Give you some privacy."

Marigold pressed the fourth name on her speed dial and he picked up before the first ring. Unless he was with a patient or in a meeting, Jonathan *always* answered her calls. "Hey, where are you? Everything okay?"

"Not really. My flight was delayed until tomorrow morning because of the storm. I'm so sorry!"

"What? *Really*?" Then he took a breath and shifted into calm, problem-solving mode. "Okay, don't worry. We'll get you back in time, I promise."

"I'll look into renting a car. If I leave tonight—"

Jonathan cut her off. "Absolutely not. You can't drive through the night in this weather. Just wait until the morning, and if there's any issue with your flight, we'll have Bill make other arrangements. We'll get you here."

"I'm going to miss the rehearsal dinner," Marigold said in a small voice.

"Which will make your entrance at the actual ceremony all the more dramatic."

Marigold exhaled slowly. "Why are you so wonderful?"

"I'm just excited to marry you. And that's going to happen regardless of storms and flight schedules."

She felt a surge of affection, strong enough to overpower her guilt and worry. For the moment, at least. "I love you."

"I love you, too. Are you at home?"

Marigold looked around Hugo's office. "Almost."

"Get some rest. We'll talk tomorrow."

The moment she hung up, the guilt returned. How had she deluded herself into thinking she'd changed? That she'd *grown up*? But maybe these were just the final throes of the process? Like how you had to take everything out of your closest before you could organize it neatly? Or how diseases grew worse before they got better?

She'd tell Jonathan everything at some point. Soon. But she couldn't do it the night before their wedding—it wasn't fair. Yet that didn't mean she couldn't begin the process of becoming a better person.

She just needed to start with someone whose heart she couldn't break.

Marigold pressed the first entry on her speed dial, and they also picked up on the first ring. "Natalie? No, I'm actually . . . well, I'm in Canada . . . Yeah, Canada, the country."

CHAPTER THIRTEEN

Natalie

"You okay, Bumpy?"

Natalie wheeled around, phone still pressed against her ear, to see Jonathan staring at her. She froze, terrified that he'd somehow overheard her conversation. That he'd heard Marigold say, "I was married before and I'm technically still married." It's not that Jonathan was some kind of traditionalist who'd object to dating a divorced woman; it was the secrecy, the deception. He wouldn't have cared if she'd told him up front. But he'd very much care that she'd hidden an entire first marriage from him, let alone secretly flown to another country to finalize the paperwork.

The day before their wedding.

And honestly, Natalie wouldn't blame him. *She* felt stung by the betrayal—by the fact that her best friend hadn't ever thought to share this information with her. But keeping it from Jonathan was a whole other level of subterfuge.

She scanned Jonathan's face for any sign of shock or anger

but found nothing—just curiosity and mild concern at her evident distress. There was no way he'd heard Marigold's side of the call. Natalie had struggled to hear Marigold over the sound of the rain beating down on the windows of the Sandpiper Island Yacht Club, where the wedding party was gathering for the rehearsal. The actual ceremony would take place on the bluff outside, but due to the storm, the rehearsal was being held in the main lounge, a wood-paneled room that looked more like a library with its framed vintage maps, clusters of upholstered armchairs, and bookcases full of antique almanacs and sailing manuals. Natalie loved the black-and-white photos of sailing teams from years past, especially the ones from the '20s and '30s with the smiling young men in striped shirts who looked like F. Scott Fitzgerald characters.

"That was Marigold," Natalie began, well aware that every good lie began with a kernel of truth. "Her flight was delayed because of the storm. She might not make it back until tomorrow morning."

"Yeah, I know. She just called me." Jonathan shook his head. "Poor Marigold. She sounded like she was freaking out. She said she was going to call her parents, but I'd better go find them, just in case. Will you update Tess?"

"Sure, no problem." Natalie didn't relish being the one to tell the high-strung wedding planner that the bride wouldn't arrive until tomorrow, but this unpleasant task seemed to fall squarely in maid of honor territory.

Jonathan left to track down Marigold's parents while Natalie returned to the lounge, where the other bridesmaids were waiting. She wasn't in any particular rush to find Tess, whom she'd been avoiding ever since Natalie had received her "Countdown to the Big Day!" email, which had been rife with "tips" that had ranged from offensive ("Leading up to the wedding, you may want to cut down on high-sodium foods that cause bloating. A juice fast is a great way to keep your energy levels up *and* ensure your bridesmaid dress fits perfectly") to the utterly deranged. ("Schedule a root touch-up no more than ten days before the wedding, to keep any grays from making a surprise appearance. Your appearance on the big day is a reflection of your love and respect for the happy couple.") Natalie had assumed that the bridesmaids had all received the same email, but when she'd texted Hannah to complain, she'd been mortified to discover that Hannah's email hadn't said anything about juice fasts.

Hannah was on the phone with her mother, growing increasingly agitated as she explained that Westleigh wasn't allowed to eat anything that'd been prepared with black plastic cookware. "Then you'll have to throw it out and start over!" Hannah hissed. Liesl and Bri had cornered the recently arrived Richie, who was even more striking in person, with startingly wide-set eyes that gave her an otherworldly, almost alien look. As Bri peppered her with questions about her skin-care routine, Richie shot Natalie a desperate *please rescue me* look, but Natalie knew that small talk with a famous actress was beyond her capabilities, so instead she wandered toward one of the tall windows that faced the ocean.

The yacht club was on the east side of the island, where, in contrast to the relative serenity of the bay that cradled the west side, enormous waves crashed against the jagged, rocky coastline. It was still technically dusk, but the thick storm clouds blocked the remaining light, and during the uncomfortable golf cart ride, it'd been difficult to see anything apart from the shadowy silhouettes of the few trees hardy enough to withstand the winds that ravaged the side of Sandpiper Island exposed to the North Atlantic.

"Natalie!" She turned to see Tess striding toward her, her blond bob as sleek as always, despite the weather. "Where's Marigold? We need to get started or we'll be late for dinner."

Before Natalie could respond, Lulu hurried up to them looking drawn but animated in a dark blue, glittery tunic with a matching, flapper-style turban. "I assume you heard that Marigold is stuck in New York! I can't believe she flew down there for her birth certificate when we could've had someone pick it up for her."

"I'm sorry, *what*?" Tess asked, looking from Lulu to Natalie. From the couch, the bridesmaids looked up with interest.

Ignoring Tess, Natalie turned to Lulu. "Yeah, I think because of the safe?" she said, guilt twisting her stomach. It was one thing to lie on Marigold's behalf to Jonathan; it was another to lie to Lulu. She'd become something of a surrogate mother to Natalie over the years, making sure that Natalie always had somewhere to spend the holidays when she couldn't fly home to Arizona, helping her line up tutoring clients, and taking her on shopping trips for her birthday.

"Marigold isn't here," Tess said to herself. "Right, okay." She began typing furiously on her phone, muttering to herself. Bri ran over from the couch to whisper something to Hannah, who promptly ended her call.

Lulu sighed, looking suddenly more tired. "I know she'll make it back in plenty of time. I just hate that she's missing all the fun! Olivia too. It's so strange that she's not here yet. Have you heard from her? She hasn't answered any of my texts, and we know she's *never* away from her phone."

"I'm sure she's on her way. The golf carts were a bit late getting to the inn."

"Thanks, hon." Lulu squeezed her arm. "You've been a wonderful friend to Marigold. To all of us. You're part of the family."

"Okay," Tess said, then took a deep breath and smiled. "Okay, it's fine. We just need a Marigold stand-in for the rehearsal. Natalie, as the maid of honor, that's your job."

Natalie stared at her, startled. "Is that really necessary?"

Tess nodded emphatically. "Absolutely. The procession might *look* simple, but that's because it's all very carefully choreographed. We can't skip any part of it."

"Okay . . . but the maid of honor is *part* of the procession. Can't we find someone else to stand in for Marigold so I don't miss my own rehearsal?"

Natalie looked at Lulu, who shrugged. "Tess is the boss."

A few minutes later, Natalie found herself standing in between Lulu and Bill. She'd never felt more mortified in her entire life. Standing in for Marigold felt like a mockery of Natalie's singleness, as if she'd begged to try it on to know what it felt like to be a bride. She cringed as she glimpsed Bri take a photo of her, then show it to Liesl, who shook her head with a smirk.

Natalie couldn't bear to look up at Jonathan, who was standing at the other end of the room next to the officiant, a junior senator from Maine who also happened to be a good friend of Lulu and Bill's. Tess had bustled them all into their places so quickly, she hadn't had time to tell Jonathan that she'd been roped into this against her will.

To her horror, the familiar opening notes of Pachelbel's Canon began to play from hidden speakers. Natalie whipped around to see Tess fiddling with a panel of AV controls on the wall. "Please, no," she whispered, breaking away from Bill and Lulu. "This is too much. We don't need the music."

"I agree," Richie said in her trademark husky voice. "This is just for blocking, right?" She either hadn't yet changed for the rehearsal dinner—or else had put her own spin on the dress code with her slouchy black pants and cropped, ribbed white tank top—but there was a gravitas to her that Natalie found both surprising and impressive.

"Yes, we do need the music," Tess said with a too-bright smile, like a kindergarten teacher who'd reached her breaking point with a troublesome child. She'd clearly become immune to the power of celebrities over the course of her career. "There are specific musical cues. Now if you could just return to your place . . ."

Natalie slunk back in between Lulu and Bill. "Don't worry." Bill elbowed her playfully. "Everyone knows we're only doing this because Tess is a control freak."

Natalie gave him a weak smile.

At Tess's beckoning, the bridesmaids and groomsmen proceeded down the makeshift aisle two by two, with Jonathan's mother standing in for Olivia, who still hadn't returned.

"And now the bride," Tess called out, motioning for them to start moving.

With a sigh, Natalie let Lulu and Bill guide her forward. She kept her eyes on the ground for the first few steps before she found the courage to raise her head. She braced for a look of confusion on Jonathan's face, or worse, the awkward smile of someone trying to mask their deep discomfort. But instead, she found him grinning at her, just like he used to when he caught her eye in class to acknowledge some shared joke. She felt herself relax and didn't resist when Jonathan reached for her hand as she reached the end of the "aisle."

"And now let's have the bride and groom face each other," Tess called.

Jonathan took Natalie's other hand, and his smile widened as their eyes met. Her chest filled with the familiar warmth she always associated with his touch, and for a brief moment, the room seemed to fade away. For the first time in years, Natalie allowed herself to admit how much she wanted this. How there was a parallel universe in which this scene wasn't a farce—it was real. A universe in which she'd had the courage to confess her true feelings for Jonathan long before he met Marigold.

And then it was over. Following Tess's orders, Jonathan dropped Natalie's hands and turned back to the senator to continue some discussion about new pharmaceutical regulations.

Without a word to the rest of the wedding party, she hurried out into the hall, where the first wave of guests were making their way toward the dining room. She just needed a minute to compose herself before returning to the fray.

"Natalie!" Hannah ran after her with a frown. "Is it true Marigold's not coming at *all* tonight?"

"She's . . ." Natalie froze, suddenly unable to sort through the tangle of lies she'd been tasked with delivering. She fanned her face as if she were flushed. "Wow, it's really warm here, isn't it? I've probably sweated off all my makeup. I'd better go freshen up."

Natalie hurried off into the large powder room, locked the door, and slumped against the wall, not even bothering to turn on the lights. She didn't care about her makeup. Or her hair. Or how she looked in the four-hundred-dollar dress Lulu had paid for. She had no idea how the rest of this weekend would play out, but one thing was certain—someone she cared about deeply would leave this island furious with Natalie.

Her phone buzzed, and Natalie fumbled for it frantically. But it wasn't Marigold. Or the weirdly MIA Olivia.

It was Mrs. Friedlander.

natalie ive called you multiple times. monday is no good esme has dance class. can you talk to esme 2morrow? i know you have the wedding but it won't take long thanks.

"Oh, go fuck yourself," Natalie muttered. She shoved her phone back into her purse and stomped out of the bathroom, suddenly desperate for a drink. She spotted a caterer holding a tray of champagne glasses, took one with a grateful smile, and went to find somewhere to drink it in peace. She ducked around the corner and slipped into one of the smaller rooms she'd heard referred to as the "office," where members could work on their laptops or hold business meetings. All the lights were out, and Natalie breathed a sigh of relief before she realized that the room wasn't actually empty. Jonathan stood in front of the large bay windows, staring out at the stormy sea. He seemed so lost in his own world that Natalie felt uneasy about disturbing his solitude. She started to back out of the room, but somehow sensing her presence, he glanced over his shoulder. "Oh, Bumps, it's you." Something had shifted since their exchange right before the rehearsal; he sounded suddenly weary and drained.

"It's me." She paused for a moment, then went over to join him at the window, which looked over the frothing gray-blue waves. "Quite the view."

"We need to get you a yacht club membership. I bet you'd write incredible books in this room."

"Thanks, but I'm not sure the room is the issue for me. A great writer should be able to work anywhere, right?"

He didn't answer and slumped onto the cushioned window seat.

"Are you okay?" Natalie asked.

"I just get the sense that there's something going on with Marigold. Apart from the flight delay. Is she freaking out about the wedding? Do you think she's having second thoughts?"

"Absolutely not," Natalie said firmly, glad that this part at least was true. Marigold was going to extraordinary lengths to keep the wedding on track. She wasn't running away. "She loves you so much, you know that. And you love her."

He fell silent and turned back to stare at the black, churning sea. "That's not always enough, though, is it?" he said quietly. "A good marriage takes more than love. It requires trust, honesty, communication. Do you really think Marigold and I have that? Are we making the right decision?"

"Of course you are," Natalie said with the same calm certainty she always employed when speaking to Jonathan or Marigold about their relationship, the tone she'd perfected to mask the pain and remorse she'd been carrying since that ill-fated night when she'd thrown Marigold into his arms.

Except that tonight, her words didn't sound smooth and confident.

They sounded as fake and desperate as she was. Because for the first time in years, Natalie couldn't silence the voice in her head telling her that Jonathan was making a mistake. Tonight, the voice didn't sound like an extension of Natalie's selfishness or delusions.

Tonight, it sounded like the truth.

CHAPTER FOURTEEN

Olivia

"Want me to drive?" Zack said as he eyed Olivia's bandaged foot, which she'd shoved, painfully, into a strappy sandal. After ensuring that the Varicks were able to secure a room at the inn under the wedding rate, she'd rushed to her own room and showered and changed in record time, but they'd still missed the last chauffeured golf carts and would have to drive themselves to the yacht club. Thankfully, the storm had abated for the moment, although the forecast showed that it'd return with a vengeance later in the evening.

"Nope." Olivia slid into the driver's seat and turned the key, barely waiting for Zack to settle into the passenger seat before she slammed her foot down on the accelerator.

"Whoa!" Zack yelped. He grasped at the handle as Olivia made a sharp turn onto the bumpy dirt road that served as the island's main thoroughfare, tires squelching through the mud. She'd been navigating these roads since she was a kid—standard practice on Sandpiper Island, where parents were delighted to let their children serve as designated golf cart drivers. "Where's the fire?"

"I already missed the rehearsal. I can't be late to the actual dinner." She could only pray that Marigold had materialized during Olivia's absence, that the New York story had turned out to be true, regardless if Marigold was mistaken about needing her birth certificate. But when Olivia had finally charged her phone back in the room, there hadn't been any new messages from her sister.

Olivia pressed all the way down on the gas until the cart reached its top speed of twenty miles per hour. The rain had slowed down, and after her hot shower, the cool, damp air felt more bracing than bone-chilling.

The cart's headlights did little to illuminate the dark road, but Olivia knew the landscape better than the back of her hand, a part of her body she tried not to look at these days since it seemed resistant to her antiaging sunscreen. She turned into the yacht club's drive with practiced ease, relishing the familiar spray of gravel followed by the satisfying crunch under her tires. "Nicely done," Zack said as she parked to the side of the entrance. He hurried around to help her out, but she ignored his hand and limped up the front path on her own. "So . . . where do the yachts park?"

"A yacht is just a boat longer than thirty feet. None of the members have one of those superyachts you're imagining. This is more of a sailboat crowd."

"Ah yes, a mere thirty feet. How embarrassing for them. So what about the whiskey tasting your buddy mentioned last night? Didn't he say that was on a yacht?"

Olivia snorted. "They'd never let Ed Growler join."

"Why not? Is he Black? Jewish? *Catholic?*"

"What? No! They don't have rules like that here."

"Anymore."

"Bill is Jewish, you know."

"And they wouldn't have let him in forty years ago, right?"

Olivia didn't answer.

"Your silence speaks volumes."

"I thought you'd decided to be nice to me? You know, to make up for stranding me at sea for eight hours and making me miss my sister's wedding rehearsal." *And offering to pretend to be my boyfriend,* Olivia added. She was certain Zack had been mostly joking, but she couldn't help but imagine how it'd feel to walk into the rehearsal dinner as part of a couple. Whether Zack had been right about Andrew needing a little competition to catch his attention . . .

"Sorry, you're right." Zack cleared his throat and made of show of offering Olivia his arm. "May I escort you inside, my lady?"

She swatted his arm away and pushed the door open. Warm light and the sound of happy chatter spilled out into the dark lawn, and Olivia froze on the threshold. Everyone who'd witnessed her humiliating show last night would be there, along with all the recent arrivals who'd undoubtedly already heard all about it. Andrew was somewhere cozying up with Emerson. And then, of course, there was Lulu. What had the last few hours been like for her with both her children missing in action?

"It's going to be okay," Zack said, dropping his faux-courtly act. "Come on." He placed a hand on Olivia's back, and this time, she didn't shake it off.

Thankfully, the guests had just started serving themselves

from the long line of chafing dishes that Olivia knew contained the trademark French-Vietnamese fusion of a famous chef who'd come up from Boston for the evening. Olivia smile-nodded at a few people as she made her way toward Lulu, whom she'd spotted sitting at the table they'd reserved for the family, stopping to say a proper hello to Lulu's best friend and Olivia's de facto godmother, Paula, and their family friend Susan, a well-known editor who'd let Olivia intern for her during high school summers, before she'd set her sights on law.

"There you are!" Lulu cried as she approached, rising to her feet to pull Olivia into a tight hug before catching sight of her bandaged foot. "What happened? Are you okay? You weren't answering your phone."

"I'm fine. It's a long story, I . . ." She trailed off, suddenly realizing that she'd been so focused on finding Marigold, she hadn't come up with an excuse for her own absence.

"It's completely my fault." Zack appeared at her side. "I begged Olivia to take me out on the boat and then, like an idiot, I ended up losing the key. It took us ages to get back, and of course, we didn't have cell reception. I'm really sorry."

"Oh my!" Lulu looked from Zack to Olivia. "You poor things. And all that was during the storm? I'm just glad you're both okay. Zack, you'd better get something to eat before the line grows too long. You're probably starving." When he was out of earshot, Lulu lowered her voice. "I assume you know all about Marigold?"

"Yeah . . ." Olivia said slowly, unsure how much her mother knew or suspected. "Is she . . ."

"Stranded in New York because of the storm. I spoke to her and she said she'll be on the first flight tomorrow morning. She must be at her wits' end. I feel just awful for her. For both of you! It doesn't sound like either of you are having the weekend you imagined."

Olivia felt a twinge of guilt. Maybe Marigold *had* been telling the truth about going home to get her birth certificate. She might've misunderstood Bruce's instructions about the paperwork and panicked. Or, hell, maybe Bruce had given her bad information. It wouldn't shock Olivia to learn that his knowledge of Maine marriage law had some gaps in it. Her *Gilligan's Island*–esque outing might've been delusional as well as fruitless.

"Honestly. You know Marigold gets overwhelmed by too much attention. She was probably glad to have a little break before the big day. And I'm fine." She wiggled her foot. "It looks worse than it actually is."

Lulu seemed to perk up. "Why don't you go get some food yourself? Before the Paulsons fill the Tupperware you know they're hiding in their bags?"

Olivia made her way across the room, hoping that a few more people would join the line and serve as a buffer between her and Andrew, but she had no such luck. "Here, you go ahead of me," Zack said.

"Please, no, I'm fine."

At the sound of her voice, Andrew spun around. "There you are!" he said brightly. "I haven't seen you all day. How'd your toast go last night?"

"It was . . ."

"It was *brilliant*," Zack cut in. "Everyone laughed, cried, experienced the full spectrum of human emotion."

"That's great." Andrew extended his hand. "I don't think we officially met yesterday. I'm Andrew."

"Zack."

"So where's Emerson?" Olivia asked in what she hoped was a light, friendly tone.

"She has friends who live on the island, so she's having drinks with them first. She'll probably meet me here later." Andrew turned back to Zack. "You look really familiar—were you at HBS?"

"HBS?" Zack repeated with what Olivia knew was feigned confusion.

"Harvard Business School," Andrew clarified.

"Nope. But I'm Jonathan's best man, so I guess that makes me a very, very local celebrity."

"No, it's not that . . . What's your last name?"

"Greenberg."

"Wait, are you Zack Greenberg the writer?"

"That's me."

"No way! I just preordered your book. I was a big fan of your Substack."

Olivia could feel her brain struggling to make sense of this. "*You* read his blog? The one where he argued for massive wealth redistribution and claimed that billionaires belonged in jail?"

"That's a *bit* of an oversimplification," Zack said.

"You work at a hedge fund," Olivia continued, stating the obvious.

"That doesn't mean I don't appreciate opposing points of view, especially well-written, well-reasoned ones," Andrew said pleasantly.

"Well, how about that." Zack grinned at Olivia. "Your friend is a fan."

Something flickered in Andrew's eyes, and his smile seemed

to fade just the slightest bit. "I didn't realize . . . Are you two . . ." He made an awkward gesture with his hands.

"Together?" Zack supplied.

"Yeah," Andrew said sheepishly. "Sorry. I know there's no real polite way to ask that question."

"I'll let the lady answer. She's the one who's weird about labels." Zack turned to Olivia and winked.

Olivia forced a laugh to stall for time. Zack's plan had sounded outlandish when he'd proposed it earlier today, but now it seemed, well, less outlandish. Maybe she was just imagining it, but Andrew did seem a little ruffled. Perhaps Zack's reductive explanation of the male psyche had been spot-on. "Well . . ." She looped her arm through Zack's. "We were hoping to keep it under wraps this weekend, since it's so new. But I guess that was silly. You can't hide—"

"A love like ours," Zack said, moving his arm to her waist.

"I was going to say, you can't hide anything with your friends and family around, but yeah, sure."

"Cool," Andrew said. "Yeah, cool. That's awesome." He placed his empty plate back on the stack at the end of the table. "I just realized, I should check and see if Emerson needs a ride. Will you excuse me?"

"Wowwww," Zack said quietly as Andrew strode off. "I didn't expect it to work *that* quickly. My man is pissed!"

"Oh, come on." Olivia rolled her eyes but couldn't suppress the tingle of excitement coursing through her body. "Okay, you can let me go now."

"You sure? He could come back at any minute." Zack tightened his hold. "He's probably just running to the bathroom. Mr. HBS probably has IBS."

Olivia looked away so Zack wouldn't see her laugh; she didn't want to give him that satisfaction. Across the room, she spotted Lulu watching them with a curious smile.

"Okay," Olivia said, turning back to Zack. "You're on. Let's try out your ridiculous pretend dating plan. But just for the weekend. Then we'll 'break up.' Okay?" That would give Andrew enough time to realize he'd made a terrible mistake. And possibly convince Lulu that she didn't have to worry about *both* her daughters this weekend.

Zack nodded. "You got it, babe."

"And definitely never call me *babe*."

"Honey?"

"No."

"Sweet cheeks? Babycakes? What's that French phrase? *Ma petite choue?*"

"Little cabbage. So romantic."

"*Ma petite choue* speaks le French! Oooh la la!"

Olivia groaned and pushed him away. "This is never going to work. No one will believe I'm dating such a cheeseball." But then she stole a quick glance back at Lulu, who whispered something to a smiling Bill, then stepped back, beaming. It was the happiest Olivia had seen her mother look in a long time.

I guess it's worth a shot. She took Zack's hand and thought, *As the French say,* courage.

CHAPTER FIFTEEN

Marigold

Marigold wondered if there was a word for the strange feeling that came over her as Hugo parked in front of Viana's Tavern. It wasn't déjà vu because, of course, she'd been here before. But the familiarity felt more like something left over from a dream than an actual memory.

Hugo had agreed to let her crash at his place but explained that he'd already made plans to do pub trivia that night. "That's fine," Marigold had said. "Just drop me off at your house first. I can hang out there."

"No, you should come. My friends would love to see you."

He'd sounded convincing back at the shipyard, and Hugo's friends had made her feel welcome and comfortable during their whirlwind romance. But now that she and Hugo had arrived, Marigold felt a lot less confident. Inside the bar were the closest friends of the man she'd run out on. Hugo seemed to have gotten over it, but it seemed unlikely that his buddies would've been quite so quick to forgive and forget. And now she had to face them at trivia night, of all places.

Trivia was Marigold's kryptonite; it made her feel far more exposed than any of the tiny outfits she'd been paid to model over the years. Jonathan was part of a team that competed at a famously difficult pub quiz in the Village where NYU grad students duked it out against what remained of the downtown intelligentsia. Marigold attended occasionally when she couldn't come up with a convincing excuse to skip out and had consistently mortified herself until she decided it was safer to stay mute. No one ever made fun of her or even expressed frustration when she supplied a wrong answer, but somehow, their kindness—Jonathan's in particular—stung more than an eye roll.

"How much did you tell everyone about why I'm here?" Marigold asked as she unclipped her seat belt.

"I said you'd come to sort out some divorce paperwork. I didn't mention that you're getting married tomorrow. That didn't seem like my news to share." Hugo opened the driver-side door, then paused. "Ready?"

Marigold nodded though she felt anything but ready.

The bar looked the same as she'd remembered, with its cracked vinyl booths, enormous jukebox, old beer ads, and fishing paraphernalia on the walls. The crowd was the usual mix of locals in windbreakers and work boots, and tourists who were easily identifiable in the brand-new sweatshirts they always bought in town when the temperature dropped in the afternoon. Hugo led her over to a table where four people were already seated: Hugo's cousin Jay, and Jay's girlfriend, Ruby, who also happened to be Hugo's high school sweetheart ("It's not as weird as you think," Ruby had explained once. "In a town this small, you're lucky to avoid your own cousins, forget about your ex's cousins"), and his friends Wes and Lauren.

"You guys remember Marigold," Hugo said evenly.

Marigold raised her hand in greeting. "Hi."

"Marigold!" Ruby stood and pulled Marigold into a tight hug. "It's great to see you." The others remained seated but gave her warm smiles.

"What do you want to drink?" Hugo asked her.

"I'll get this round," Marigold said. "I insist." She'd rather let the group whisper about her in her absence than try to make small talk without Hugo.

When she returned with her and Hugo's beers, Wes was writing their team name on their answer sheet: *Stay Marigold, Ponyboy*. "We're usually *Trivia Newton-John*, but we change it up when we have special guests," he explained.

"I'm honored," Marigold said, although she didn't fully understand the pony thing. Was this a jab about her being rich?

To her relief, Hugo squinted at the sheet and said, "I don't get it."

"From *The Outsiders*!" Wes said. "You know that famous line, 'Stay gold, Ponyboy'?"

"Oh, right." Hugo nodded. "That's a good one."

Wes gave him a curious look, but before he could say anything, the quiz began. It was just as difficult as Jonathan's, maybe even more so because so many of the pop culture questions—the only category in which Marigold ever dared attempt an answer—were skewed toward Canadian references. Even those were few and far between, though, with more esoteric subjects taking precedence. Hugo seemed undaunted, easily summoning answers like "the Second Punic War" and "*Ode on a Grecian Urn*."

No one seemed to notice, let alone care, that Marigold wasn't providing any answers. It wasn't that Jonathan ever seemed frustrated, exactly. But whenever a question came up that he thought Marigold should know, he'd prod her like an encouraging teacher. "We saw this painting at the Met, remember? When we went for that exhibition?" Or, worse, "Didn't you say you'd read this one?" about a book Natalie had summarized for her.

Instead of debating the answers until the last possible second, Hugo's team would discuss, write down a response, and then go back to whatever they'd been talking about: Ruby's latest work drama (the owner of the veterinary practice had been caught stealing drugs), Wes's home brewery, the camping trip they were leaving for on Sunday, or whether Lauren's American boyfriend was using her as a route to Canadian citizenship. "That's one thing we can't accuse you of, Marigold!" Jay said, prompting a look from Ruby. "What? What'd I say?"

"Just ignore him," Ruby said with a sigh. "He knows not what he says."

"I don't get it," Jay continued. "I meant that she clearly *wasn't* one of those Americans looking for Canadian citizenship or else she never would've run off!"

Marigold shot a nervous glance at Hugo, but he'd gone around to the other end of the table to work on some physics equation with Wes and was thankfully too engrossed in the math to notice.

"No, you're right." Marigold flashed a smile at Jay. "That wasn't on my mind. Though if I'd had a crystal ball, it might've been."

Jay nodded. "Because Hugo's business ended up taking off."

"What? No," Marigold said quickly. "Because of the political situation in America. With all those sociopaths trying to destroy the country?"

"Come on, Jay," Lauren said. "Marigold didn't even know about Hugo's business. He started that after she . . . He started that later."

"That's right," Marigold agreed. "I didn't know. But I'm really impressed!"

Lauren waited until Hugo went up to order from the bar, then turned to Marigold and lowered her voice. "He was like a man possessed. He'd always wanted to switch from repairs to design, but it's a big leap with a lot of financial risk. And then, one day, he just sort of . . . went for it. He enrolled in a bunch of night classes, then he got a loan, switched to part-time at the dock, and started designing."

"And this was sometime after our . . . thing?" Marigold asked.

"*Right* after," Jay said. "Like, the next week. Guess he needed something to take his mind off you." A cheer went up from the table next to them as the quizmaster read out the latest scores. "Uh-oh, *The Algebraic Functional Alcoholics* are catching up. I hate those guys. I'm going to go try to distract them."

As Jay approached his rivals' table, Lauren leaned in to whisper to Marigold. "For what it's worth, I don't think it was a distraction—I think he wanted to impress you."

"Oh." Marigold wasn't sure how to respond to this. Why would Hugo want to impress the person who treated him so poorly? And who'd done her best to cut off contact? It didn't make any sense. "I doubt it had anything to do with me. It was all his accomplishment."

Lauren and Ruby exchanged a fleeting look and seemed to agree it was time to change the subject. "Do you still live in

Manhattan?" Ruby asked. "I thought all the hip people lived in Brooklyn."

"Hip?" Lauren repeated. "I'm sorry, that's so cringe, I just died a little inside."

"Okay, *cringe* is a LOT worse than *hip*. Tell her, Marigold."

"Wait, it *is* her," a voice said. Marigold looked up to see Jay coming over with two of the girls who'd been sitting at the next table, one with dark brown hair in long braids, and another with a dyed purple pixie cut.

"Told you," Jay said smugly.

"Um, hi?" Marigold gave them an uncertain smile, wondering if "her" meant "that New York bitch who broke Hugo's heart" or "that influencer I follow."

"I think you're amazing," the girl with braids said, then tilted her head toward her friend. "So does Chelsea."

"I don't follow you," Chelsea, the purple-haired girl, said, looking embarrassed.

The girl with braids shot an exasperated look at her friend. "Yeah, but I've sent you, like, hundreds of her posts."

"Sorry for the spam," Marigold said with a smile while secretly wishing she could disappear. No one ever approached her in New York, where she was small potatoes compared to real celebrities like Richie.

"What are you doing up here?" the girl asked eagerly. "Is it for a campaign?"

"Um, no . . . I . . ."

"Hey, Mare?" Hugo appeared at her side and tossed his keys onto the table with a clang. "I think I left my phone in the truck. Do you mind checking?"

"What?" Marigold looked from the keys to Hugo in surprise.

"Oh yeah, sure. No problem." She excused herself and headed toward the door, doing her best to maintain a casual pace that belied her desperation to get outside. She stepped into the chilly evening air and took a few bracing deep breaths before walking over to Hugo's truck. She unlocked the door and looked around, but there was no sign of his phone, so she went around to the other side and began rooting through the glove compartment.

"What are you doing?" Marigold turned to see Hugo standing next to the truck.

"Looking for your phone?"

Hugo smiled. "It's in my pocket. It just seemed like you were maybe ready for a break, so I made up an excuse."

Marigold stared at him, feeling a surge of warmth despite the nippy air. That's exactly what Natalie would've done for her. Except that, in Marigold's experience, no one else—not even her family—could sense when she needed a few minutes alone to recenter herself. "Thank you."

Lauren stuck her head out the door and called to them, "Hugo, come back! There's another literature category coming up."

"One sec!" He turned to Marigold. "You ready to head back in? Or do you need more time?"

"I'm ready." She closed the glove compartment and shut the door. "I didn't realize you knew so much about literature. Was that your major? Before you dropped out?"

"No, ecology and engineering. I just like to read."

Marigold came to a stop right before they reached the door. "Wait. You recognized that quote from *The Outsiders* right away, didn't you? You were just pretending so I wouldn't feel stupid."

"What are you talking about?"

She jabbed him in the ribs. "The 'stay gold, Ponyboy' thing!

You didn't want me to have to admit I didn't get it, so *you* pretended not to get it."

Hugo flashed her a smile. "Since when did you become such a conspiracy theorist?" He opened the door and placed a hand on her back, guiding her inside. "Let's go, pony girl."

CHAPTER SIXTEEN

Natalie

The break in the rain didn't last long, but Natalie waited until the last possible moment before heading back into the yacht club. If Marigold had been there, Natalie would've summoned the strength necessary to feign excitement about the wedding. But right now, the thought of fake-smiling through hours of small talk with people she'd never see again felt too daunting.

A message popped up from Tess.

Only ten minutes until your speech.

That was Tess-speak for *You'd better get your butt back in here now.*

"There you are!" Hannah said brightly. "I was just grabbing my sweater from the golf cart and I saw you standing here all by yourself. You looked so lonely, I had to come join you!"

"I wasn't *lonely*," Natalie rejoined, then smiled. "I was just getting some air." She generally found Hannah the easiest to talk to out of all the bridesmaids—she'd grown up in Maine and didn't have Bri's or Liesl's jaded hauteur—but she didn't have much of a sense of humor, either. Whenever Natalie told a funny anecdote about a bad date, Hannah would place a hand on Natalie's arm and say something like, *I'm so sorry that happened to you*, like Natalie had just spent two weeks in the ICU instead of two hours at a wannabe dive bar with a stony-faced aspiring comic who, instead of laughing at her jokes, pulled out a notebook and said, "That's funny. I'm gonna use that."

"You know, I really admire you," Hannah said. "I'd never be brave enough to go to a wedding without a date."

"Oh, I didn't even think about bringing a date. It wouldn't have been fair to him, you know, given how much I have to do as the maid of honor." *That, and I had no one to ask.*

Hannah perked up. "So are you seeing anyone special?"

"Oh, you know, I'm having fun, keeping my options open." Natalie tried to sound playful and coy, but of course, Hannah was having none of it. She placed her hand on Natalie's arm and said, "You'll find someone eventually. I'm sure of it. You know, it always happens when you least expect it. That's what happened with me and Kevin! Once I stopped looking, I got my happily ever after."

"You sure did!" Natalie's husband, Kevin, was perpetually sweaty—even in the winter—and laughed at his own unfunny jokes, an act that generally left him with a bit of white spittle in the corner of his mouth. "Will you excuse me? I need to go freshen up before my toast."

Natalie had been dreading this moment ever since Marigold asked her to be her maid of honor. She'd always hated public speaking, but the thought of even momentarily becoming the center of attention in this crowd was particularly terrifying.

She was happy with what she'd written, and grateful for the professionally applied makeup, but none of that was enough to give her the unwavering self-assurance that marked those raised in Marigold's world. Natalie couldn't remember ever seeing Marigold's New York friends blush or stammer; they never seemed self-conscious or embarrassed. Their money functioned as a form of social armor. If they spilled on their shirt at lunch, they could buy a new one at the boutique next door, even if it didn't stock anything under three hundred dollars. If they made a gaffe during a job interview, their parent could smooth it over with a phone call to the VP, their roommate from Exeter. If they noticed a pimple emerging the night before a big event, they could summon a concierge doctor to administer a steroid shot. The idea that self-confidence came from within was complete and utter bullshit—it came from trust funds and founder shares.

Natalie ducked into the bathroom to confirm that her teeth were still lipstick-free, then headed into a stall. As she tried to decide whether she had to pee badly enough to justify wiggling out of her Spanx, a group of women swept in with a rustle of swishy skirts and animated whispers. Through the crack in the door, Natalie could see Liesl, Bri, and a friend of theirs named Isadora, examining their reflections. "So what's *really* going on with Marigold?" Isadora asked, rummaging through a tiny beaded clutch before producing a tube of Chanel lip gloss. "The whole situation is kinda sus, right?"

"I don't know." Bri leaned forward to examine her eyelashes in the mirror. "I wonder if Olivia did something to her wedding dress. She seems like the type, doesn't she?"

"Her toast last night *was* kind of unhinged," Isadora agreed. "But I don't think she's reached that level of jealous. I'm pretty sure she's hooking up with the best man. They looked very cozy during dinner."

"You mean *Zack*?" Liesl scoffed, either skeptical that Olivia would go for Zack or irritated that the only single groomsman had set his sights on someone else. Not that Liesl had any interest in Zack—she dated photographers with man buns, trust funds, and a tendency to describe themselves as "humanists" instead of feminists—but she needed to confirm that Zack was attracted to her before she could dismiss him.

Isadora ignored her, probably because she knew Liesl's next move would be to disparage Olivia, and Isadora had a craving for bigger prey. "Even if her flight was really delayed, it's still super weird that Marigold's missing the rehearsal dinner," she continued.

"I wonder if she and Jonathan had a fight," Bri said with a touch too much excitement. In an Uber back from the bachelorette party, Bri had burst into tears and told Natalie how unfair it was that Marigold had gotten engaged before her. "When's it going to be *my* turn?" Bri had asked in between sobs. "I should be the one marrying a doctor—I majored in nutrition studies!"

"It's so Marigold to miss her own rehearsal dinner," Liesl said with a sigh. "You know I love her, but sometimes it feels like she manufactures drama. Do you think it's because she was worried about being upstaged by Richie?"

A flare of anger blazed through Natalie's chest. These women were supposed to be Marigold's closest friends—her *bridesmaids*. She straightened her skirt, unlocked the door, and stomped out of the stall, expecting to see Liesl, Bri, and Isadora turn red with shame. But of course, they barely gave her a second look.

"See you all out there," Natalie said brightly when she finished washing her hands.

"See ya," Bri said. Liesl and Isadora didn't turn away from the mirror.

Natalie took some deep breaths as she entered the hall, but still felt herself fuming. Bri and Liesl were old childhood friends and were justified in saying that it was "so Marigold" to miss her rehearsal dinner—they'd witnessed more mishaps than Natalie had over the years. But there'd hadn't been an ounce of sympathy or concern in their voices.

Marigold deserved better; she *was* a good friend. Natalie's best friend! Who else would've gone to four different delis so they could taste-test different matzo ball soups when Natalie had the flu? Who else would've given Natalie a key to her apartment so she could crash there even when Marigold was out of town? And raid her closet before a date? Marigold was the most generous person she'd ever known. But moreover, she was generous of spirit. She was loyal, a great listener, and the only person Natalie had met as an adult who made her laugh hard enough to spit out her cocktail. It wasn't Marigold's fault that Natalie had never gotten over her college crush. And it certainly wasn't her fault that Natalie had spent years deluding herself into thinking she had a chance with Jonathan, despite all evidence to the contrary. It had been Natalie's choice to set them up, even if it'd been a knee-jerk reaction in a moment of panic. If Natalie had any regrets about how things had played out, that was on her. It was time to stop moping and be the maid of honor Marigold deserved.

Natalie headed into the dining room and was relieved to discover that she no longer felt all that nervous, as if her anger at the bridesmaids had swallowed up her anxiety. "There you are!"

Tess said, hurrying over to thrust a microphone in Natalie's hand. "You're up."

Natalie turned it on and braced for the ear-piercing whine of the speakers before remembering that she was at Sandpiper Island Yacht Club, not the ballroom of the Cleveland Airport Marriott. The members shelled out fifty thousand dollars a year to protect themselves from all manner of irritants, from eardrum-bursting AV systems to watery martinis to servers who cleared your plate before others had finished eating. "Hi everyone," Natalie said, her voice echoing throughout the room. "I'm Natalie, Marigold's maid of honor. Marigold is devastated not to be here tonight, but we're recording the toasts so she doesn't miss anything. And just to be clear, the storm was an act of god. There was nothing Marigold could've done to prevent it." Natalie paused for dramatic effect. "Not like the time she arrived at the airport, only to discover that you need six months of passport eligibility to enter Indonesia." Everyone laughed good-naturedly. "That's how I knew she was serious about Jonathan—unlike with previous boyfriends, she'd start getting ready for their dates *before* she was actually due at the restaurant. Shocking, I know." There was more laughter, still knowing and affectionate, which was a good sign. So far, no one seemed to be deeply offended by or suspicious of Marigold's absence. "But as a second-year resident, Jonathan's free time was very limited, and Marigold didn't want to miss a moment with him. They say love can perform miracles, and trust me, I've seen it happen. I saw love turn Marigold Harding—the girl who's *missed* more flights than most people take in a lifetime—into a punctual person. It's a privilege to watch two people you care about fall in love. I've known both Jonathan and Marigold a long time and witnessed the rise and fall of many relationships, but I knew from the beginning that their connection was something special. Sometimes looking for love feels like sending radio waves into the darkness of space—you can go years without any response, and then just when you start to wonder if we really are alone in the universe, you hear that voice. That someone who's tuned to your exact frequency. That's what it's like with Marigold and Jonathan." A chorus of *awwws* drifted up from the tables, and Natalie looked around the room until her gaze landed on Jonathan, who was staring at her with a blank expression, his shoulders oddly rigid. "So let's raise a glass to Marigold and Jonathan," she continued hastily, eager to relinquish the spotlight. "Thank you for making us believe in true love."

Natalie made her way to her table, blushing and nodding her thanks at the handful of people who mouthed *Great toast!* or raised a glass as she passed. By the time she slid into her seat, Jonathan was smiling again, seemingly relaxed, and Natalie was able to convince herself that she'd merely imagined the strange look on his face.

CHAPTER SEVENTEEN

Olivia

By the time dinner was over, the rain had finally stopped, which meant that the after-party could take place on the beach as planned, bonfire and all. The storm was apparently no match for Tess's "manifesting."

The bonfire was near the yacht club, on the east side of the island, the portion that faced the ocean. If you set sail from the beach, you wouldn't strike land again until you reached the South of France. The thought of that vast emptiness usually made Olivia shudder, but tonight the surf seemed strangely calm in the wake of the storm, and the crash of the glassy waves sounded more cheerful than ominous.

Olivia drove Zack, Andrew, and Natalie over in her golf cart, joining the caravan of chauffeured carts that'd been booked for the evening. The path down to the beach was too steep for carts to take them all the way, so the wedding guests all got out at the top of the bluff and shuffled down the dark, rocky path—no small feat considering how much most people had had to drink at the rehearsal dinner. *This is a lawsuit waiting to happen*, Olivia thought as she slid out of her cart.

Andrew eyed the steep, narrow path before them. "Are you going to be okay getting down there? Need a hand?" Olivia's brain raced to perform the cost-benefit analysis she applied to nearly every decision. Was Andrew more attracted to tough, independent women or was he the type who liked to rescue a damsel in (very mild) distress? Then he extended his hand, and Olivia's body went into autopilot, unwilling to forgo the chance to lean against him. He wrapped his arm around her so she could keep her weight off her injured foot and guided her down toward the beach. Up close, he smelled faintly of scotch and salt; Olivia had to resist the urge to inhale.

"I'm surprised you signed off on this location," Andrew said. "Seems like a lawsuit waiting to happen."

"*You* try convincing Marigold that something's a bad idea." The bonfire had been the only part of the wedding weekend agenda Marigold had insisted on, leaving the rest up to Lulu and Tess. "She said she'd 'seen it all in a dream,' but I think it's more likely she stumbled across something on Instagram."

"It's remarkable what wedding planning does to people's brains. My sister made it her whole personality, then went through this weird withdrawal phase after. Like postparty depression."

"Yeah, that doesn't seem uncommon."

"I can't see you losing your mind over napkin rings."

"Because I'm *famously* laid-back and chill."

Andrew laughed. "I'd never call you 'chill.' But you expend so much energy on stuff that matters, it doesn't feel like you'd have much left over to worry about trivial shit. Those bridezilla types are the ones with too much time on their hands."

"'Stuff that matters,'" Olivia repeated with a smile. "That's nice. Zack thinks I've been 'tricked into believing moving money from one corporation's account to another is a matter of life and death.'"

Andrew stopped walking. "He said that?" he asked with a mix of surprise and concern. "I'm sorry, but that's really not cool."

Shit, Olivia thought. She'd forgotten that Zack was supposed to be her boyfriend. "He was just joking," she said quickly. "You must know his humor, since you read his work."

"Okay, good. Otherwise he's an idiot who doesn't deserve you." The conviction in his voice made Olivia's stomach flutter with a combination of excitement and guilt; it was thrilling to think that Andrew felt protective of her, but she didn't want to unfairly cast Zack as the type of man who'd belittle his girlfriend.

They stepped onto the sand and Andrew waited what felt like an extra beat before letting go of Olivia's waist. Up ahead, the catering staff had built a huge bonfire and erected folding tables covered with ingredients for s'mores, and guests were already swaying in time with the steel drum band, drinks held aloft in the air. *Marigold would've loved this*, she thought with more wistfulness than frustration. She still wasn't sure what was going on with her sister—whether she'd actually gone to fetch her birth certificate or if something more serious was afoot—but there was nothing Olivia could do about it now, not without creating even more tension and drama. She just had to hope Marigold got on that flight tomorrow so that everything could continue as planned.

Andrew glanced at his Apple Watch. "Excuse me. I should call Emerson back. I think she needs directions."

As he pulled out his phone and headed down the beach, Lulu shuffled toward Olivia, beaming from the depths of a full-length puffy coat. She'd always gotten cold easily, and these days anything under seventy degrees left her shivering. "Sooo . . ." she said, eyes flashing with delight. "How long has this been going on?"

"Nothing's going on!" Olivia said, watching Andrew out of the corner of her eye. *At least, not yet.*

"Really?" Lulu's face fell slightly. "Andrew told Bill that you and Zack were an item."

"Oh, right. Me and *Zack*. Well, it's new. And not really official or anything."

Lulu brightened again. "Got it. I promise not to ask probing questions. But I'm so happy, Livvy. Zack's such a sweet boy. Remember that care package he sent last time I was in the hospital?"

"Um, no?"

"I went into the hospital a few days after he and Jonathan came over for Thanksgiving, and Zack sent me a bunch of the books we'd discussed at dinner. And some fancy tea and cookies."

"You . . . definitely never mentioned that." Olivia imagined all the steps that would entail: going to the bookstore and the gourmet grocery store, finding the right-sized box, texting Jonathan for the room number at the hospital, standing in line at the post office. It was a lot of work to cheer up a person he'd only met a handful of times.

"Well, he's a good egg, as my grandmother would've said."

"He is," Olivia agreed, though she was certain that if Lulu had discovered that Olivia was dating Andrew, she'd be singing his praises instead. *She just wants me to be happy and loved*, Olivia thought.

As if confirming her suspicions, Lulu continued, "I know I've been a pain in the ass about encouraging you to date. I never thought of myself as one of those mothers. And I know you don't *need* anyone—you have a rich, wonderful life, and I'm so proud of you. But there's a special kind of emotional support that comes from having a partner, and I think even you might appreciate that when things . . . get hard."

"Maybe," Olivia said, eager to change the subject.

"Why don't you go join him?" Lulu nodded at the circle of cushions around the bonfire, where Zack had been roped into a conversation with Dylan, a high school friend of Marigold's who was currently taking a "gap year" after dropping out of his MFA program. "Looks like he might need rescuing."

"I think I need a drink first," Olivia said, eyeing them. She took two beers from the bar and made her way to the bonfire, where she gingerly lowered herself onto the empty cushion next to Zack, wincing when her injured foot hit the sand.

"You okay?" Zack asked. "Is it your foot?"

"Yeah, but I'm fine. I'll take some Advil later."

"Want me to go find some now?"

"Thanks," she whispered. "But if you leave me alone with these people, I'll kill you."

Zack gave her a tight smile, then said loudly, "Dylan was just telling me about his novel."

"I needed to get away from academia to really *write*, you know?" Dylan tossed his head back to swig his beer, his wavy, light brown hair brushing against his shoulders. "It was such a suffocating environment—all those self-righteous twenty-three-year-olds. Believe me, the kids are not all right."

"I don't know about that." Zack accepted a beer from Olivia

with a grateful nod. "I teach college kids, and I'm consistently impressed with them."

"Dylan, hi!" Bri took a few unsteady steps toward them, then collapsed on the sand with a giggle. Liesl followed with her usual saunter before lowering herself to the ground. With languorous, catlike movements, she folded her legs into a lotus position, causing her loose white shorts to slide up her thighs.

"How was Bali?" Bri asked, leaning toward Dylan. "Your photos were incredible."

"It was pretty chill," he said. "I wanna go back, but I promised my buddy I'd meet him in Berlin."

"I *adore* Berlin," Liesl said in the vaguely European accent she affected from time to time. She turned to Zack. "It seems like a city you'd really enjoy. It's the only place I've been that feels full of *really* free thinkers, you know?"

"I'll take your word for it," Zack said pleasantly.

A shadow of irritation flickered across Liesl's face. This clearly wasn't the reaction she'd hoped for. She decided to try a different tact. "Everyone also feels so liberated sexually as well. Liv, what's your favorite city for a one-night stand?" Liesl asked, well aware that her friend's older sister wasn't one for overseas flings.

"Sandpiper Island," Zack answered for her, wrapping an arm around Olivia. "Though I'd be pretty bummed if this turned out to be a one-night stand."

Liesl stared at him, though this time, it wasn't part of her act. But it took just a second for her to regain her composure. "You two are together? Oh my god, that's so cute." She flashed them a sweet smile, tossed her long, dark hair over shoulder, and turned to face Dylan.

"You're putting on quite a show," Olivia whispered. "I didn't realize you were such a good actor."

"Anything worth doing is worth doing well. Besides, this is a perfect place to pretend to be in love, isn't it? At a beach bonfire on a starry summer night?"

"Sure, I guess."

"You *guess*?"

"It's kind of cold. The sand is itchy. And I've never understood the allure of a bonfire. It falls into the same category as fireworks, this spectacle we've been socialized to think is special and beautiful. But is it? Does it really move something inside us? Or are we just conditioned to believe it does?"

"Holy shit," Zack said with a grin.

"Yes, I'm just as cynical as you imagined."

"No, that's not it." He reached down and rolled up his pant leg to reveal a tattoo above his ankle: a short sentence in the shape of a cresting wave.

"What does it say?" Olivia asked, squinting for a better look.

"'It's not pretty.' From that Bukowski poem *I Met A Genius*. You know, the one with the kid on the train who points to the ocean and says, 'It's not pretty'?"

"No idea."

"It's about the exact question you just asked, about whether we're conditioned to find certain sights beautiful regardless of the emotion they conjure. It was my favorite poem as a kid." He rolled his pant leg back down. "Super douchey as a tattoo, though," he added sheepishly.

"Not gonna argue with you there."

Zack laughed and shrugged out of his blazer before placing it over Olivia's shoulders. "I can't make the sand less itchy, but I can make you less cold."

"Thanks." Olivia felt a surge of warmth that had nothing to

do with the new layer of fabric. She pulled it around her, then grimaced. "God, this is itchier than the sand! What the hell is this material?"

"It's wool!"

"Who the hell wears wool to a July wedding?"

"Not everyone can afford a new suit for every event, Miss Manners."

She scratched her arm. "I think it gave me fleas."

"You've lost jacket-wearing privileges. I'm taking it back."

Zack tugged on the sleeve, and Olivia pulled it toward her with a laugh. "No way! I'm freezing."

"Guess you'll learn a lesson for next time, then." He yanked it again, but Olivia held on tighter. They played tug-of-war for a few seconds before Olivia let go, sending Zack tumbling backward into the sand.

"That's it," Zack said, wiping sand off his face. "You asked for it." He wrapped his arm around Olivia's waist and started to pull her down toward him.

"Stop it!" She laughed and tried to wriggle free. "I'm wearing silk!" As she squirmed in a half-hearted attempt to get away, she caught sight of Andrew watching them. He was standing alone, a drink in his hand, surveying Olivia and Zack with an expression that was hard to discern from a distance. A flicker of some emotion crossed his face, though perhaps it was just a shadow from the bonfire.

CHAPTER EIGHTEEN

Marigold

Marigold wasn't surprised that she fell asleep during the short drive back to Hugo's house. It had been one of the most physically and emotionally draining days of her life—in the past fourteen hours, she'd learned she'd potentially sabotaged her own wedding, flown to another country without so much as a toothbrush, spoken to her ex-husband for the first time in four years, and had an embarrassing fan encounter at pub trivia, all while lying to everyone she loved most. She could've fallen asleep at a death metal concert. But there was something particularly soothing about sitting in the passenger seat of Hugo's truck at night, watching him drive with one hand on the steering wheel, the other resting lightly on the gearshift. Knowing that she was in such safe hands.

"Let's get you to bed," Hugo said as he opened the passenger door to help her out. She followed him up the front path while Humphrey ran circles around them, barking excitedly. "Just ignore him. He thinks it's time for his walk. I'll take him out after I show you to your room."

"I'll go with you," Marigold said. The sharp scent of the sea had revived her like old-fashioned smelling salts. "I'll sleep better after a little beach walk."

"Let's see how you feel in a few minutes." She followed him inside, through the living room, and into the small room she remembered being used for storage. The last time she'd seen it, it'd been stuffed with suitcases, broken furniture, and battered cardboard boxes, but since then it'd been transformed into a proper guest room, with a cast-iron bed covered in a blue-and-white patchwork quilt, a wooden rocking chair with hand-embroidered cushions, and a small antique dresser with a vase of dried flowers on top.

What had precipitated all this? She remembered what Lauren had said about the intense efforts Hugo had devoted to his abrupt career change: *He was like a man possessed.* Did that have anything to do with his sudden interest in interior decorating? "Wow," Marigold said. "It looks great in here."

"Thanks, yeah, I thought about renting it out on Airbnb at some point, but the idea of strangers sleeping here just felt too weird."

Marigold nodded seriously. "You gotta be on your guard around those *Anne of Green Gables* tourists. Who knows what they're capable of?"

"Easy for you to say—they're not staying in *your* house." Hugo shuddered. "All those fake braids attached to those straw hats . . ."

"You know, it does sound kind of kinky, when you think about it. You're right, I wouldn't want them doing some Anne and Gilbert role-play in my bed."

Hugo covered his ears. "No more, please!"

Marigold flung herself on the bed with a laugh. "Call me *Carrots*," she said, trying to make her voice as husky as Richie's.

Hugo dove onto the bed next to her, face down with his hands still covering his ears. "I don't want to know what that means," he said into the pillow.

Marigold sat up and stared at him. "Don't tell me you've never read the book."

"Nope," he said, rising up onto his elbows.

"Your loss. It's one of the only books I remember truly loving as a kid. My mom read the first two aloud to me and Olivia, back when we shared a room. Then we moved in with Bill, and I read the rest of the series on my own. They were my mom's favorite, too, when she was growing up."

Hugo watched her for a beat, then asked, "How's she doing?"

"Great!" Marigold said automatically. "She's starting this new miracle drug."

But for some reason, the words didn't give her the boost they normally did, and Marigold felt the familiar stirring in her chest, the one she'd become adroit at neutralizing with some kind of distraction—an extravagant shopping spree in SoHo, an impromptu drive to Montauk at two a.m., an evening that started with drinks at the Carlyle and ended with a sunrise photo shoot on an abandoned pier in New Jersey.

The dark thoughts only slipped past her defenses when things were still and silent, when she was afraid of waking Jonathan up after a long day. She recognized the irony; there was no one better equipped to listen to her fears than an empathetic oncologist trained to have the most difficult conversations imaginable. He wouldn't flinch at the questions that filled the silence between heartbeats when there were no other sounds to drown them out.

Marigold pulled her knees up to her chest, and a moment later, Hugo sat up and scooched over so he was sitting next to her, just close enough for their upper arms to touch. Without thinking, she leaned into him and stayed like that for a long moment, feeling the warmth of his body seep into hers. Knowing that he wouldn't move until she did, wouldn't speak until she did. After a few minutes, the knot in her chest began to loosen, and she felt she could breathe again.

The door creaked open, and Humphrey burst into the room, nails skittering on the hardwood floor. "Let's take him out," Marigold said, rising to her feet. "Can I borrow a jacket?"

They headed to the closet by the front door where Hugo produced a fleece for Marigold, and a black hoodie for himself. She watched him zip it up, then burst out laughing. "What?" he asked, confused.

"I didn't realize you were such a big Nickelback fan."

"Who isn't? They're one of Canada's greatest treasures."

"You have got to be kidding me. Tell me you're kidding."

"It was in the lost-and-found box at the boatyard for a long time, and I was cold one day, so I took it."

"Hugo, you cannot wear that."

"Why not?"

"It's literally the most embarrassing sweatshirt I've seen in my entire life."

"I literally couldn't care less. It's really warm, and I wear it to walk my dog. Who's gonna judge me?"

"Oh, trust me, even Humphrey's embarrassed."

Hugo opened the door and Humphrey dashed out to run a

few circles on the lawn while he waited for them to catch up. "You coming?"

"Yes," Marigold grumbled. "But I'll have you know, that sweatshirt alone is grounds for an annulment."

"Who are you worried about impressing?"

"No one. I'm just giving you a little friendly fashion advice."

Hugo began to sing quietly. "Save tonight, and fight the break of dawn. Come tomorrow, tomorrow I'll be gone . . ."

"Okay, that's not Nickelback."

"No? Who is it, then?"

"Eagle-Eye Cherry, I think?"

"Guess I should probably get one of their sweatshirts."

"Oh god, please don't."

"So what's Nickelback's big song?"

"I truly have no idea."

"And yet you somehow find it embarrassing. That makes sense." Hugo pulled out his phone and opened Spotify. "Aha, here we go." The opening chords of a vaguely familiar song rang out as Hugo murmured along. "It's not like you . . . ba doo dum . . . say sorry . . ."

Marigold covered her ears. "Please stop."

". . . this is how you remind me," Hugo sang in that deep, slightly scratchy voice that had captivated her that night on the beach. Suddenly, Nickelback didn't seem all that embarrassing.

But Marigold refused to let him get off that easily and made a show of running ahead.

"I refuse to stay within earshot of that," she called over her shoulder.

Hugo's singing got louder as he approached the chorus.

"I DO NOT CONSENT TO HAVING MY EARS

ACCOSTED BY NICKELBACK," Marigold shouted, though in truth, she'd happily listen to Hugo sing anything. His rich, gravelly voice was still one of her favorite sounds in the world. She sped up, laughing as Hugo chased after her. Without thinking, she turned around the side of the house and ran down the dirt path that led to the beach, guided by muscle memory and the scent of the sea.

"YOU CONSENTED THE MOMENT YOU LANDED ON CANADIAN SOIL!" Hugo rejoined, then started to sing again, even louder.

"Stop it!" Marigold tried to speed up, but her laughter kept throwing her off-balance. She couldn't remember the last time she'd laughed this hard. This wasn't the practiced, coquettish giggle she could produce on command—this was wild and genuine and was probably doing unattractive things to her face, but she didn't care.

When the path began to slope down, she slowed to a walk, though she was still laughing too hard to catch her breath. Her lungs burned, but the rest of her body felt strangely light. Hugo fell in step next to her while Humphrey sprinted ahead, though he kept whirling around and running back to sniff Marigold, confirming she hadn't once again vanished into thin air.

For Marigold, stepping onto the sand was like stepping back in time. Her skin tingled with the memory of emerging from the water—lost and shivering—until she'd been enveloped by the warmth of a fire, and the welcoming smile of a guitar-strumming stranger.

As though reading her mind, Hugo said quietly, "I think about that night every time I come down here."

"How often is that?"

"Every day."

Marigold came to a stop and closed her eyes as something in her chest tore open. The world seemed to swim around her, as if the stars themselves had slid out of the night sky and come tumbling down to earth.

"I'm so sorry," she whispered.

"Why'd you leave, Mare?" Her eyes were still closed, but she could feel him standing next to her.

"I don't know," she said, voice cracking under the weight of all the other words left unsaid, the ones she'd been afraid to utter, even to herself. The truths she'd buried to protect her heart, even when it meant breaking his. Because deep down, she did know why she'd run away after the two happiest weeks of her life. She'd always been told that she was reckless, that she didn't consider the consequences of her impulsive decisions. That she depended on others to clean up her messes. And so, when she'd married a stranger after two weeks, it'd felt like she was proving everyone right. But that was only half of it. The truth was, she'd been blissfully happy and utterly terrified at the same time. She'd felt free with Hugo in a way she never had before; there'd been no pressure to maintain the charming party-girl persona that had defined and exhausted her back home. But that'd also made her feel incredibly vulnerable—she'd never gone that long without her armor, and was terrified that Hugo would eventually lose interest once he realized she was just a girl like any other.

But how could she tell him all this? It sounded trite and ridiculous in her own head; how could she possibly say any of it aloud? "Those two weeks felt like a dream," she said finally. "It was hard to believe that kind of happiness could be real. I figured I'd ruin it at some point, and you didn't deserve that."

"I thought . . ." Hugo's shoulders slumped. "I assumed you regretted marrying someone like me. No degree, no real career. I thought you were ashamed of me."

"Hugo, *no*." The word tore through her, propelled by shame. "You're so completely, totally off base. I didn't think I was good enough for you! You're brilliant and kind and handsome, and I was this flighty girl who couldn't stick with anything."

She turned away, unable to bear the pain in Hugo's eyes. "So that's why you started the business? Redid the house? To prove you were 'good enough' for me?"

He reached out for her arm and gently pulled her around to face him. "I don't regret any of it," he said quietly. "Even if I was . . . misguided. It put me on the right track. And I'll always be grateful to you for that."

"Don't say that." Marigold shook her head just as tears began to trickle down her cheeks. "I don't deserve that."

"Mare . . . You don't need to beat yourself up. There were a million reasons why it never would've worked. Just because I didn't see them at the time doesn't mean you weren't right."

"Right to run off? And leave you a *note*?"

"No," he said, wincing. "That wasn't right. But you were scared and made a mistake. I forgive you."

"I'm not sure I'll ever forgive myself," Marigold said, voice trembling.

Hugo reached out to wipe the tears off her cheek, then ran his fingers along the side of her face until his hand cupped her chin. Gently, he lifted her face toward his. Marigold's whole body went still except for her heart, which began to thump as manically as Humphrey's tail. This was it. The moment she'd longed for and feared since he'd first opened the door.

She closed her eyes and held her breath, then felt his lips brush against her forehead.

She wasn't sure whether she was more disappointed or relieved.

Hugo let out a long breath, then wrapped his arms around her, pulling her toward his chest, this time kissing the top of her head. "You have to," he whispered into her ear. "We gave it a shot. Now it's time to move on."

Marigold didn't answer. She leaned into him, pressing the side of her face into his shirt. Letting him hold her as they swayed to the rhythm of her last few sobs, and then when she'd finished, the crash of the waves against the shore.

CHAPTER NINETEEN

Olivia

Olivia trudged back up the rocky path, wincing with every step. She seemed to be the only person making the ascent alone—everyone else trekking from the beach up to the golf carts did so in pairs. She wasn't sure where Zack had disappeared to. He'd done an impressive job pretending to be her boyfriend all night and was entitled to a break, but his unexplained absence stung more than it should. Here she was, once again, leaving a party alone.

Most of the time, Olivia was totally fine with being single. Her demanding job and full social calendar left her very little time to feel legitimately lonely, but she was hit by occasional waves of wistfulness. Sunday afternoons were tough: those hours between boozy brunch with friends and evenings at home with takeout and whatever prestige drama was on HBO. Sometimes she'd bring work to do in the park, but it was hard to focus with so many seemingly happy couples around, some lying with the their heads in their partners' laps, other chasing after dogs or pushing baby strollers. But special occasions were the worst—there was something about leaving a festive event by herself, the jarring disconnect between the lively party chatter and the heavy silence of the Uber, that served to emphasize Olivia's aloneness.

She felt it more keenly tonight than she had at all the other weddings and galas she'd attended this year. After her almost-date with Andrew, she'd spent hours fantasizing about spending this weekend with him. And then when that dream had dissolved, she'd taken comfort in Zack's attentions, not caring that it'd all been an act. It'd been enough to make her feel wanted, *chosen*.

By the time she made it to the top, most of the chauffeured golf carts had left, leaving just a few locals like Olivia who'd driven themselves. Thank goodness she hadn't had much to drink and was fit to get behind the wheel. It was a relief not to have to make any more small talk, but she couldn't help but wonder what would've happened if her foot had kept her from completing the climb. How long would it have taken someone to notice that she hadn't made it back to the inn?

She limped over to her cart and was about to start the engine when someone called her name. A moment later, Dylan jogged up and launched himself into the passenger seat. "Can I get a ride?"

Olivia suppressed a groan. "What happened? The inn was supposed to send enough golf carts for everyone staying there."

"I hung back on purpose. I needed to make sure that Bri girl didn't try to follow me up to my room."

The words "that Bri girl" rankled her. Bri wasn't Olivia's favorite person by a long shot, but she was objectively pretty, smart enough, and more fun to talk to than a lot of Marigold's friends. Certainly more fun than Dylan. "Oh yeah?" Olivia said, muscle memory compelling her to glance over her shoulder before she pulled onto the road, despite the fact that there was no sign of traffic. "Why? I thought you were single."

"Does that mean I have to sleep with every girl who throws herself at me?"

"No offense, but she definitely didn't seem to be throwing herself at you. She was just drunk and flirty."

"Fine, whatever. I'm just getting tired of hookups, you know? I want to fall in love."

"No, I get it," Olivia said, softening. "It's tough out there."

"Yeah, and I'm so over the apps."

"Same. The gaslighting makes me feel truly insane. Like, sir, if you liked me enough to make out with me outside my building, why wouldn't you want a second date? It doesn't make any sense! I get ghosting after you've slept with someone. I mean, it's shitty, but I understand the logic. But if you're attracted to someone, why would you disappear *before* you've even had sex? Have you ever done that?"

"Done what?"

"Made out with a woman on a first date and then ghosted her."

Dylan shrugged. "Yeah, probably."

"But *why*? Explain it to me. If you like her enough to kiss her at the end of the first date, why wouldn't you want to go on a second date?"

He didn't exactly scratch his head, but he ran his fingers through his long hair. "If she's hot, I'll kiss her. Because kissing is fun. But that doesn't mean I necessarily want to see her again."

Olivia eased up on the gas as they entered a stretch of road covered by a canopy of trees that blocked most of the moonlight. There was a small pothole up ahead that sometimes caught her by surprise in the dark. "But if she's hot and you had fun—and you say you're looking to fall in love—why wouldn't you want to see her again? That's how this works."

"Because I don't want to waste my time when it's not the extraordinary, life-changing kind of love I'm looking for."

"How can you know that after one date?"

"Trust me, I know. When I meet the right woman, it's going to feel electrifying. I'm not gonna go home after to scroll on my phone and jerk off. I'll stay up all night writing the best short story of my life, then go for a run at sunrise."

"That's not love. That's cocaine."

Dylan turned to glare at her. "Real love *is* a drug.

"Dude, no woman is going to make you feel *high*. Especially not on a first date. You're looking for some manic pixie dream girl that doesn't exist."

"I'm not gonna apologize for having high standards." He paused then said, "So what's the deal with Emerson?"

"What about her?" Olivia asked flatly.

"Is that guy she's with her boyfriend?"

"I'm not sure," Olivia said, torn between her urge to burst Dylan's bubble and her desire for him to lure Emerson away from Andrew. Dylan was almost as good-looking as Andrew. He might have a shot, if he never opened his mouth.

"A supermodel lawyer," Dylan said with a wistful sight. "I guarantee no one is ghosting *her* after a first date."

The pothole was up ahead, but instead of slowing down, Olivia reached for the roof handle and stepped on the accelerator. The golf cart launched into the air and landed with a heavy jolt that nearly sent Dylan flying out of his seat. "Fuck," he yelped.

"Whoops! Sorry about that."

They spent the rest of the short drive in silence. Olivia pulled off the road next to the long set of wooden steps that led from the beach up to the inn. Dylan jumped out before she had time to kill the engine. "Thanks for the ride," he said curtly, then jogged up the stairs two at a time.

Olivia slid out of the driver's seat, testing her injured foot before putting her full weight on it. It was still throbbing from the walk from the beach, and the prospect of another steep flight of stairs was daunting. *Don't be a baby*, she told herself. *Think of what Mom has gone through. You can deal with a hurt foot.* She grabbed on to the railing and started to hoist herself up the first step when she saw a figure hurrying down the stairs. "Hold on!" a familiar voice called. It was Andrew.

"Let me help," he said, wrapping his arm around her waist.

"Thanks," she said gratefully. She leaned into him as he helped her hop up the stairs one by one, keeping the weight off her bad foot. When they reached the porch, Olivia collapsed into a wicker chair with a heavy sigh. "I need to take a break, but you go ahead."

"I'm in no rush." He sat down in the chair next to her.

"Isn't Emerson waiting for you?" Apparently, her aching foot wasn't enough for her to meet her pain threshold for the evening.

"She's still out with her friends." He sounded slightly uncomfortable. "What about Zack?"

"Oh . . . he goes to bed early so he can get up to write." She prayed that Andrew wouldn't find Zack in the hotel bar with some woman he found genuinely attractive, who he hadn't just decided to flirt with as a favor.

Andrew turned to face the ocean. "He's not exactly what I would've expected for you."

"I thought you were a fan?"

"I am! He's a really interesting writer. Just not someone I would've picked out for you."

"Why not?"

"Just a vibe."

"Oh, come on. Tell me what you mean!"

"I'm not gonna talk shit about your new boyfriend."

"He's not my *boyfriend*, exactly. You can tell me what you think. I promise I won't get mad."

"Right, because that's always such an easy promise to keep."

"Don't worry, I don't actually care what you think. I'm just curious."

Andrew made a show of surveying her. "That's probably true. You don't seem like someone who can be easily swayed one way or the other."

"So you're trying to sway me?" Her lighthearted tone belied the excitement fizzing in her chest. Zack had been right. Everything seemed to be going according to plan. How often did that happen in real life?

"No, no swaying," Andrew said with a smile. "I was just surprised. Zack seems like a nice guy. And he's clearly really smart. But there's also something sort of naïve about him. From what I can tell, he has a black-and-white, binary way of looking at the world. And you're more realistic; you get that things are messy and complicated, that it's not always about right vs. wrong."

"That doesn't really sound like a compliment."

"It is, I swear! You're someone who understands nuance. I would've thought that his anticapitalism shtick would've struck you as a little . . . unsophisticated."

"Ah, I see." Olivia nodded. "And here I was thinking that you were judging him for his breach of fashion etiquette."

"That jacket *was* a bold choice."

"Now you're just being mean."

"Oh, I know you'll spruce him up once you make things official. I'm sure the next time I see him, he'll be in Thom Browne."

"What about Tom Ford?" Olivia asked, eying Andrew's suit knowingly.

"Let's not get carried away. That'd be too much of a shock to the system."

"Like how you can't give a starving person too much food at once."

Andrew raised an eyebrow. "That sounds like something your not-quite-boyfriend would accuse us of—denying starving people food for their own good."

"So where does Emerson fall on this continuum? Is she closer to Zack or has she veered over to the dark side with you?"

"Hard to say. We don't really have those kinds of conversations."

"Really? So, what? She gets back from the Hague and wants to talk about *Love Island*?"

"Maybe not *Love Island*, but definitely not social stratification and the wealth gap."

"How funny. That's Zack's kink," she said, taking a page out of Liesl's book. Why not invite Andrew to think about Olivia having sex?

"Arguing about economic policy in bed?"

"Sure, what's wrong with that? Though now I draw the line when it comes to dressing as Marx. That was just too weird."

"Oh yeah? Who wore the costume, you or him?"

"We liked to switch it up."

Andrew laughed and patted her on the arm. "I always forget how funny you are when you're relaxed." She expected him to remove his hand, but he left it there, resting lightly just above her elbow.

"Trust me, I'm the furthest thing from relaxed at the moment."

"Why? What's wrong?"

"Oh . . . you know, family weddings are always stressful, aren't they?" *Especially when the bride is missing.*

"Anything I can help with?" He squeezed her arm, and her breath caught in her chest.

"You've already done more than enough. I'd still be trying to get up those stairs if you hadn't come to my rescue."

"I'm a little pissed that Zack went back to the inn without you."

"I told him it was fine."

"I wouldn't have listened," Andrew said quietly, leaning toward her.

Oliva raised her chin ever so slightly, certain she was about to feel his lips brush against hers. Her mouth tingled with anticipation, and she was just about to close her eyes when Andrew stood up. "I'd better get to bed. It's later than I realized. Do you need help getting up to your room?"

"No thanks. I'm on the first floor," she lied. There was no way she'd let Andrew help her up any more stairs. She couldn't press her body against him knowing that he was heading to wait for Emerson. Dylan was right—it was perfectly possible for men to flirt shamelessly with women who fell far short of their standards.

"Have a good night." Andrew patted her shoulder in a decidedly platonic fashion and then headed inside.

Olivia pulled her knees up to her chest and squeezed, trying to staunch the spread of disappointment and embarrassment. What had she been thinking? Even if she hadn't imagined the vibe between them, Andrew wasn't the kind of guy who'd make a move on a woman with a boyfriend, especially when his own date was en route to meet him. In their shared room.

Her phone rang, and she sighed as she rummaged through her purse. It was Lulu. "Mom?" Olivia answered, suddenly trembling for an entirely different reason. She'd never forget the sound of her mother wheezing that time she'd called Olivia in the middle of the night, choking and terrified, unable to breathe when Bill was out of town. "Is everything okay?"

"Yes, don't worry." Lulu sounded tired but otherwise fine. "I'm so sorry to call this late, but there's been some mix-up with the rooms. Apparently, the Varicks somehow convinced the front desk into giving them Aunt Harriet's suite. She just tried to check in and was told they're completely booked."

"Oh god," Olivia said. *Fucking Varicks.* She'd instructed the inn to give them one of the standard rooms. "I'm sorry, I told them . . . Don't worry about it, okay? I'll figure it out."

"It's so late. I was wondering—do you mind crashing with Zack and letting Aunt Harriet sleep in your room? I know you booked separate rooms to keep the rest of us off the scent, but now that the secret's out . . ."

Oh, fuck my life, Olivia thought, suppressing a groan. How the hell was she supposed to wake up her fake boyfriend and ask if she could sleep in his room? She didn't even have his number. "No problem. That's a good solution," Olivia said.

"Wonderful. I'll tell Aunt Harriet. Good night, hon."

"'Night, Mom. I love you." She'd started saying it every time she hung up, just in case.

"I love you too."

CHAPTER TWENTY

Natalie

This can't be how Jonathan imagined the night before his wedding, Natalie thought, looking around the lounge area that contained the inn's after-hours honor bar, a beautiful, library-esque room with built-in bookshelves, a fireplace, and leather club chairs where some of the guests had gathered for a nightcap. Jonathan and Natalie's actual friends had all gone to bed—save for Zack, who'd left on a quest to find an open pharmacy—and now they were stuck with Hannah and her husband, Kevin, both of whom defied the laws of nature by growing duller the drunker they became.

"Dinner was delicious, wasn't it?" Hannah said. "I had the chicken and the salad, and a little bit of the beef, but I didn't try the fish, which is a shame because later at the bonfire, this woman was *raving* about the fish. So I asked Kevin if he'd tried it, but he said he couldn't remember, and I told him he'd remember really exceptional fish, so either he didn't have it, or else it wasn't as special as that woman thought it was. But I was bummed about missing out, so I googled the chef and it turns out his restaurant is going to have a booth at the food festival in my parents' town, the same weekend we'll be visiting next month. Isn't that ironic?"

"*So* ironic," Jonathan said before flashing Natalie a quick smile. It was one of their many shared linguistic pet peeves, when people erroneously used *ironic* instead of *coincidence*. They also shared a mutual dislike for *back east* (back from where?), *yummy* (cloyingly cutesy), *fine wine* (corny and meaningless), and *curl up with a good book* (why would anyone curl up with a *bad* book?) Jonathan typed something on his phone, and a moment later, Natalie's buzzed with a text.

This isn't how I pictured the night before my wedding.

This is what you get for coming to my rescue, Natalie wrote back. The lounge had been empty when she'd snuck in to grab a nightcap from the honor bar, but instead of heading straight back to her room, she'd made the error of sitting down for a moment. A minute later, Hannah had bustled in, hair damp from the rain. "Goodness, here you are all alone again!" she'd said, fixing Natalie with a pitying smile while Kevin headed wordlessly to the bar. "I'm exhausted, but I'll sit here for a bit while you finish your drink."

"I'm fine, really," Natalie had said. "I could actually use a few minutes by myself."

"Don't be silly! You should never drink alone. Especially single girls. It can be a slippery slope, you know. That glass of wine before bed turns into two, and pretty soon you're downing a bottle a night."

Kevin ambled over with the enormous water glass he'd filled to the brim with scotch, ignoring the neat row of appropriately sized whiskey tumblers. "I think you forgot to sign for that," Natalie had said.

"What are you talking about?" Kevin grumbled.

"It's an honor bar. You're supposed to sign for it on the sheet there."

Kevin sniffed. "What kind of wedding doesn't have an open bar?"

Natalie stared at him incredulously. "This isn't the wedding. This is a hotel."

Hannah continued, ignoring the whole exchange, "You know, I have a cousin in New York you might like. Well, he lives in New Jersey, but he comes into the city whenever he has a doctor's appointment."

That's when Jonathan had wandered in with Zack and another groomsman, Chris. They'd planned to end the night at a dive bar in town, but had arrived to find it closed due to flooding from earlier. "Here's the man of the hour!" Hannah had said. "I was just telling Natalie that it's not good to spend so much time alone, and that she *has* to meet my very eligible cousin."

"Natalie's a writer. She needs to spend time alone," Jonathan had said, signing for the bourbon he'd poured for himself and his groomsmen. "She's not one of those people who talks more than they think." Zack laughed and then started to choke on his drink until Jonathan pounded him on the back.

A few other guests had joined for a bit, but the impromptu after-after-party had wound down, leaving just Natalie, Jonathan, Hannah, and Kevin. Natalie was more than ready for bed, but it didn't seem right to abandon the groom. Jonathan's ceiling had started to leak during the storm, and the inn's handyman was still in his room, patching it up.

Finally, Kevin topped up his drink, once again ignoring the notepad where guests were meant to sign for their drinks, and he and Hannah retired for the night.

“You don’t have to wait here with me,” Jonathan said to Natalie after they left. “You look exhausted.”

“Thanks for pointing that out.”

“Not *bad* exhausted. I just know you’ve had a long day. I don’t know how we’ll ever repay you for everything you’ve done. You’d win the maid of honor Olympics, hands down.” He stood up, walked over to the bar, picked up a pen, and began to scribble on the notepad.

“What are you doing?” Natalie asked.

“I’m marking down Kevin’s drinks . . . and billing everyone else’s drinks to his room.”

“No, you’re not.”

“I absolutely am.”

“Jonathan! Stop it. That’s fraud.”

“Fraud?” Jonathan repeated with a smile. “Right, of course. I’m talking to the girl who told the registrar that they’d given her *too* much financial aid.”

“It was a mistake! I wasn’t being a Goody Two-shoes. It would’ve come back to bite me in the ass at some point.”

“Fine. I won’t make Kevin the cheapskate pay for a few drinks. Let see . . . I’ll sign the book as . . . Amanda Hugginkiss.”

“Yeah, sure you will . . .” Natalie said, rolling her eyes.

“Just did.”

“No, you didn’t.” She got up and walked over to the book. Sure enough, “Amanda Hugginkiss” had signed for two whiskeys.

“You’re such a doofus,” she said, unable to stifle a giggle.

"Come on. You're creating extra work for the poor employee who'll have to sort this out."

"Oh, it's fine. I already told the front desk that I'd cover the drinks from tonight."

"Well, in that case . . ." Natalie took the pen, scratched out her own name, and replaced it with *Dr. Anita Cox*.

Jonathan stared at it, wide-eyed, and they both burst out laughing. Then, with a mischievous smile, he added "Biggs" as a middle name, and Natalie laughed so hard she lost her balance and had to collapse back into her armchair. "I don't know why I'm having this reaction," she said, wiping tears from her eyes. "It's really not *that* funny." Perhaps it wasn't the juvenile joke; maybe it was the surprise of seeing Jonathan's goofy side remerge. She hadn't seen him like this in years—it'd been a long time since she'd felt this giddy energy with him, the kind she remembered from their early days in New York, when they'd gorge on all-you-can-eat sushi in the East Village, then meet some of their college friends for karaoke in Koreatown, where, if she'd had enough to drink, Jonathan could persuade her to sing TLC's "Waterfalls" with him.

"I think you're regressing," Natalie said, still giggling. "It's probably the stress of the wedding. I haven't seen you like this in ages."

Jonathan sank back down into his own chair, his expression suddenly contemplative.

"It's not a bad thing!" Natalie continued. "I didn't mean that you were doing anything wrong."

"No, I know. I just . . . I guess I didn't realize how much I'd changed."

"I don't think you changed. You just grew up—we all did.

And that's a good thing. No one wants a doctor who signs his charts as *Amanda Hugginkiss*."

"For many reasons," Jonathan said with a small smile. "But I miss the way I used to joke around, you know? Blow off steam. Now it's like . . . I don't know."

"What do you mean?"

"That's not the guy Marigold fell for," he said quietly, then took a long sip of his drink. "Not that it's her fault! It's just . . . when we started dating, she kept saying how different I was from the other guys she'd been with. How I was 'mature' and 'responsible' because my job actually meant something. And I guess I leaned into that without even realizing it. And then, after a while, it just felt like . . ." He exhaled. "Like if I let the other parts of me show, it'd mess with the version of me she fell in love with."

"Come on. You think Marigold's only marrying you because you're a doctor?" Natalie scoffed, though she wasn't sure who her incredulity was meant to protect, whether she was bolstering Jonathan's confidence or defending Marigold.

"No. I think I didn't give her the chance to get to know the real me."

"You're being ridiculous. You make jokes around her all the time."

"Certain kinds of jokes. Not stupid, goofy ones."

"Then we all owe Marigold a huge thank-you."

"Come on, Bumpy. You know what I mean. You just pointed it out!"

"It sounds like you just have cold feet."

"Well, I *was* just out in a rainstorm." He leaned back in his chair and smiled. "Remember when Anna had a panic attack the night before her wedding?" About a year after graduation, they'd gone to the first of their college friends' weddings. The night before the ceremony, the bride, Anna, had begun to freak out, and when she'd complained of chest pains, Natalie had summoned Jonathan, who, although only a first-year med student, seemed best equipped to deal with the situation.

"Oh god, yes," Natalie said with a laugh. She raised her voice to imitate Anna: "Of course I'm having a heart attack! I'm about to marry a man who takes so long to shit in the morning, he takes his laptop with him. And his *coffee mug*." She shook her head. "At least Marigold doesn't do *that*."

"How would you know?"

"We were roommates!" She took a sip of water then spat it out. "This is someone else's drink. Ew, ew, ew. Am I going to get herpes? Can you give me something to prevent it?"

"Oh my god, I thought you said your germophobia was getting better."

"It is! I can hold the subway pole now."

"I'm very proud of you. Now, what about ketchup bottles?"

"No comment." Back when they used to have dinner together regularly, before she introduced him to Marigold, he'd noticed that she never put ketchup on her fries and eventually she'd admitted that the communal bottles freaked her out; too many people had touched them. That night, he'd poured ketchup onto her plate as a joke, but then he did it the next time she ordered a burger, and the time after that. Soon, it was automatic—as soon as their food arrived, Jonathan would add the appropriate condiment to Natalie's plate without a word.

"You need exposure therapy. ASAP."

"You're not a psychiatrist."

"Any port in a storm."

"That's not what that means," Natalie said with a smile.

Jonathan shrugged. "When in Rome."

"Gotta strike when the iron is hot."

"It'll be like killing two birds with one stone." It was one of their old bits—slipping random clichés into conversation where they didn't belong. "I'm not letting you leave this wedding without conquering your fear of germy hands. Come here." He reached out and grabbed her arm.

"Stop it," Natalie said, laughing.

"Now close your eyes and imagine allllll my germs seeping into your skin."

"You sound like you're trying to *hypnotize* me. I'm going to have you disbarred."

"That's for lawyers."

"Fine. I'm going to have you dis-doctored."

"Now take a deep breath in . . . and a deep breath out . . ."

"This isn't exposure therapy. I'm not freaked out by you touching my arm."

"Right. Hmmm . . . Let's see, didn't you once say that you could never get a facial because you didn't believe anyone had clean enough hands to touch your face?"

Natalie pulled back. "You wouldn't."

"Now, just relax . . ." Jonathan tightened his hold on her arm and brought his other hand to her cheek.

"Jonathan! Come on," Natalie giggled, squirming away. He brushed his hand across her cheek, and she went completely still, momentarily stunned by the current of electricity buzzing across her skin. The pleasure was short-lived, swept aside by panic that he'd noticed the effect his touch had on her. "It's your fault for enabling me all those years," she said with forced playfulness.

"What choice did I have? You looked so helpless, staring longingly at the ketchup."

"Helpless. Great."

"Helpless and adorable. I couldn't stand to see you in distress. I had such a crush on you back then."

Natalie's heart slammed against her sternum, as if pressing itself against her rib cage to hear better. "What?"

"Oh, come on," Jonathan said, smiling. "Don't pretend like you didn't know."

What the hell was going on? Had she gone through the looking glass? Entered Bizarro World? There was no way she'd just heard . . . No, it wasn't possible.

Jonathan had had a crush on *her*?

Her mind reeled as she thought how hard she'd worked to conceal her feelings for him. The drastic measures she'd taken to cover her tracks lest she make him uncomfortable or ruin their friendship.

Or just embarrass herself. Because that's what it'd really come down to, hadn't it? She'd been afraid of looking foolish. And so she hadn't gone after the one thing she'd wanted most of all.

Tell him, a voice screamed from the back of her head. *Tell him that you've been head over heels in love with him for years. Tell him right now.* Maybe it wasn't too late to make things right. He'd admitted he was worried about marrying Marigold. Maybe he *wanted* a reason to call things off.

Natalie took a breath, willing herself to speak, but no sound emerged. Words still escaped her.

Jonathan rose from his chair with a heavy sigh. "I'm gonna try Marigold again. I won't be able to sleep until I hear her voice and know she's okay."

Natalie felt something inside her clatter, a tiny scaffolding of hope she'd never had the right to build in the first place. No one would ever choose her over Marigold. Maybe Jonathan had had a crush on her once, but he would've dropped Natalie as soon as he set eyes on her gorgeous, charismatic roommate. Natalie had only accelerated the inevitable by introducing them. Jonathan was never going to be hers.

" 'Night, Bumpy."

"Good night."

He lifted his whiskey glass from the table, gave her head an affectionate pat, then left to call the woman he truly loved.

CHAPTER TWENTY-ONE

Olivia

Olivia took pride in her fearlessness. Or at least, her ability to master fear. When they'd still lived in their old apartment, she'd stomped on cockroaches the size of playing cards while Marigold cowered. She'd stood up to sexist law school professors and taken down some of the city's most feared litigators. But the thought of knocking on Zack's door somehow felt more daunting than any of these encounters. Would he really believe that Lulu had given Olivia's room away? Or would he assume that she'd gotten carried away by their fake-dating scheme and was no longer able to distinguish between reality and fantasy?

Olivia had a spreadsheet with all the guests' room assignments, but she felt weird about rolling up with no warning. Yet the thought of texting Jonathan and asking for Zack's phone number at one a.m. was even more mortifying. She had his email address, but there was no guarantee he'd check before bed. She supposed she could drive the golf cart back to the cottage, but then who would believe that she and Zack were in a relationship? The last thing Lulu needed right now was proof that her older daughter couldn't hang on to a man for more than twenty-four hours.

Finally, she steeled herself and knocked on Zack's door. He opened it a few moments later. It didn't seem like she'd roused him from sleep, though he'd clearly been getting ready for bed. He had on flannel pajama pants but wasn't wearing a shirt, and it took all of Olivia's well-developed self-control not to stare. His lanky body had a lot more lean muscle that she would've expected, including defined biceps and abs approaching a six-pack. An image flashed into her head of Zack doing weighted sit-ups with a one-thousand-page copy of *Das Kapital*.

"Hey," he said. "Everything okay?"

She explained the conundrum with her aunt's room and told him about Lulu's request. "But only if you feel comfortable," Olivia added quickly. "I can easily find somewhere else to sleep." *Like the front porch. Or maybe the golf cart.*

"Yeah, sure, no problem." He stepped to the side and held the door open for her. He sounded a bit flat. Maybe he had been asleep? Or perhaps he just resented having women he barely knew showing up with their luggage in the middle of the night.

Zack's room was a bit smaller than hers but decorated similarly, with antique wooden furniture—or excellent reproductions—a scratchy hooked rug under the brass bed, dainty floral wallpaper, and framed nautical prints. But whereas Olivia had been living out of her suitcase, Zack's belongings were everywhere: a few pair of shoes lined up neatly next to the dresser, a stack of books on the desk, a pile of used workout clothes in a heap next to the bathroom, and a night table covered with all manner of pill bottles, hand cream, toiletry bag, reading glasses, ChapStick, and tissues. Olivia hadn't seen anything like the nightstand since she'd last visited her great-grandmother in her nursing home.

"I'll sleep on the floor," Olivia said, eyeing the queen-sized bed.

"It's okay. I can take the floor."

"That's ridiculous. It's your room, and you're the one doing me a massive favor."

"You have a big day tomorrow. I just need to avoid getting too drunk to stand during the ceremony."

"Those sound like my marching orders as well." Olivia took a throw blanket from the end of Zack's bed and laid it on the floor. "I'm fine here, I promise. Okay if take a pillow?"

Zack handed her one, along with the quilt. "Use them both. I'll be fine with just the top sheet. I run hot."

When it came time to take her sleepwear out of her suitcase, she hesitated. She'd had Andrew in mind when she'd packed her nightgown, a sexy black slip that came to midthigh, but if she were trying to assure Zack that her *my aunt took my room* story wasn't a ruse, this outfit wasn't going to help her case. But the other option would be a T-shirt and underwear, which was objectively worse.

Perhaps she wasn't as fearless as she'd thought.

She went to the bathroom to brush her teeth and wash her face, then changed into her nightgown. There was no full-length mirror, of course. These old-timey inns never had them. Perhaps it was for historical accuracy. After all, the colonists didn't have to make sure their nightgowns covered their ass cheeks. In an act of desperation, Olivia stepped onto the toilet and tried to examine her reflection that way. She frowned; it was definitely on the edge of inappropriate, but still her best option.

When she came out of the bathroom, she made a beeline for her makeshift bed, eager to get under the blanket as quickly as possible. "Good night," she said, avoiding Zack's eyes. "Thanks again for this."

"No problem." He switched off the lamp on the nightstand. For the first few minutes, an unnatural silence filled the room, as though they were each taking care not to move at all. Olivia's shoulder ached on the hard floor, but she felt weirdly self-conscious rolling over. *I would've been more comfortable in the golf cart.*

"Seems like the plan is working," Zack said finally.

"What do you mean?" Olivia asked, tensing, convinced that Zack thought she'd concocted a plan to get into his room.

"You and Andrew looked really cozy on the porch."

"You were watching us?"

"I wasn't *watching* you. I saw you when I came back from my walk."

"Our little adventure earlier today wasn't enough exercise for you?"

"I went to buy an Ace bandage for your foot. But the stores were all closed."

A strange kind of warmth seeped through her chest. She wasn't used to people going out of their way to care for her like that. "Yeah, everything in town shuts down at eight. That was really nice of you, though." She imagined Zack wandering from store to store, squinting at the locked doors through the storm.

He didn't answer, and for a second, she thought he'd fallen asleep, but then he said, "What happened to Emerson?"

"Andrew said she was out with friends who live on the island."

"I guess that answers the girlfriend question."

"Couples don't have to spend every second of the day together."

"No, but they don't canoodle in the dark with other people unless they're total shitheads."

"Do you really think that counted as canoodling?" Olivia's skin tingled at the memory of Andrew's hand on her arm.

"Seemed like it, though it was hard to tell in the dark." A smile crept into his voice. "But, of course, it depends on whether you're measuring it on the American or European scale."

"I didn't realize you could measure canoodling with both the imperial and metric systems."

"Oh yes. What I saw seemed like a three in European canoodling, and an eight on the American scale."

"It's really hard to scandalize Europeans, isn't it? Especially the Germans. They're so much *freer* than us, aren't they?"

"That Liesl is something else. I'm glad Jonathan warned me about her."

"Really? What'd he say?"

"Just that she'd probably hit on me, not because she was actually interested, but because she needed assurance that every man around wanted her."

"He nailed that one on the head," Olivia said. "It's fascinating—she's been like that since she was twelve."

"Kind of sad, isn't it?"

"That's one word for it."

"I'm a little disappointed I cut her off so quickly. I mean, how far does it go?"

"Dunno. You should call her bluff and tell her you want to try some move you learned in a German sex club. A kaiserschnoodle or something."

Zack laughed. "A king poodle?"

"Don't laugh at my sexual proclivities. I thought you were supposed to be the open-minded one."

"Oh, I am. It's just that the kaiserschnoodle is too tame for me. I prefer a glockenspieltergeist."

"So . . . a glockenspiel ghost?"

"There's no English word for it. But trust me, your boy Andrew wouldn't be able to pull it off."

"I'll keep that in mind."

They fell silent, and Olivia assumed this meant it was time to sleep, but just when she was certain Zack had drifted off, he said "Weinerfraude."

Olivia giggled, then buried her face in her pillow. "Okay, enough! I get it!"

This time, the silence lasted longer than before, and it was nearly five full minutes before Zack shouted, "Get the schnitzel away from my pickle!" He sat up, and in the darkness he mimed wiping sweat off his brow. "Sorry, I think I was having a nightmare."

Olivia burst out laughing and couldn't stop. "Oh my god, I can't breathe."

"I'll stop now," Zack said. "I know you're trying to sleep."

"It's okay. It normally takes me hours to fall asleep."

"Why?" he asked, his voice suddenly serious.

"I don't know . . . It's hard to turn my brain off sometimes."

"I get that. Anything in particular at the moment?"

"It's . . . it's hard to relax. I feel like if I fall asleep, something bad will happen." *My mom will call me again and I won't hear my phone. She'll be scared and in pain, and I won't get to her in time. Every time I close my eyes, I brace for the sound of the world crumbling around me.*

"That sounds awful."

"There are worse things."

"I'm sorry." He paused and then, tentatively, with the care of someone stepping onto thin ice, he said, "Is it about your mom?"

"Yeah, mostly . . . She told me about the care package, by the way. That was really thoughtful of you."

"I was happy to. Your mom's awesome. Jonathan won the mother-in-law lottery."

"He did." Her voice shook slightly. What if Olivia didn't meet her future husband until after . . . well, after it was too late? How could she marry someone who'd never known Lulu? Who only thought of her as a whimsically dressed character in photos instead of a living, breathing, dancing, art-creating being?

"Are you worried right now?" Zack asked quietly.

Olivia hesitated. Even the giddiness of her laughing fit hadn't been enough to dispel the weight that settled in her chest every night, growing heavier and heavier with each passing minute until it felt like it'd crush her bones. "Yeah, it doesn't really go away until dawn. That's when I can finally relax. Of course, that's also when I have to get up and go to work, so that sucks."

"Does talking about it help?"

"Not really." She didn't know how to make any of those feelings word-shaped.

What if this treatment doesn't work?

I'm worried I'll also disappear.

How can I ask her if she's afraid to die?

I don't know if I can be the brave one this time.

A sob escaped her before she realized what was happening.

"Olivia? Are you okay?"

Tears began to stream down her face. Tears for Lulu, who

had to say goodbye to everyone she loved, who'd never meet her grandchildren. Tears for Marigold, who wouldn't have time to prepare. Tears for Bill, who loved his wife as fiercely and tenderly as a man could, who would've given up his own life if it meant that Lulu could have even a year more of hers. And for the first time, tears for herself.

Without another word, Zack got out of bed, lowered himself to the ground, and wrapped his arm around her.

You can't tell him, Olivia thought. *You promised you wouldn't tell anyone.* But the secret felt so spiky inside her body, she'd give anything to release it, if only for a moment. "My mom is stopping treatment. Only my parents and I know. No one's told Marigold."

Zack was silent for a long moment. "Fuck."

"Yeah."

"I'm so sorry," he whispered. He held her like that until her sobs subsided, the pressure more comforting than words could ever be. Then he gently lifted her to her feet and guided her toward the bed. "I'm taking the floor. No arguing."

"Okay," she said, too weary to push back.

"You can sleep," he said. "I promise, nothing bad will happen tonight."

"You can't promise that."

"Would the creator of the glockenspieltergeist lie to you?"

She was struck by how much she already missed the weight of his body. As he turned away, she asked softly, "Will you lay with me for a minute?"

Without a word, he climbed into the bed next to her. She turned onto her side to make room, and he wrapped his arms around her, pulling her backward against his chest. "Is this okay?" he whispered in her ear. "Just tell me what you need."

"This is good." Her voice was still shaky, but not as if she were about to cry. She was hyperaware of the fact that Zack wasn't wearing a shirt, his skin warm against her own mostly exposed back. She was even more aware of the contact between their lower halves; her nightgown had ridden up so there was nothing separating the front of his pajama pants from the rather insubstantial back of her black lace underwear.

He tightened his hold but didn't move his hand, which stayed in the safe zone between her breasts and her waist. The message was clear—he wasn't going to make any kind of move, not when she'd just tearfully confided in him about her dying mom. But for the first time in a long while, those worries felt suddenly far from her mind. Her body had taken over, and all that seemed to matter was staying as close to Zack as possible. She tilted her hips back, a movement so subtle, he might not have noticed, had the extra contact not made her inhale sharply. The fingers on her torso twitched, and soon Zack was running his hand along her stomach. She felt his breath on her neck, her ear, then she turned to face him. There was nothing tentative about the kiss—her lips parted to make room for his tongue, which explored her mouth with the same gentle urgency as the fingers roaming her body. Zack's hand ran down her back, slowly tracing her spine all the way to the bottom before squeezing her ass.

Every point where their bodies met—their hands, their cheeks, their thighs, their tongues—tingled to the point of aching. An ache Olivia was suddenly desperate to satisfy. As if reading her mind, Zack brought his hand to her thigh, lightly stroking it, his fingers dancing slightly higher each time. She couldn't see his face, but she could almost imagine him smirking as she shuddered, taking the same pleasure from teasing her like this as he did from their verbal banter. Her body pulsed with anticipation until it became almost too painful to endure.

He began to rub her underwear in just the right spot, the sensation so intense and surprising that she almost jerked away. He paused for a moment, then resumed with less pressure. "Better?" he whispered.

Olivia could only manage a nod.

Normally, Olivia would try to move things along at this point. One-night stands were never satisfying for her, and once the novelty wore off, she was keen to get to the next stage of the proceedings. But the thought of Zack stopping his current activity felt unbearable. Every time her breathing became more regular, when he felt her body relax, he increased the pressure slightly.

"Any chance you packed a condom in addition to eight different brands of hand cream?" she finally whispered. She felt so close to the edge, she had to pull herself back.

He laughed, his breath tickling her ear. "Yeah, I'll get it in a minute."

"Get it now."

"You're not the boss right now, counselor." He slipped his hand into her underwear and found the spot again. Before her brain shut down completely, Olivia had the fleeting thought that she should perhaps do something to reciprocate, but as Zack's hips rubbed against her, it became increasingly clear that he didn't need any additional assistance.

Her breathing grew ragged, and just when she thought she couldn't hold on any longer, he reached for something in the toiletry bag on the nightstand. He fiddled with the wrapper briefly, and then gently shifted her over so she was lying on her back. He lowered himself on top of her and pressed forward, her body yielding. As her breath caught, he paused and brought his face to hers, kissing her mouth, her neck, her ear, before returning to her lips, kissing her even more deeply as he pushed himself fully inside her. She gasped and clutched his back as he began to move, slowly but with purposeful intensity.

She wriggled and positioned herself so that every thrust made her nerves tingle. He followed her lead and adjusted accordingly. Olivia felt pressure building at a rate she'd never experienced before.

The world melted away. No one else existed; nothing else mattered except for the feeling of Zack. There wasn't room for any other thought, any other sensation. The last thing Olivia remembered before falling asleep a bit later was the sound of her own contented sigh, and the warmth of Zack's breath on her skin. As she drifted off, she felt certain he'd keep his promise to make sure nothing bad happened. At least, not tonight.

CHAPTER TWENTY-TWO

Marigold

The guest room door creaked open, and Hugo stuck his head in. It was just before five a.m., but his long hair was damp and combed, a detail Marigold could spot easily because light had begun streaming through the blinds an hour earlier; this far north, the sun didn't set for more than a few hours in the summer. She'd seen it rise after a restless night—despite her physical exhaustion, it'd been almost impossible to fall asleep. Every time she closed her eyes, she imagined Jonathan lying in bed alone. She hadn't answered when he'd called last night, terrified that some noise in the background would betray her true location: the crash of the waves, Humphrey's nails skittering on the hardwood floors, the tread of Hugo's boots. When those thoughts dissipated, she thought about her mother, who surely hadn't slept much, either, torn between anxiety for Marigold and frustration that her heedless daughter had created so much unnecessary chaos.

And then there was what Hugo had said to her on the beach:

"We gave it a shot. Now it's time to move on." The resignation in his voice had seeped into her, sadness spreading like mildew beneath her skin. Was he *that* certain it never would've worked between them? Did he remember those magical two weeks differently than she did?

"Time to get up," Hugo whispered. To emphasize this point, Humphrey barreled in and jumped onto the bed.

"I'm up," Marigold said hoarsely.

"Coffee's ready. We should leave in twenty minutes."

"I'll be out in a sec." It wouldn't take her long to get ready; she had nothing to pack, no outfits to choose from, no grooming to undertake besides brushing her teeth with the toothbrush Hugo had found for her. When Hugo left, trailed by Humphrey, she reached for her phone, willing herself to ignore the dozens of texts and missed calls that'd poured in once news of her absence had begun to spread.

But there was one text she couldn't ignore. She reread the first line, and her heart stopped. Flight 2891 Delayed.

No. This couldn't be happening. Not again.

We regret to inform you that Flight 2891 from Charlottetown to Halifax, has been delayed due to mechanical issues. Your new departure time is 11:09 a.m. We sincerely apologize for the inconvenience.

"Motherfuckers!" Marigold shouted. Alarmed, Humphrey careened back to the room and leaped onto the bed, ready to defend Marigold against whatever had threatened her.

"What's wrong?" Hugo called, appearing back in the doorway.

"My flight's delayed until eleven." Saying the words aloud was enough to fill her body with cold dread. "I'm screwed. There's no way I'm going to make my connecting flight to Portland."

"Oh, shit." Hugo began to pace around the room. "Okay, don't panic . . . Let's see . . . can't you charter a plane? Isn't that an option for super-rich people?"

Marigold climbed out of bed, too distracted to care that she was only wearing a tank top and underwear. "I can try." She logged back into Bill's NetJets account and held her breath as she entered her desired itinerary. "No," she said, on the verge of tears. "There aren't any jets available within a thousand miles."

"Okay, don't panic." Hugo pulled out his phone, fingers flying over the screen. "My friend James has a plane. It's a small one, but I think it can get you to Halifax in time to make your connecting flight to Portland."

"Really?" Marigold said, brightening. "Do you really think James would do that? I'll pay for everything—fuel, a hotel if he wants to stay over in Halifax, whatever."

"Should be fine. I'll explain the situation. Just give me a second." Hugo pressed a few buttons on his phone, brought it to his ear, and stepped out of the guest room. "Hey," Marigold heard him say quietly. "I'm sorry for calling this early, but I have a friend in a right pickle." The rest of the conversation was inaudible; he must've gone into another room.

Marigold texted Natalie with an update on her travel plans. It's gonna be tight, but I'll make it back. Wish me luck. Then she brushed her teeth, slipped into her jeans, and went to find Hugo, who was pulling on his boots by the front door.

"All set. We're gonna meet at the airfield."

"Really?" Marigold squealed. "Oh my god, amazing. You're the best! Your *friend* is the best."

"You're staying here, Humph," Hugo said. He scratched the dog's head while his tail thumped eagerly.

"Guess I need to say goodbye, then." Marigold bent down to give Humphrey a pat. "I'll miss you, buddy," she said, laughing as he licked her cheek. When she went to put on her shoes, Humphrey began to whine, clearly aware that they were about to leave without him. "I'll see you soon, okay?" she said, hoping his doggy heart couldn't tell it was a lie.

The island looked even more beautiful than it had yesterday. The road to the airfield curved along the ocean, which sparkled in the early morning light. As they left the small town behind, the clapboard houses and fishing shacks gave way to patches of woods that opened up into fields of wildflowers.

Neither of them spoke. Perhaps it was the earliness of the hour. But it wasn't an easy silence, the air in the truck heavy with everything they were too afraid to say.

"Why did you never tell Jonathan you were married?" Hugo said finally.

"I don't know . . . I guess I was embarrassed."

"Ah, right." Marigold saw Hugh's jaw tighten.

"Not by *you*," she clarified quickly. "But who marries a stranger they met on the beach? After knowing them for two weeks? It'd just confirm all his fears about me—that I was too impulsive and unpredictable for him to take seriously. But now I realize how ridiculous that was. I feel like shit lying to him, and even worse about making Natalie lie for me." Marigold sighed. "I need to tell him before the wedding. He deserves to know the truth."

"Yeah, I think so."

Marigold took a deep breath. "What's your guess, then? How would you react if you were in his shoes?"

"I'm not sure. What kind of shoes do pediatric oncologists wear?"

"Hugo, come on! I'm being serious."

"I'm treating this seriously! I'm trying to get into character." Hugo shook his shoulders like an actor preparing for a warm-up exercise. "Okay, so I'm Jonathan, celebrated throughout the world for curing sick kids. Especially the cute ones. People burst into tears every time I enter a room as they thank me for my service. I'm not actually that good-looking, but my saintlike aura enhances my features."

"Are you done yet?"

"Sorry," Hugo said with a smile. Then his expression grew serious. "I'm Jonathan, and I feel like the luckiest man in the universe because I'm about to marry the most beautiful, funny, charming woman I've ever met. Then right before the ceremony, she admits that she kept this huge secret from me. And I . . ." His brow furrowed, and he pressed his lips together as if trying to sort through a jumble of tangled, uncomfortable thoughts. "And I'm hurt that she didn't trust me. And pissed that she waited so long to tell me. But I can see the pain in her face, and I know she's truly sorry. And I know I'll do whatever it takes to make her feel safe and happy again. Does that help?" Hugo waited a beat and then turned to look at her. "Mare?"

"Sorry," Marigold said, voice breaking as she blinked furiously. "Yeah, that's helpful." She brushed her eyes with the back of her hand. "Thank you, Hugo. For . . . everything."

He nodded, not taking his eyes away from the road.

A few minutes later, they pulled into the private airfield. Hugo drove straight onto the runway and pulled up next to the smallest plane Marigold had ever seen. It looked like something that'd belong in a museum, not waiting to carry human beings thousands of feet into the air. "So . . . your friend's a pilot?" Marigold asked. In her excitement and relief, she'd forgotten to ask who exactly would be flying her to Halifax—a professional aviator or a weekend hobbyist.

"Oh yeah, really experienced. She takes tourists up into the bush for hunting and fishing. She's got thousands of hours of experience."

"She?"

Before he could answer, a truck even older and louder than Hugo's rumbled up, and a woman jumped out with more energy and a bigger smile than Marigold believed was humanly possible this early in the morning. She was tiny—a good six inches shorter than Marigold—with creamy skin covered with a smattering of freckles that matched her reddish, goldish, brownish hair, that perfect, striking color people always spent a fortune trying to replicate to no avail. Not that Marigold could imagine this woman spending hours in the salon every six weeks; she wore baggy jeans stuffed into muddy rubber boots, and a raggedy navy woolen sweater that set off her hair and matched her deep blue eyes. She was stunningly beautiful in the most natural, effortless way Marigold could imagine, like Riley Keough cosplaying as Anne of Green Gables. With a pilot's license, apparently.

"Hi," she said, bounding over. "I'm James."

"James," Marigold repeated. "Sorry, I wasn't expecting . . ."

James's smiled widened. "Yeah, I get that a lot. James is short for Jamesina. My mom read it in an L. M. Montgomery book when she was a kid, and now I'm stuck with it.

Nailed that one, Marigold thought. "Nice to meet you! Thank you so, so much for doing this. You're a literal lifesaver. I'm not sure how much Hugo told you about my . . . situation."

"He said you'd be right hooped if you didn't get to Halifax by nine a.m.!"

"Sorry, what?"

"She doesn't speak Canadian," Hugh said. "*Hooped* is like *screwed*."

"Oh," Marigold said. "Yeah, I'll be beyond hooped. I'm really grateful."

"No worries! I'm happy to help. Can't have you missing your wedding." James turned to Hugo. "You coming with? We can spend a few hours in Halifax before we head back. Maybe check out that restaurant we tried to go to last time, the one that ended up being closed for construction?"

"Yeah, I'm coming," Hugo said. "I want to make sure Marigold makes her commercial flight."

"I'll be fine! You definitely don't need to come." Marigold had inconvenienced Hugo enough already—she didn't need to add to the chaos by making him fly five hundred miles round trip to escort her the half mile from the private airport to the commercial one. Especially when he was supposed to leave for his camping trip the next day.

"I'm seeing this mission through," Hugo said.

"I'm just gonna do my preflight check and then we'll have you on your way." James bounced off toward the plane, leaving Marigold and Hugo to wait by the trucks.

"You didn't mention that James was a woman," Marigold said in what she hoped was a light, casual manner.

"Does it matter? Women can fly planes, too, you know."

Marigold ignored the sarcasm. "So you two went to Halifax? Together?"

"Would've been weird to travel separately. And expensive."

"Hugo, come on. Why are you being so cagey?"

"Because you're not entitled to full details about every aspect of my life. You can't just show up on my doorstep after four years of radio silence and then demand full briefing on everything you missed."

Marigold looked away, face flushing with shame. "You're right. Sorry."

Hugo let out a long breath. "No, I'm sorry. That came out wrong. James and I dated for a bit a while back. But we're just friends now."

"Oh, right. That's great!" Marigold said, a bit too brightly. "I mean, the fact that you dated. Not that you broke up. She seems really cool. So . . . you guys took lots of trips together? Like to Halifax? Guess that's the perk of a girlfriend with a plane."

"That was for a friend's wedding. We'd mostly head into the bush, spend the weekend camping and hiking."

"That sounds fun." In fact, it sounded like Marigold's version of hell. Her idea of quality time in the great outdoors was cocktails on a nice patio. Or maybe a hot tub at a luxury spa where you could stare up at the stars for a bit, don a fluffy robe, and then head back to your suite to sleep on eight-hundred-thread-count sheets, as god intended. She'd been such a fool to even entertain the idea of staying here with Hugo—she hadn't just broken his heart; she was an impediment to the type of life he wanted to lead. He belonged with that milk-fed, nature-loving, plane-flying woman over there. (Or at least someone like her.

If Marigold had her druthers, fate would hand Hugo someone equally nice but just a tad less striking.)

James jogged back over, auburn waves bouncing. "All set! You two ready to go?"

"Ready," Hugo said. "Mare?"

Marigold glanced at the red cliffs that led down to the white-capped waves. She could still smell the faint scent of the fields of wildflowers they'd passed mingling with the scent of the sea. She thought of the comforting rumble of Hugo's truck, of Humphrey waiting at home by the door, tail thumping in anticipation of her.

She took a deep breath, as if trying to inhale enough of the island to take some of it back with her. It was time to say a final farewell to the fantasy she'd been secretly harboring in her heart and return to real life.

To real love.

"I'm ready."

CHAPTER TWENTY-THREE

Olivia

Olivia snuck out of Zack's room at dawn. Waking up next to him had felt warm and comforting, a sensation that had lasted about thirty seconds before cold dread set in. Her thudding pulse sounded an alarm: *Danger, get out. Danger, get out.* A frantic metronome that kept time as she scurried silently around the room, throwing her stuff into her suitcase.

As she opened the door, Olivia glanced over her shoulder at the bed. In the dim light, it almost looked like Zack was smiling in his sleep. She hesitated in the threshold, wondering if he'd feel hurt or relieved to wake up and find her gone. It took her a split second to land on relieved. The sex had been great, no question. Had this been a normal one-night stand, she'd have had fewer compunctions about facing him the next day. But it's what happened *before* that made Olivia flush with shame. Weeping in front of a man she barely knew. Climbing into bed with him after confessing her feelings for someone else. She flinched as she remembered the look in his eyes when she told him about her mom, the kindness but also the pity. And then when he'd offered what he'd probably envisioned as platonic comfort (near-nakedness aside; after all, it wasn't his fault that she'd burst into his room when he was already dressed for bed), she'd been the one to escalate things.

She was sure he hadn't *minded* sleeping with her—actually, she was pretty certain he'd enjoyed it—but the idea that it'd started as an act of emotional charity, a fear of offending an already-crying woman, made Olivia want to sink into the ground with embarrassment. She needed to go into damage-control mode, immediately.

Stepping into the hallway, she pulled out her phone, opened an email to Zack, and typed:

> Hey, I'm really sorry if I made things weird last night, or put you in an uncomfortable position. I promise—I won't mention it again and we can pretend it never happened.

She reread it. It seemed a little harsh, so she pushed through her resistance and added a smiley face at the end.

Olivia sighed with relief as she hit "send." Everything was fine. She just needed to find a place to compose herself and get dressed properly. Aunt Harriet would be up soon, and then Olivia could camp out in her room until it was time to get ready with the other bridesmaids. For now, she just needed to disappear.

Olivia went downstairs and dragged her suitcase out to the porch. She slumped into an Adirondack chair and stared out at the water sparkling in the early morning sun. This was normally her favorite time of day in Maine, when everything was clean and quiet and damp, like the world had just emerged from the shower, refreshed and renewed. The pine trees were wet with dew that made their crisp, sharp scent even stronger. She loved hearing the seals hunt in the harbor while birds skimmed just over the surface of the water, preparing to dive for fish. *This is a safe place*, the animals seemed to announce as they emerged from wherever they sheltered at night. The worries that kept Olivia awake late never felt quite as insurmountable at dawn in Maine. At least, they hadn't until now.

Fragments from last night flashed through her head, a destabilizing mix of some memories that made her skin tingle, and others that made her feel itchy with shame. The tenderness with which Zack had kissed her, the way his touch had made her whole body shudder. The gasp he'd let out at the end. But then she remembered how she'd randomly appeared at his door and asked to crash in his room, how he'd said yes without asking any questions despite her fake-sounding explanation. The way she'd started to cry without warning, then *asked him to lie in bed with her* before essentially grinding against him.

Oh god, oh god, she thought. What the hell had she been thinking?

"Everything okay?" Olivia opened her eyes to see Andrew staring at her with concern. His hair was wet, and he had a beach towel slung over one shoulder.

"Did you go *swimming*?" she asked incredulously. Swimming this far north was never for the faint of heart, let alone at six a.m.

"I'm training for a triathlon. Didn't I mention that?"

"You didn't, actually, which is deeply odd," Olivia said, grateful to focus on something other than her behavior last night. "You must be the first human in history to train for a triathlon without bringing it up in every single conversation. Like people who can't go five minutes without mentioning their gluten allergy. Or the fact that they're polyamorous."

Her attempt at banter felt forced, her slightly flat tone belying her exhaustion. But Andrew smiled at it anyway. "I'd be curious to see that Venn diagram," he said with a smile. A server who'd been folding napkins nearby came over and asked if they wanted anything. Olivia ordered coffee. Andrew asked if they had green juice and, after being told they only had orange and grapefruit, ordered an iced coffee.

"Green juice?" Olivia shook her head. "You're a long way from Tribeca, my friend."

"Don't try to shame me. You're the one staying at the inn instead of with your parents because it has better Wi-Fi." His expression turned serious. "So, what's going on? Why are you out here so early? With your suitcase."

The absurdity of the situation combined with her lack of sleep made her feel suddenly loopy, and she had to suppress a hysterical giggle. What on earth was she supposed to tell Andrew? *Everything's fine! I'm just thinking how I made a complete fool of myself last night, seduced the best man, and now I'm spiraling!*

"Um . . ." Olivia stalled. "Zack and I had a big fight last night, so I left before he woke up. I guess it wasn't the most mature thing to do, but I needed some space."

"Oh," Andrew said, sounding strangely animated. Then he seemed to catch himself and modulated his tone. "I get it. It's smart to clear your head before you do anything rash."

Wait, Olivia thought as her brain raced to take stock of the situation. Was he . . . excited that she and Zack were on the rocks? Was this her chance to make something happen, finally?

The prospect had extra appeal at the moment, given that Andrew only knew the cool, composed Olivia, a far cry from the hot mess who'd jumped into Zack's bed. And Zack would probably be *relieved* to see her with Andrew. That way, he'd know he didn't owe her anything, that he could forget about sleeping with her and move on. "I think I need to accept that we're just really different people who want different things."

"I'm with you. At our age, it's just not enough to have fun, you know? You want to date someone with similar values, someone you could imagine being with long term."

"It seems like you hit the jackpot with Emerson, though. It's like you asked AI to create the perfect girlfriend."

"Oh, she's not my girlfriend." Andrew sounded slightly sheepish. "I probably shouldn't have brought her, but she already had plans to visit friends on Sandpiper Island this weekend, and since she'd heard so much about Marigold's weekend, she sort of asked if she could be my plus-one."

"Bold move," Olivia said, trying to contain the grin threatening to spread across her face. Zack had been right. Andrew and Emerson *weren't* a couple.

"Yeah, she's not afraid to ask for what she wants."

"I could learn a lot from her."

"You could," Andrew said with a smile. "I'm sure there a lot of people who'd be happy to oblige."

It's on, Olivia thought. She felt the same surge of satisfaction she experienced just before she closed a deal, when she could feel her opponent giving in. That moment was often sweeter than the actual victory, the anticipation of victory about to come.

She'd spent so much time convincing herself that Andrew and Emerson were perfect together that she'd failed to consider the possibility that maybe, just maybe, she'd been wrong. Maybe Zack had been right. Maybe Andrew *wasn't* as serious about Emerson as she'd thought.

Maybe she still had a chance.

"That's nice of you to say," she said, returning his smile.

He ran his hand through his wet hair, looking endearingly bashful. "I should head inside and change. I'll see you later?"

"Definitely."

But as he walked off, Olivia's smile faded slightly. Emerson wasn't his girlfriend—great. She'd sort of invited herself to the wedding—even better. But that didn't mean they weren't sleeping together. She recalled how physically affectionate Andrew had been toward Emerson at the welcome drinks. Was she in the same situation as Olivia? Confused by the cues he was giving? Hoping for more?

As Olivia tried to chase the thought from her head, lest it ruin her burgeoning good mood, she heard another voice. "Hey."

Startled, Olivia turned to see Zack. He'd put on a T-shirt, but was still wearing his pajama pants, and his hair stuck out in all directions. Something about his appearance reminded Olivia of a little boy who'd woken up on Christmas morning and run straight downstairs, too excited to bother with teeth-brushing or hair-combing. However, his face contained no hint of festive glee. "I got your email. You don't need to apologize for anything."

"Oh," she said with an awkward laugh. Great. In trying to smooth things over, she'd just made things even weirder. "Okay. I just wanted you to know that we don't need to make a big deal out of last night. It was just . . . one of those random wedding hookups, you know?"

"Relax, Olivia," Zack said with a smile. "Everything's fine.

Last night was really fun, and I know it was just a onetime thing. I promise, I'm not going to start stalking you."

She felt herself blush. "I thought you'd worry *I'd* become obsessed with *you*."

"Most women do."

Olivia laughed. "Alright, you're not *that* good."

"Oh, really?" Zack raised his eyebrows. "I feel like I have some evidence to the contrary."

"Okay, okay," she said, raising her hands in surrender. "Let's change the subject."

"Sure . . . I saw you talking to Andrew."

"Yeah, he was on his way back from a swim and wanted to know what I was doing up so early, with my suitcase."

"I think taking a predawn swim in the North Atlantic is weirder than walking around a hotel with a suitcase."

"He's training for a triathlon!"

"Of course he is. My man is definitely the 'work hard, play hard' type. Go on."

Olivia ignored the jab and continued, "Well, I panicked and told him that we'd had a fight. And he kind of seemed . . . happy?"

Something flickered across Zack's face. "Oh yeah?"

"You don't sound surprised."

"I told you. You were underestimating the simplicity of the male brain."

Olivia considered her options for a lighthearted retort—like how maybe that explained why Zack hadn't minded sleeping with a woman who'd just been hysterically crying—but something about his carefully blank expression made her pause.

"So," Zack said, "I guess that means we should initiate phase two? Operation fake breakup?"

Olivia hesitated. That *was* the plan, right? Now that she knew Andrew was interested, this was what she wanted. "Sure, that makes sense."

"I'll start spreading the word," Zack said. "Zack and Olivia are history."

Olivia nodded. "RIP," she said, surprised to find that her throat felt a little tight. "Thank you again. It was a lot—showing up in the middle of the night, taking your bed, breaking down in tears. I know you said not to apologize, but—"

"Olivia," Zack cut her off, and something in his voice made her breath catch. "You don't have to apologize for being human."

She forced a smile. "Well, don't worry. My human emotions will be someone else's problem soon."

"I'm glad to hear it. I guess I'll see you later, then."

"See ya."

He headed toward the door, then paused and turned around as if about to say something else. Then he shook his head and continued out of sight.

Olivia watched him go, her heart suddenly pounding for an entirely different reason. *This is what you wanted*, she reminded herself.

So why did it feel wrong?

CHAPTER TWENTY-FOUR

Marigold

As soon as they landed at the private airport in Halifax, James let Marigold and Hugo out near the terminal so they could call a cab while James handled the postflight paperwork. She and Hugo arranged to meet up at a brewery in town after he dropped Marigold off at the commercial airport. Marigold could just imagine them sitting side by side at some charmingly rustic picnic table, James's russet hair sparkling in the sun as she happily sipped one of those hoppy beers that always turned Marigold's stomach. She knew it was unfair to feel any weirdness—she was getting *married* today, for the love of god—but there was a part of her that wished she didn't have a visual of the woman Hugo was going to hang out with after she left, even a lovely one who'd provided a massive favor.

"What's the best way for me to pay James?" Marigold asked as the taxi pulled away from the terminal. "Can you text her and ask for her bank details so I can transfer the money right now?"

"I'll figure it out with her later and let you know," Hugo said. "You just worry about getting to your wedding."

My wedding, Marigold thought. She'd been so laser-focused on making in back to Sandpiper Island that she hadn't really thought about what would happen after she arrived. The frantic rush to change into her dress, get her hair and makeup done (if there was even time), and then composing herself in time to walk down the aisle while hundreds of people looked on, whispering with surprise or relief that she'd finally shown up. Because no matter how skillfully Natalie covered for her, guests were certainly speculating about Marigold's whereabouts, wondering whether the notoriously impulsive party girl had had a change of heart. The thought of all those eyes on her made her skin crawl.

"So what happened with you and James?" Marigold asked, half out of desire for distraction, half out of morbid curiosity.

"What do you mean?"

"Why'd you break up?"

"It didn't work out."

"Come on!" Marigold hit his arm. "I'm freaking out. I need some gossip to take my mind off things."

"A painful period from my life counts as gossip?"

"Fine. When you put it that way . . ."

Hugo sighed and looked away. "She dumped me."

"She dumped *you*?"

"Yes. Why do you sound so surprised?"

Marigold considered this. James had definitely been giving off *I'm still into you* vibes. She'd been borderline flirty all day, affectionately teasing Hugo when he got nervous during takeoff, and then spending the rest of the flight reminding him of funny stories from their past. But perhaps she'd simply realized she'd made a mistake breaking up with Hugo. She wouldn't be the first. "Who'd break up with you?" Marigold said, aware she was venturing into dangerous territory.

Hugo sniffed.

"Okay, I mean, what *normal* woman would break up with you?"

"I did something dumb. She found out and dumped me. Pretty standard stuff."

"What'd you do?" Marigold couldn't imagine Hugo doing anything shady, like texting other women, let alone cheating. He was one of those impossibly, almost exhaustingly moral men, like Jonathan. It was probably what they had most in common—a strong code of personal ethics from which they never deviated.

"I didn't . . . communicate as well as I should've."

"Something I know a little about."

The taxi turned off the highway and onto the road that led to the airport. Marigold thought about what Natalie always did before getting out of a cab: confirm that her phone was in her pocket, slip her purse over her shoulder, and then look around to make sure nothing had fallen onto the seat. Her constant vigilance had always struck Marigold as amusing or exhausting, depending on her mood, but that's why Natalie had never misplaced her phone, let alone fled to a foreign country to finalize her secret divorce the day before her wedding.

The taxi pulled up in front of the terminal, where dozens of people were taking suitcases out of bags, fetching trolleys, and hugging their loved ones goodbye. A veritable mob scene compared to the private airfield they'd flown into. "Thanks again for taking me all this way," Marigold said. "It's a lot more than I deserved."

"You can't get rid of me that easily. I'm not leaving until your plane takes off."

"You know you can't wait with me at the gate, right? Even Canada isn't *that* laid-back."

"I'll wait in baggage claim. Your flight doesn't leave for forty-five minutes. That's a long time in Marigold world. Anything could happen. Weather delays, random drug search, a sale at Gucci."

"There's definitely no Gucci in this airport. And what do I look like? A suburban mom desperate for tacky status sunglasses?"

"Gucci's tacky?"

"Never change, Hugo." Marigold paid the fare and then she and Hugo headed into the terminal and made their way toward the security checkpoint.

She couldn't believe they'd pulled this off; she was actually going to make her flight to Portland! She still had a long way to go, but by the end of the day, she was going to be married. Yet despite her eagerness to get on the plane, she found herself wishing the security line weren't quite so short so she could have a few more minutes with Hugo. It felt unlikely that they'd ever see each other again.

"I hope you work things out with James," she said. "I think you two would be good together."

"You do? She's training to be a moose oncologist, you know."

"The noblest Canadian profession."

"Text me when you get home, okay? I want to know that everything . . . worked out."

Marigold nodded, worried that her voice might crack if she spoke. She reached up to give Hugo a tight hug. "Bye," she whispered.

"Bye."

Marigold stepped toward the end of the security line as Hugo turned away. She forced herself to wait a few moments, then glanced over her shoulder. Hugo had taken a seat in the cluster of gray pleather chairs under the departures board, apparently making good on his promise to wait until her plane took off. He sat with his elbows on his knees, head resting in one hand. His hair had come loose from its bun, making him look so much like a forlorn folk singer on an album cover that Marigold would've smiled had the slump of his shoulders not made something in her chest ache.

"Passport and boarding pass, please." Marigold spun around to see a security officer frowning at her.

"Oh, sorry, here." Marigold extended her documents, then pulled her arm back. "Hold on, I just need to—"

"Mare!" Hugo had risen from his seat and was jogging toward her.

"Sorry," Marigold said to the security officer. "I'll be right back." She scooted past the five people in line behind her and waited for Hugo. "Everything okay?" she asked.

He paused to catch his breath, although it seemed strange that a ten-meter jog would've left him winded. "I don't really know how to say this . . . I know I *shouldn't* say this. But I need to tell you what really happened with me and James." He inhaled like a nervous kid preparing to give a speech in front of his whole class.

"I never should've dated her to begin with. I wasn't over you. A few weeks after we got together, I went to New York to look for you. I lied to her and told her it was a work trip. But I was really trying to track you down. James found out and realized I was still in love with you." He paused and met Marigold's eye. "That I *am* still in love with you."

Marigold stared at him, wishing she could press "rewind" and listen again. She needed to confirm that she'd understood him correctly, that her brain wasn't playing a trick on her. She wasn't sure if these were the words she'd been waiting for or the ones she'd most feared. It was unclear what was making her heart race—was it dopamine or adrenaline? Joy or terror? "You . . . you really came to New York to look for me?"

"Yeah, I did. I obviously tried calling first, but you never picked up or called me back."

"I . . ." Marigold winced, remembering the missed calls. How she'd panicked and just erased her call log. "I'm sorry. I didn't know what to say without making things worse."

"Well, I didn't have your address, either, but I went to all the restaurants you'd mentioned, all the places you posted on Instagram. I spent three days combing the city before I ran out of money and had to fly home."

Marigold pictured Hugo wandering the streets of a city he'd never visited before, navigating crowds and buildings as foreign as anything he'd ever seen. His hopeful expression each time he saw a landmark he remembered from Marigold's stories. His face falling every time he walked out, no closer to finding her. "I wish . . ." She trailed off.

"What do you wish?" he asked quietly.

"I . . . I'm not sure."

Hugo still loved her. And she couldn't deny that she still had feelings for him. But what did that really mean? This wasn't a situation where she could just follow her instincts and see what happened. Marigold had to face the painful, embarrassing truth: she'd never made good decisions on her own. She'd always relied on people to steer her in the right direction: her parents, Olivia, Natalie, and now Jonathan. Her heart had never led her down the right path—her heart didn't know what was best for her. Everyone she loved and trusted believed Jonathan was the one she belonged with, the man who'd keep her safe and protected even as the world crumbled around her. What would they all say if she pulled out now? Who would ever trust her with anything again?

Over the PA system, she heard some kind of boarding announcement about her flight, but the airport noise made it sound distant and staticky.

Hugo reached for her hand. "What if I said . . ." He swallowed, closed his eyes for a second, then tried again. "What if I asked you to . . ." Then he shook his head and smiled ruefully. "Forget about it. I'm being ridiculous."

"No, please. Ask me what?"

He squeezed her hand. "Nothing. I don't need to make this any harder for you." Then with a sigh, he dropped her hand and reached out to stroke her hair. "It wasn't meant to be. This is the happy ending you deserve."

"Flight 7319 to Portland is now boarding. We'll begin with boarding group one. Will all passengers in boarding group one please make your way to gate twelve."

"There's time. Please, we can't leave things like this." Except Marigold wasn't even sure she knew what she was asking him for.

"Go on." Hugo nudged her shoulder. "It's time. I wish you all the best, Mare. Truly."

She pressed her lips together and nodded, knowing that if she opened her mouth, she'd only make things worse. With a final smile, she turned and headed back to the security checkpoint. And this time, she didn't look back.

CHAPTER TWENTY-FIVE

Natalie

By noon, Natalie felt like she'd spent half her life in the bridal suite. They'd already ordered room service three times: breakfast, lunch, and a second lunch for Liesl, who explained that her body couldn't process too much food at once and therefore had to eat numerous smaller meals throughout the day. She and Bri were also clearly pissed that Richie had gotten her makeup done first and then opted to go back to her room rather than hang out for the rest of the day. "I wouldn't be surprised if she's one of those woman who can't have genuine relationships with other women. You know, who sees everyone else as competition," Liesl had said with a sniff.

At this, Natalie had shot an *is she serious?* look at Olivia, but Olivia didn't seem to notice. She'd spent all morning lost in her own world, frowning at her phone or staring into the distance, looking troubled. Almost as if *she* were the one whose entire reality had been shattered last night.

Natalie still couldn't quite believe that Jonathan had had a crush on her. And that she'd been too dense and insecure to realize, let alone do anything about it. The regret she felt would be almost too much to bear if she didn't keep reminding herself that Jonathan had never actually made a move. How strong could his feelings have been if he'd never acted on them?

This isn't about you, Natalie reminded herself. *That's all in the past. Right now, you have to focus on being the best maid of honor you can be.*

Except that while she was convinced Jonathan loved Marigold, was she as certain about Marigold's feelings for Jonathan? Not telling him that she'd been married before was a *big* deal. And yes, she was probably just trying to protect him, but would that be her MO going forward? Would they have a marriage built on deception?

"So we're going to meet Marigold over at the venue?" the makeup artist, Crystal, asked as she cleaned her brushes.

"Yup! That's the plan!" Natalie said, too cheerily. Was this what it felt like to go insane? She had that strange, disoriented feeling that casinos tried to create by removing all clocks and blocking all natural light so that gamblers would lose track of time, no longer knowing or caring whether it was day or night. She'd had three mimosas but didn't feel drunk, just kind of detached and dizzy. She supposed she was in limbo, in a way. Natalie truly had no idea whether Marigold would actually arrive in time for the wedding, if her ridiculous plan would actually work, or if it'd all come crashing down around them.

"Then you're next, Miss Maid of Honor." Crystal smiled at Natalie and gestured at the chair next to her workstation. "What are you thinking?"

"Oh, you know . . ." Natalie said vaguely. *Whatever will give me the best shot of hooking up with the most attractive single guest in a fruitless attempt to distract myself from the fact that I blew my chance with the only man I've ever truly loved.* "Polished but natural, I guess."

Hannah pulled a chair up next to Natalie's. "I'll keep you company!"

"You don't need to do that," Natalie said. "I'm happy to just zone out."

"It's no problem!" Hannah turned to Crystal, who'd started to apply taupe shadow to one of her brushes. "Could you do some contouring on her so her face doesn't look so round?"

"I'm not trying to change my face shape," Natalie said through gritted teeth.

"No, of course not. You're so pretty! It's just that all the other bridesmaids have more oval faces, which will make yours look a bit rounder by contrast when we're all up there. And then you have to think of the photos. They'll be great for your dating profile, won't they?"

"I've never been on the apps," Liesl chimed in. "But I totally get the appeal, for a certain type."

"Like who?" Hannah asked, walking straight into her trap. Natalie always wondered what kind of person actually signed up for high-interest store credit cards at Banana Republic, accepted rides from random men posing as taxi drivers at baggage claim, or made eye contact with anyone talking about Jesus on street corners. But now she knew it was people like Hannah.

"Like, anyone who's just a little socially awkward." At that moment, Natalie would've chopped off her left arm in exchange for the power not to blush. "Oh, Natalie, I'm not saying it's a bad thing!" Liesl said with exaggerated contrition. "I just mean, not everyone was taught how to comport themselves in public. I always forget that it's a form of privilege, really. How people like me, Marigold, and Bri were raised in a world that values manners and social graces. It's a hard thing to learn as an adult."

Olivia finally looked up from her phone. "What sort of manners and social graces were on display that time you threw up in a planter outside Per Se?"

"You know I had food poisoning," Liesl said coolly.

"Food poisoning. Sure. From one of the best restaurants in the world."

Natalie shot Olivia a grateful smile, but she'd already returned to her phone. A moment later, Natalie's own phone buzzed with an incoming call. "Do you mind if I take this quickly?" she asked Crystal. "It's Marigold." The other bridesmaids watched curiously as Natalie scurried into the hall.

"Hey," Natalie whispered once she'd made it far enough to be out of earshot. "Where are you?"

"I'm at the Halifax airport. My flight's on time, so it looks like I'll make it back just before the ceremony, thank god. How's everything going there? Is anyone growing suspicious?"

"Yeah, people have been asking a lot of questions, but I think as long as you show up in time to walk down the aisle, it'll be okay."

"You're the best. I feel awful putting all this on you. It was way too much to ask."

"It's fine," Natalie said automatically. "I'm happy to—"

Marigold cut her off. "No, it's not okay. It was ridiculously selfish to ask that you cover for me. This was my mistake, and I should've owned it instead of lying to everyone. You've always been such an amazing friend, and I shouldn't have taken advantage of you. I love you so much."

"I love you too," Natalie said, softening.

"I know. And I'll make it up to you, I promise."

"Honestly, I can't think of anything that'll make up for stranding me with Liesl for this long."

Marigold laughed. "She's really the worst, isn't she? I probably shouldn't have made her a bridesmaid, but she's literally my oldest friend, and I didn't want to deal with the drama of leaving her out. What's she doing now?"

"Where do I begin? Before you called, she was explaining that dating apps were only for awkward normies who didn't learn social graces as children."

"Are you serious?" Marigold scoffed. "That girl's been on dating apps for *years*. I have screenshots of her profile. Jonathan's friend Mark matched with her just last week. Hold on, let me see if I saved the photo . . . Yes, here it is . . . She describes herself as 'omnivore, artist, wanderer, always in search of the perfect word and the perfect martini.'"

"Wowww . . . You know what perfect word I'm searching for? Something that blows *pretentious* out of the water."

"You know she's just jealous of you, right?"

"Thanks, Mom."

"I'm serious!"

"There's no way in hell that Liesl is jealous of a tutor who lives in Sunset Park."

"She *is*. You know how she fancies herself a writer. She lost her mind when you had that piece published in *The Cut*."

"I wrote about rich clients who didn't let me use their bathrooms. So glamorous."

"It went totally viral! And I'm always talking about how you're such a great writer, which drives her nuts."

"You're my biggest fan," Natalie said with a smile. She thought about how Marigold had posted the link on all her social media accounts and even had two copies of the essays framed—one a gift for Natalie, one for Marigold, which she displayed proudly on her living room wall. Not even Natalie's parents had done that. That was the thing about Marigold—she could be flighty and a little self-absorbed, but no one loved more fiercely than she did. She wouldn't be marrying Jonathan if she didn't love him deeply, and it was time for Natalie to stop pretending otherwise. Marigold was her best friend—the most loyal person Natalie knew—and she couldn't betray her like this, indulging in stupid fantasies and obsessing over what might've been.

"Because you're mega talented! And if you keep standing in your own way, I'm going to have to take drastic measures."

Standing in my own way, Natalie thought. *You have no idea . . .*

It was too late to figure out what might've been with Jonathan, but that didn't mean Natalie had to give up on all of her dreams. "Noted," she said.

"Oh, wait, hold on . . . I have to go. I'll text you when I land, okay?"

"Okay. Love you."

"Love you."

"What'd she say?" Natalie looked up to see Olivia watching her. Natalie panicked briefly as she reviewed her conversation with Marigold before assuring herself that she hadn't said anything incriminating. Olivia knew that Marigold was about to board a flight to Maine. She didn't know from where.

"Flight's on time, so all good!"

Olivia gave her the penetrating look that made her such a fearsome litigator, but Natalie didn't balk. Then she sighed and said, "I guess I'm not surprised she called you instead of me. I probably would've said something that sounded 'judgy.'"

"You? Judgy? *Never*," Natalie said.

"Okay, I deserved that. And I'm sorry for giving you such a hard time the other day."

"Thanks," Natalie said. "I appreciate that."

"I know I can be a bit of a control freak. But I'm working on it." Natalie raised her eyebrows, and Olivia laughed. "Fine, I could try harder. But trust me, this weekend has only served as a reminder that the more I try to control things, the worse they become."

"Yeah, I get it," Natalie said. "I think I do the same thing. But you're just a lot better at it."

"Trust me, I'm not." She paused. "I suppose I need to accept that you can't make people do things. Or *not* do things. You can only manage your own reactions."

"If that's the best insight you're getting from your four-hundred-dollar-an-hour therapist, you're getting ripped off," Natalie said with a smile.

"Who said my therapist was four hundred dollars an hour?"

"Most people would've responded to that with 'who says I have a therapist?'"

"Not in New York." Olivia smiled back. "We should head back to your antique-filled prison. The inmates are getting restless. We need to distract them from the fact that Marigold's MIA."

"I'll be there in a sec. There's something I need to do first."

Natalie found Susan Denver on the patio, surrounded by a stack of manuscripts. "Oh, hello there," she said as Natalie approached. "You probably think I'm nuts, schlepping up here with all this paper. But I can't edit on a computer. I've accepted that about myself."

"No judgments here. I have six books in my suitcase. And a Kindle."

Susan smiled. "I told my husband the story about you flying down to Florida with the horse, and we both cracked up. It's such a great visual."

Do it, Natalie told herself. *Tell her about your book!* She imagined Marigold giving her a big thumbs-up and mouthing, *You've got this!*

So what if she came across as pushy? She'd spent far too much of her life worrying about what other people might think about her. It'd already cost her Jonathan, and she sure as hell wasn't going to let it cost her a potential book deal. "You know, I should've mentioned this the other day, but I'm actually querying a novel about an Upper East Side tutor. I've been pitching it as *The Nanny Diaries* for tutoring."

"Really?" Susan's eyes lit up. She opened her purse and rummaged for a bit before producing a business card. "Will you send it to me? I'd love to read it."

CHAPTER TWENTY-SIX

Olivia

Olivia couldn't believe it was only one p.m.—there were still three hours until the wedding party was supposed to gather at the yacht club. Four hours until the actual ceremony. But it felt like she'd lived multiple lifetimes since waking up in Zack's room that morning.

Lulu had driven over to the inn to meet her friends for lunch and had asked Olivia if she wanted to join. Although Olivia felt like she'd been eating and drinking nonstop since dawn (she didn't even want to imagine what the room service bill for the bridal suite would look like), she refused to turn down any chance to hang out with Lulu. She already regretted all the opportunities she'd squandered—family dinners she'd skipped for work, vacations she'd bailed on to travel with friends instead. She wasn't going to miss out on whatever time they had left . . .

The lobby was even more packed than it'd been earlier in the day, and Olivia felt a bit self-conscious walking around in full makeup, hair-sprayed updo, and a floor-length bridesmaid's dress. No one seemed to take much notice of her, however. There was a strange, slightly manic energy in the inn: a long line stretched out from the check-in desk, bellmen rushed around with piles of luggage, and guests exchanged loud, jubilant greetings. She avoided eye contact with Mrs. Varick, who stood in front of the concierge desk, speaking animatedly to a young man with a tight smile. Olivia caught the words "sloppy presentation" and "if you're going to work in this country, you need to speak English" before hurrying on.

A man with a laptop sat in one of the leather armchairs, shouting to be heard in what appeared to be a Zoom meeting. "You gotta trust me, Craig. I know this market, and there's huge upside here for anyone with the balls to withstand a little turbulence . . . It's up to you. But you have to move fast or else—" He cut himself off to glare at an older woman struggling to answer her loudly ringing phone. "Seriously?" he muttered.

"You could always go up to your room," Olivia said sweetly. "You know, the one with the walls and the doors? It could be helpful." She sauntered off, recalling Zack's words from the day before. *Not all of us have been tricked into believing moving money from one corporation's account to another is a matter of life and death.* God, he'd really gotten into her head. It was for the best that he hadn't wanted anything more than a one-night stand—if they'd actually started dating, Olivia probably would've ended up moving to Brooklyn and getting into heated arguments about the Park Slope Food Co-op newsletter.

"Hey," Andrew said, emerging from the inn's small library. "Have you seen the honor bar ledger? Look what these doofuses did." Then he did a double take and whistled. "Wow . . . you look amazing."

Olivia brought her hand up to her elaborate updo and posed. "What? This? I just threw it up so it'd be out of my face when I went for my run." She extended a foot to show off her strappy sandals. "I can probably do four or five miles in these."

"I don't doubt it," Andrew said with a grin. "So your foot's okay?"

"Miraculously healed. So what did you want to show me?"

Olivia followed him inside the library, where he pointed to a bunch of hastily scribbled names from the night before. "Amanda Hugginkiss?" she read. "I thought she'd RSVP'd no."

"It's a joke from *The Simpsons*. You know, like, a man to hug and kiss?"

"Yeah, I know. And I don't think *The Simpsons* invented it."

"Sorry." Andrew shook his head. "I can't believe I just tried to mansplain that joke to you."

"You're forgiven. You haven't reached your mansplaining quota for the weekend."

"Oh yeah?" He gave her a knowing look. "You're right. I doubt I'm the worst offender."

"What do you mean?"

"Sorry," Andrew said, almost sheepishly. "I just heard that you and Zack broke up, and I thought . . ."

"Yes . . . ?"

"I'm being stupid, sorry. I assumed that part of the trouble was that he's so pompous, and I figured you were tired of being lectured." Before Olivia could interrupt him and explain that Zack wasn't pompous at all, that he was actually pretty humble and open-minded when you got to know him, Andrew continued, "And then here I was, trying to ask you out, and *I* ended up lecturing you. The irony, right?"

Olivia waited for the rush of excitement she'd been waiting for, but it never came.

"Totally ironic," she said, forcing a smile.

He surveyed her for a moment, then said, "No pressure if it's too early. We can always put a pin in it until you feel ready."

A weird, perverse part of her wished Zack were here so she could see him react to "put a pin in it."

Stop it, Olivia chided herself. *Zack doesn't want to date you. Andrew does. Focus on the one real thing you have going on.* "No, not at all. We were never official; it wasn't that serious."

"And it's not too tacky to ask out a woman who just broke up with her boyfriend?"

Olivia affected a playful shrug. "I don't know. You should probably consult Emily Post first."

"Of course." Andrew turned to inspect the bookshelves behind him. "Hmmm, let's see," he said, running a finger along the spines. "It looks like mostly whaling chronicles and Stephen King novels . . . Oh, wait. Here we go." Andrew pulled out a book that clearly wasn't an etiquette manual, flipped to a random page, and pretended to read. "If a man and a woman have never presented themselves to society as a couple, one may ask the woman out on a date after a twelve-hour grace period." Andrew closed the book and replaced it on the shelf. "I think I'm good. Olivia, will you go on a date with me when we're back in New York?"

"I thought you'd never ask."

"Is that a 'yes' then?"

"Yes . . . but I just want to make sure . . . I know Emerson's not your girlfriend, but are you guys . . ." Andrew gave her a funny look, and she trailed off. "Sorry, it's none of my business. Especially in light of my own recent situationship."

"Just relax," Andrew said with a smile. "I promise, everything's under control."

Olivia returned his smile and then excused herself to go find Lulu, trying not to wonder what bothered her more: the fact that Andrew had told her to relax, or that he hadn't answered her question.

Olivia found Lulu at a table on the patio with her best friend from art school, Paula, and Paula's wife, Karen. It was unclear whether the two women were already dressed for the wedding. Ruffled sequin skirts, layers of pearls, and cowboy boots constituted casual wear for Paula, who'd gotten her start as a fashion designer in New York in the '80s before moving to New Mexico to teach art. And Olivia couldn't remember ever seeing Karen in anything other than jeans and western shirts.

"Look at you!" Karen exclaimed as Olivia approached. "You look *gorgeous*." Olivia did a little twirl before she sat down.

After the update from Natalie, Olivia had called Lulu and assured her that Marigold would arrive in time. Apparently, she'd been convincing, because Lulu seemed perfectly relaxed, beaming at her friends and her daughter. "I was just telling Paula and Karen about my conversation with Jonathan's aunt Nancy last night," Lulu said.

"Oh god," Olivia groaned. "What'd she do this time?"

"She spent quite a bit of time telling me about alternative cancer treatment, like juice cleanses and sound therapy."

"*Sound* therapy?"

"Apparently, gong vibrations can interfere with the replication of cancer cells."

Karen nodded. "You know, I did read something about that."

"So how did you respond?" Olivia asked.

"I told her it sounded interesting and that I'd look into it."

"Why are you always so nice to these people?" Paula asked, shaking her head.

"They're just trying to help." Lulu paused. "But then Aunt Nancy started talking about a friend of hers who'd been told she had six months to live, and then her tumors completely vanished through the power of positive thinking, and that did rankle me a bit, because I consider myself quite positive. So then I took out my phone and showed her photos of those pieces I did recently. You know, the ones where I took my scans and painted flowering vines growing out of the tumors? They always make me smile."

Olivia smirked. "And how'd that go?"

"She went a bit pale and excused herself. It's strange how often people find those pieces upsetting. I think they're so cheerful."

"Cheerful. Right." Paula turned to Olivia. "How's Marigold?"

"She's good. Excited. It means so much to her that you're both here. We know it wasn't the easiest trip." At least, that's probably what Marigold would've said, if she hadn't disappeared. Karen had an intense fear of flying, so she and Paula only traveled by train. It'd taken the better part of a week for them to make it to Sandpiper Island.

"We wouldn't have missed Marigold's wedding for the world," Paula said. "And we'll do the same for your wedding someday."

"What if it's in Hawaii?"

"Then we'll take an outrigger canoe."

The firmness in Paula's voice made Olivia's chest twinge. She was making a promise in that moment, an assurance that she'd always be there for Olivia. That even if Olivia's mother didn't live long enough to see her get married, she'd be there in spirit, carried in the heart of the woman who knew her best, and loved her daughters as if they were her own.

"Olivia might not want to get married," Karen said, giving her wife a reproachful look.

"Tell that to the seven-year-old who would force the goats to be the 'ushers' when she came to visit me on the ranch. Do you remember those little bow ties we made for them?"

"Yeah, they did *not* like that," Olivia said.

"I always thought it was funny." Paula's voice grew slightly wistful. "You were such a serious little thing at that age, but you loved pretending to be a bride."

"I wonder what that was about." Lulu sounded suddenly sad, as if worried what too much probing would reveal. "You had too many responsibilities when you were young. Maybe you fantasized about getting swept away by someone who'd take care of *you*."

"I don't think it's that deep, Mom. It was probably just about the dress. And the cake."

A server came to take their order. Olivia had lost track of what meal she was supposed to be on and asked for a side salad and an iced coffee. "Are you one of those women who loses a bunch of weight after breakups?" Paula asked worriedly.

"Breakup?" Olivia repeated.

"We heard about you and Zack."

"Oh? Yeah. I guess? I mean, we were hardly dating, so I'm not sure it counts as a breakup. I didn't think many people knew we were even together."

"I'm sorry, it's my fault," Lulu said. "I was just so happy, I probably spread the news a bit too widely. He's had a crush on you for ages."

Olivia whipped around to face her mother. "Wait, what?"

"He admitted it once, that time he and Jonathan came over for Thanksgiving. I think he was a little drunk. It was very sweet."

"Why didn't you tell me?"

"He made me promise not to say anything. He sounded so scared and earnest, what could I do? I knew he wasn't your type, so it didn't seem worth breaking his confidence."

"That Thanksgiving was almost two years ago," Olivia said, her mind reeling. She'd been deeply annoyed when Jonathan invited Zack, and even more irritated when she'd ended up seated next to him. They'd debated student loan forgiveness, as she recalled. And universal basic income, which Olivia had called a beautiful fairy tale for bleeding-heart liberals who'd studied the history of anarchist zines instead of economics. (Something she didn't actually believe; she just wanted to push his buttons.) Even after dinner was over, he'd followed her around the penthouse, trying to bait her into another argument. At the time, she'd assumed it was all fodder for his blog, but perhaps it'd been his version of playground teasing. "Why'd you think he wasn't my type?"

Lulu gave her an *are you serious?* look.

"Fine, you're right. I wish you'd told me, though. I wouldn't have been so mean to him." *And I wouldn't have agreed to pretend to date him.*

She replayed the events of the past twelve hours, except this time, she forced herself to look at them objectively, not letting her misguided shame and insecurity color anything. Maybe he hadn't hooked up with her out of pity. Maybe he'd actually been excited that something was finally happening. And then he'd woken up to find Olivia gone and an email on his phone saying that it'd all been a mistake.

What if he'd suggested the fake breakup to give *her* an out?

No wonder Zack had looked so disappointed when she'd told him Andrew was acting flirty. He'd been rejected by a woman he had feelings for and watched her go after someone else.

How had she been so clueless? And so cruel?

"I don't think he thought you were being mean," Lulu said. "He liked bantering with you. I'm glad he got his shot, even if it didn't work out."

By the time their food arrived, the conversation had moved on, but Olivia had trouble feigning interest in the scandal that'd roiled the New Mexico art museum where Paula worked part-time as a docent. If she'd known about Zack's crush on her earlier, would she have behaved differently? Would she have risked hurting his feelings just to increase her chances with Andrew?

Would she have thought about Andrew at all?

Lulu, Karen, and Paula burst out laughing. Olivia hadn't been paying attention well enough to understand the joke, but she smiled nonetheless, grateful that her mother was still able to laugh with such abandon.

"Ladies," a man's voice said. "The management received some noise complaints. I'm going to have to ask you to keep it down." They all turned to see Bill standing by the table, watching them fondly.

"Your humor's so cheesy, I should take Lactaid an hour before you show up," Paula said with a smile. Olivia knew that it'd taken Paula and Lulu's other friends a while to accept Bill when he and Lulu had first gotten together. He couldn't have been more different from the talented, temperamental artists she generally dated. But the clean-shaven, short-haired, earnest hedge fund manager had eventually won them all over with his clear love for Lulu and her daughters.

"I brought your pills." Bill placed a small orange bottle on the table in front of Lulu.

"Thank you," Lulu said. She tried to unscrew the cap, but her hands were suddenly shaking.

Bill opened the bottle, removed two pills, and handed them to Lulu, who took them with a sip of water.

"I can't believe I forgot my painkillers."

"Why didn't you call me?" Bill asked. "I would've brought them."

"You had that call. I didn't want to bother you. And I had the golf cart—I wasn't going to ask you to walk all the way over here." She glanced down at Bill's feet; his loafers were completely caked in mud. "Those are ruined."

"They're just shoes." Bill placed his hand on Lulu's.

Paula leaned over to Olivia and whispered, "That's the kind of love you want, sweetheart. That's all that really matters." She squeezed Olivia's arm.

And in that moment, it wasn't Andrew who appeared in Olivia's mind.

CHAPTER TWENTY-SEVEN

Natalie

There's no time like the present, Natalie thought as she reactivated her Hinge account. Jonathan and Marigold were two hours away from getting married. She'd made her peace with that. Yet there was no denying that their wedding would feel like a root canal for the soul and that Natalie needed to find some kind of numbing distraction, even if it meant exchanging messages with some guy who'd ghost before they ever met up in real life.

She was sitting on the inn's back porch, a spot that was nearly always empty since it faced a nondescript copse of trees instead of the ocean, but she still looked up every few seconds to ensure that she was still alone. The last thing she needed was for someone to spot her swiping. In a bridesmaid's dress. Right before a wedding she was attending alone. If anyone snuck a photo, it'd be meme-worthy.

The coast seemed to be clear, luckily. The lobby had emptied out as the guests returned to their rooms to get ready, though a few people had still been milling about when Natalie passed through. Some even expressed concern about not having seen Marigold yet. "She's on the island, isn't she?" Bill's cousin had asked.

"Everything's under control," Natalie had said with a smile, feeling like one of those sleazy press secretaries who refuse to answer direct questions.

The golf cart taking the bridesmaids over to the inn wasn't due to leave for another half hour, so she switched her Hinge location to New York—it'd be nice to have a date lined up when she returned to town next week—and began to swipe through the usual array of offerings: real estate brokers looking for their partner in crime, analysts who loved taking advantage of everything the city had to offer, bartender/poets seeking the mysterious lady who once bummed a cigarette on a rainy night on the Lower East Side, and podcasters proclaiming, "Hot dogs are sandwiches. Change my mind."

After a few minutes, Natalie matched with a cute, bearded associate professor at NYU named Leo and felt a flicker of excitement before remembering that she'd matched with him about five years ago on a different app. Their first date had been the best of Natalie's life—they'd met one Saturday afternoon at a West Village café where they'd both talked so much, they'd left their coffees completely untouched. Then they'd gone for a walk and ended up at a bookstore where, while Natalie was browsing, Leo had snuck off to buy her a copy of the book she'd expressed interest in reading. Then after asking if she wanted to get dinner, he took her to a Spanish restaurant hidden inside a town house on a leafy street, where they'd spent nearly three hours talking over tapas and sangria before ending the date with an epic make-out session by the subway. Natalie had been on cloud nine the next day, unable to keep herself from weaving elaborate fantasies about the relationship that would inevitably ensue: the cozy nights they'd spend cooking and drinking wine, the trips they'd take together, introducing him as her boyfriend at weddings. But Leo hadn't texted her that day, or the day after that. Finally, after a week, Natalie sent a Hail Mary text: I'm really enjoying the book—thanks so much! Any interest in a drink this weekend? Five days later, he'd responded, Sorry for the delay. Work's been intense. I really enjoyed our chat but I'm also feeling pretty picky at the moment, waiting for something that feels just right, and I'm sorry that this isn't quite it for me.

It wasn't the rejection that'd stung—she'd been on the apps long enough to become fairly immune to that—it was the way he'd framed their seven-hour, laughter-filled, multistage date as a "chat." As if *he* hadn't been the one to keep extending it, the one who'd bought her a gift and suggested dinner. Who'd initiated the kiss and let his hands roam down her back before whispering in her ear, "I can't wait to do this again."

Before Natalie could decide whether or not to unmatch, he sent her a message.

Hey there, stranger. What have you been up to?

With a sigh, Natalie closed the app and headed back inside. It was almost time to head over to the yacht club for the ceremony. Natalie just needed to run upstairs to grab Marigold's dress so it'd be there waiting for her. At this point, there wouldn't be time for her to get dressed at the cottage or at the inn. She'd texted when she'd landed at the Portland airport two hours ago but hadn't sent any updates since.

As she headed up the stairs, Natalie tried to imagine what

they'd do if Marigold was late. Like, really late. Not just Marigold late. Would they make an announcement to the guests? Or just hope that most people would avail themselves of the pre-ceremony open bar and get too sloshed to notice?

Either way, there was probably time for Natalie to touch up her makeup before she left the inn. Once inside her room, she grabbed her lipstick and headed over to the antique mirror on the wall.

Someone knocked on the door.

"Come in," she called distractedly, still focused on her lipstick. It was probably one of the bridesmaids looking for Band-Aids or bobby pins or something Natalie was known to carry with her.

"Natalie," a deep, hoarse voice said. Reflected in the mirror, she saw Jonathan standing in the door in his tuxedo, a strange look on his face.

She whipped around. "What's wrong?"

"Is it true?"

"Is *what* true?"

"Is Marigold . . . *married*?"

Oh. My. God. "What are you talking about?" Natalie asked, stalling for time. She needed to figure out how much he knew before she said something she'd regret.

He shut the door behind him, then took a few steps forward. "Please, you have to tell me the truth."

"What's going on? Did you talk to Marigold?"

"I called her Maine lawyer, that guy Bruce, to ask if all our paperwork was finally in order, and he told me that we were all set because Marigold had submitted new *divorce* papers." Jonathan shook his head as if he couldn't believe those words had just come out of his own mouth. "So tell me, is it true? Did Marigold fly to Canada the day before our wedding to finalize a divorce?"

Natalie froze in painful horror, torn between her loyalty to Marigold—her best friend, who'd welcomed Natalie into her family, who kept a set of pj's and an emergency stash of ice cream at her apartment to cheer Natalie up after bad dates—and her loyalty to Jonathan, who was, in a sense, her other best friend, and who deserved to know the truth. "Yes," Natalie said finally. "It's true. She eloped with this guy in Canada a few years ago and then divorced him. It all happened before she met you. But there was some mishap with the paperwork, so she had to meet up with him to . . . handle it."

Jonathan lowered himself onto the edge of the bed. "I don't understand. Why did she keep all this secret?" His voice was shaky.

Natalie walked over to the bed, hesitated a moment, then sat down next to him. "I'm not sure . . . but I think she was afraid. She worried that you'd think less of her, knowing she'd done this impulsive thing."

Jonathan's head jerked up. "I wouldn't have cared at all! You know that. How could *she* not know that? We've all done things we regret. But keeping a secret like that for our entire relationship? And then lying about leaving the country to see her ex the day before our wedding? That's . . ." He trailed off.

"I know it sounds bad, but she loves you so much. I think . . . I think she just got in over her head."

"I knew something was off," Jonathan whispered, more to himself than to Natalie. "Nothing about that birth certificate story made sense, but I think I was afraid to face it."

He stood and began to pace around the room. "Does she still have feelings for this guy? Did she want to see him one last time before she made *another* mistake marrying me?"

"No way," Natalie said. "I get that you're upset, but Marigold loves you. You know she does!"

"This isn't how you treat someone you love." Jonathan's pacing took on a frantic quality, like an animal trapped in a cage. "Why'd she think she had to hide this from me? She could've told me on our first date, *Hey, by the way, I've been married before*, and I would've been like, *Cool, no problem*. Hell, she could've told me a *week* ago and we would've figured it out! But keeping it from me? And then sneaking off to another country to hide the evidence? How could I marry someone capable of that?"

"Okay, just take a breath." Natalie hurried over to him and grabbed his arm. "I get that you're freaking out, but you need to breathe."

Natalie expected him to shake her off, but as he looked at her, his expression changed. "I've made a huge mistake," he said, his voice softening. "I'm marrying the wrong woman."

Natalie froze. Whatever synapse was in charge of sending words from her brain to her mouth seemed to have snapped. All she could do was stare at Jonathan. Then he lowered his head and leaned forward until his lips brushed against hers.

And then she was frozen no more. Just the opposite, in fact. Every nerve came to life as a current of heat sizzled through her body until she couldn't help but melt into him. Her lips parted as she kissed him back, sighing as her mouth yielded to his, as his hands wrapped around her and pulled her deeper into him.

"What the hell?!"

Jonathan sprang back as both he and Natalie spun to face the door, where Marigold stood, staring at them, eyes wide with disbelief. "Oh my god," Natalie whispered, while Jonathan muttered, "Shit, shit," under his breath.

Without another word, she turned and ran out of the room, door slamming behind her.

CHAPTER TWENTY-EIGHT

Marigold

Well, this is a fine kettle of fish, Marigold thought—a phrase she'd learned from Jonathan—as she ran down the stairs, out the side door of the inn, and into a small, scraggly "garden" that was mostly used to store empty flowerpots and bags of soil. She was desperate to get as far away from Jonathan and Natalie as possible. But the lobby was full of wedding guests who'd certainly notice a distressed-looking bride running out the front door, especially one who wasn't dressed for a wedding that was meant to start in forty-five minutes, so this semisecluded garden would have to do for now.

Marigold leaned back against a tall pine tree, relishing the feeling of the bark against her skin. A reminder that the world was still standing. Because nothing else made any sense. How could Natalie, her best friend, her *maid of honor*, do this to her? Had Natalie been lusting after Jonathan this whole time and Marigold had just been too dense to notice? Or had they just gotten caught up in the heat of a stressful moment during the strangest wedding weekend of all time?

But then again, hadn't Marigold just stood in an airport, half willing her ex-husband to ask her to stay? How had everything unraveled so quickly?

She needed time to collect her thoughts, but said thoughts had scattered like dandelion seeds in a strong breeze. She had no idea what she felt, what she wanted. And that was a problem, given that her wedding ceremony was due to start in less than an hour.

"Marigold!" The door swung open, and Natalie raced down the wooden steps, her hair disheveled and her face flushed. "Please, you have to let me explain."

"Explain?" Marigold laughed despite herself. "What could you possibly explain?"

"I'm sorry," Natalie said, wiping away her tears. "It didn't mean anything. Not to him, I promise."

"But to you?"

"I . . . I don't know." Natalie leaned back against the railing. "I've tried so, so hard to deny my feelings. I knew I didn't have a chance with Jonathan, and I didn't want to ruin our friendship."

"Oh my god," Marigold muttered to herself as she began to pace. It just kept getting worse and worse. Her phone buzzed, and she looked down to see a text from Olivia.

Are you on the island yet? We're heading to yacht club. Do you need me to stall?

No, Marigold thought. *I need you to find me a time machine.* But what would that even fix? Had this wedding been doomed from the start?

"Hey, Natalie?" a male voice called. Marigold gasped and

ducked behind a wheelbarrow, then peered out just enough to see her friend Dylan standing in the doorway. "The bridal party is leaving now, right?"

"In a minute!" Natalie called, her voice oddly high. "Tell them I'll be right there!"

"Is there room in the golf cart? Can I come with you guys?"

"The rest of the guests don't need to leave for another half hour. Go relax! Have a drink at the honor bar! Did you know you can sign for it using any name you want? No one cares!"

"No, I mean, I wanted a few minutes with Richie. I really think we'd vibe."

"Based on *what*, exactly?" Natalie asked skeptically. It sounded like she'd been shocked back into her senses.

"I just think we'd have a connection."

"She's a movie star. She gets paid millions of dollars to make people feel a connection with her. Now please go tell the bridesmaids I'll be there in a second."

"Come on, don't be such a—"

"DO IT NOW, DYLAN!"

He spun around, shutting the door behind him, and Marigold stood up, wincing.

For a moment, she and Natalie just stared at each other. "So what do we do now?" Natalie asked finally.

"I have no idea." Marigold shook her head, trying to figure out which revelation hurt the most. Like testing one limb at a time after a bad fall. "I can't believe you kissed my fiancé. I thought you were in my corner." Saying the words, she realized it was true: Natalie's actions stung worse than Jonathan's. Maybe it was sexist and unfair, but it was true.

"I am in your corner! I'm *always* in your corner. How many

times have I dropped whatever I'm doing to help you out of some mess—when you're locked out of your apartment, or at the airport without your passport, or being questioned by the police for trespassing?"

"Wow, okay. I'm sorry I was a burden to you!"

"You weren't a burden. You're a thoughtful, caring, amazing friend. But yeah, sometimes it felt like I was on the support staff for the Marigold show. Do you have any idea how hard it was for me to watch you and Jonathan fall in love? How it felt to help you pick the perfect birthday present and ghostwrite all those cards?"

"You're acting like I forced you to do all that!" Marigold heard her voice growing shrill but didn't care. "You loved being superhelpful Natalie. It was, like, your whole personality."

"The guilt and regret were eating me alive. I had to support your relationship."

"And that's why you kissed Jonathan? Because it's what you deserved in exchange for all your *support*?"

"Jonathan kissed *me*. He found out you were married, and was hurt and angry, and I just happened to be there."

Marigold stared at Natalie as her heart slid toward her stomach. "He knows?"

"Yeah."

"How'd he find out?"

"He called your lawyer."

"Is that *really* what happened?"

Something inside Natalie seemed to harden. She lifted her chin to look Marigold in the eye. "What are you implying? Do you really think I'd tell him?"

"I don't know what to believe anymore . . ." Marigold thought about all the ways Natalie had encouraged her relationship with Jonathan. "You basically set us up. Why would you do that if you wanted him for yourself?"

"I . . . I panicked." Natalie closed her eyes and winced at the memory. "I did something really, really stupid, and I was terrified he'd find out. So to cover my tracks, I told him there was someone I wanted him to meet." She opened her eyes and let her gaze fall to the ground. "To be honest, I never thought it'd go so far. You'd never dated anyone for more than a few weeks. I figured you'd lose interest at some point, and I'd get my chance later on, once he'd forgotten about . . . certain details."

"What are you talking about?"

"I moved to New York for him," Natalie said, so quietly Marigold could barely make out the words. "Instead of going to grad school in Scotland, I moved to New York because I thought I might have a tiny shot. I lied about having this great job, and when it seemed like he was close to figuring out the truth, I freaked out. I didn't want to seem like some unhinged stalker, so I told him I had someone in mind for him. To throw him off the scent."

Marigold fell silent as she took all this in. Natalie's feelings for Jonathan had been so strong that she'd given up her dream of living in the UK—something she'd always fantasized about—to follow him to New York. Marigold couldn't think of a time she'd wanted anyone or anything that badly. "I don't get it. So what if you moved to New York for him? Wouldn't he have been flattered?"

Natalie let out a short, dry laugh. "No, you don't get it. Not all of us can get away with stuff like that. If you did it, it'd be romantic. But I'd just look crazy."

"But *why*? What's the difference?"

Natalie shot her a look. "Are you serious?"

"Um, yes."

"Because you're beautiful and charming, and everyone falls in love with you on sight. But that's not what life is like for the rest of us."

"Bullshit." Marigold felt her cheeks growing hot. "That's a myth you've told yourself. You divide the world into the lucky and the unlucky, which allows you to give up on things before you've even started. You did it with Jonathan, you did it with your book—you let your fear of failure convince you that you're not good enough for anything, so there's no point in trying."

Natalie's eyes widened. They'd never spoken to each other like this, but now that Marigold had started, she found that she couldn't stop. "I'm not any more special or deserving than you are. I'm just not a coward."

"What on earth is going on out here?" Olivia asked as she burst through the door of the inn. She looked at Natalie, then did a double take when she saw Marigold. "Holy shit, you actually made it."

CHAPTER TWENTY-NINE

Olivia

"Here I am!" Marigold threw her hands in the air. "Did no one believe I'd really come back? Is that why I just walked in on my maid of honor and my fiancé making out?"

"I'm sorry . . . *what?*" Olivia looked from Marigold to Natalie in disbelief, waiting for someone to speak. She felt like she'd wandered onstage in the middle of a play, some absurd production she wouldn't have sat through let alone participated in. Natalie was sweaty and sniffling in a wrinkled bridesmaid's dress, and Marigold seemed to be wearing the same clothes she'd left in yesterday. But she was here, on Sandpiper Island—that was what mattered. They'd deal with the rest of it later.

"I walked in on Natalie and Jonathan kissing," Marigold said wearily.

That can't be right, Olivia thought. She turned to Natalie, certain that she'd say something to explain, to clarify. Loyal-to-a-fault Natalie was too meek to make a move like that, even if she wanted to.

But Natalie simply reddened and looked away, muttering, "Why don't you ask Marigold where she's been this whole time?"

Olivia turned to her sister. "Where were you?"

Marigold glared at Natalie before answering. "I was in Canada. I had a very short relationship I never told anyone about. We eloped, realized it was a mistake, and got a divorce, but I never signed the paperwork. That's why there was an issue with the marriage license."

Olivia could normally process new information with lightning speed, but this was too much. Her brain whined in protest like the fan inside an overheated laptop. "You were married. And you flew to Canada to finalize a divorce. Yesterday. The day before your wedding."

"Yep," Marigold said.

Olivia stared at her, waiting for her to continue. But Marigold seemed to have gone somewhere else, a distant look in her eyes. Olivia whirled around to face Natalie.

"And you knew this the whole time?"

"No, she lied to me, too, at first. I only found out she was in Canada when her flight back was canceled last night."

"And you didn't think to tell me?" Olivia said. "You just decided it'd be better to lie to my face? Lie to my *family*?"

"I promised Marigold," Natalie said quietly.

"You don't get to make that kind of decision. This has nothing to do with you! I can't believe you kept me in the dark about all—I thought we were on the same side."

"Don't yell at her," Marigold said, her focus returning. "This isn't her fault. Now will you please leave me alone so I can find my fiancé and figure out whether we're still getting married in forty-five minutes?"

"Leave you alone to figure it out?" Olivia repeated. "Of course. I'm sure that'll go well."

Marigold winced as if Olivia had slapped her. And suddenly, she no longer looked like a woman whose wedding was about to be shrouded in scandal. She looked like a little girl who'd been too afraid to tell anyone she'd broken the cookie jar, and had gotten caught hiding the pieces.

"I'm sorry," Olivia said. "That wasn't helpful. I just . . . I just wish you'd told me about this. I could've helped you. Or at least managed the situation better."

"See, that's you wanting to control everything again." Natalie clocked Olivia's irritated expression and reddened. "Sorry, not the time."

Olivia turned back to Marigold and sighed. "This is such a mess. What are we going to tell Mom? She was really looking forward to this."

"Oh, come on." Marigold looked pained again. "Mom would be horrified to hear you trying to guilt-trip me like that. She has other things to look forward to: there's that Morocco trip with Bill at the end of the summer, and Christmas in the Cotswolds. And her art show in the spring."

Each of the events Marigold rattled off plunged into Olivia like a knife. There would be no Morocco trip. By the time Lulu's art show went up, her biography would be written in the past tense. *Lulu Harding (née Levinson), 1964–2026, was an American artist . . .*

"None of that is happening," Olivia said quietly. It was time to come clean, even if that meant breaking her promise to Lulu and Bill. Marigold deserved better. *Olivia* deserved better—she couldn't carry the weight of this on her own any longer.

"Mom only has a few months to live. She stopped treatment earlier this year. I'm so sorry, Mare."

Whenever Olivia had heard the expression "the blood drained from her face," she'd assumed it was a figure of speech. She'd never actually seen anyone turn white until this very moment, as she watched the color leave Marigold's skin in real time.

"No," Marigold said in a voice that made Olivia long for the days when she could fix her little sister's problems with a Band-Aid or a bedtime story. "That's not true. You're just trying to punish me." On her other side, Natalie stood with her eyes closed, her lips moving slightly, almost as if she was whispering to herself. Or praying.

"I'm sorry," Olivia repeated. "You weren't supposed to find out this way."

"How long have you known?" Marigold asked as she slumped down to sit on an overturned tree stump.

"A few months. Mom was going to tell you after the wedding."

"And you agreed? You thought this is what I would've wanted? That I'm *that* self-absorbed?"

"I don't know what I thought," Olivia admitted. "I didn't agree with their decision, but I didn't think I had a choice. It's what Mom wanted, and I thought . . ." She lifted the hem of her dress so she could navigate the remainder of the stairs without tripping, and then made her way over to Marigold. "I guess I wanted to spare you the pain for as long as possible." She placed a hand on her shoulder, but Marigold shrugged it away.

"I wouldn't have taken so many trips . . . I wouldn't have . . ."

A sob tore through Marigold, and she buried her face in her hands.

"Mare . . ." Olivia tried again to wrap her arm around her sister, but Marigold jumped to her feet.

"Just stay away from me. Both of you." She shoved past Olivia and nearly elbow-checked Natalie on her way up the stairs.

"Wait," Olivia called after her. "You can't go through the lobby looking like that. People will wonder why you're not dressed."

"Oh, 'people will wonder,' will they? Fine." She ran back down the stairs, jogged over to the chain-link fence that separated the garden from the woods behind the inn, and began to climb.

"Marigold, come on, don't be ridiculous!" Olivia shouted. "You can't just run away . . . *again*."

But her sister was already gone.

Olivia sat in the golf cart with the engine running and absolutely no clue what to do next. Marigold had disappeared. Perhaps she'd gone home to find Lulu, or left to track down Jonathan. Or maybe she just wanted to be alone. Olivia didn't blame her. As frustrated as she was about her sister's lies, she knew Marigold didn't deserve this kind of pain on her wedding day.

Anxious to move in some direction—any direction—Olivia pulled onto the road and began to bump along with no particular destination in mind. She had a mile to decide whether to take the turn for their cottage or keep heading across the island to the yacht club where everyone was gathering for the ceremony.

She moved over to make room for a group of tweens on bikes,

some in sandals, others barefoot—their skin protected by their summer calluses—as they pedaled toward the beach. Olivia remembered days like that, leaving the cottage with nothing more than a towel and few dollars for Popsicles, returning after sunset sunburnt and sticky, her limbs heavy with the kind of contented exhaustion she hadn't felt in a very long time.

Up ahead, a man in a tux caught her eye, and Olivia sighed. It was probably a wedding guest who'd missed the last golf cart shuttle and was trying to walk all the way to the yacht club. The last thing Olivia wanted at the moment was company, but it'd be rude just to drive past. She slowed down as she approached and realized it was Zack.

"Hey," she called. Her heart lurched as she slammed on the brakes. Or perhaps it would've lurched anyway. "What are you doing? Do you need a ride?"

"I'm fine, thank you," Zack said, sounding oddly formal. "I felt like a walk."

He doesn't want to be alone with me, Olivia thought. And who could blame him after the way she'd toyed with his emotions, albeit unknowingly?

"The yacht club is more than three miles away. You'll never make it in time." *That is, if there's even a wedding to make it to.* "Come on, hop in."

Zack gave her a meaningful look. "I think we both know this wedding isn't going to start on time."

"Oh . . ." Olivia faltered. "I guess you've talked to Jonathan."

"Yeah, he's pretty upset."

"So upset that he had no choice but to kiss Natalie?"

Zack raised his hands. "Hey, I'm not passing judgment here! I'm just reporting the facts."

"Sorry, I know. What a mess, huh? This is turning out to be the wedding weekend from hell."

"Oh, it could be a *lot* worse. I read about this wedding that took place on a cruise ship, and everyone got norovirus. You know, the one where you simultaneously—"

"Yeah, I know," Olivia said, cutting him off. "No need to get into the nitty-gritty."

Zack shook his head and made a *tsk, tsk* sound. "You put on a fancy dress, and suddenly you think you're too good to talk about diarrhea."

Olivia laughed. "You're right, I have some nerve. Now let me give you a ride. I could use the company."

Though what she meant was, *I could use* your *company*.

Zack was the person she wanted by her side as she struggled to sort through the mess she'd made with Marigold. Over the past few days, Zack had been privy to the messy emotions she always tried to hide, and he'd never seemed uncomfortable or overwhelmed. But it felt supremely unfair to lean on him like that now, after he'd already endured so much for her—"fake-dating" the woman he wanted to date in real life, then watching her blithely strike up a flirtation with another man.

As if reading her mind, he said, "It's probably better if we keep our distance. We worked hard to convince Andrew that we were dating, and then that we broke up. We should try to keep things clean moving forward. That way, you'll have a better chance of getting what you really want."

He smiled, but the look in his eyes was nearly as painful as Marigold's had been. Olivia hadn't realized she'd had such a talent for causing so much suffering.

She'd been pulled in so many directions this weekend, she

didn't know which instincts to listen to and which to ignore. She couldn't let Zack believe that last night hadn't meant something to her—it had. But she also couldn't tell him the questions that'd been consuming her all day. She'd put Zack through so much already; she couldn't keep playing with his feelings before she was positive about her own.

"Zack, listen, I don't want you think . . . I mean, I'm not going to lie, I felt something with you too."

"It's fine, I swear. You don't have to spare my feelings. I can take it."

"I'm serious!" Olivia insisted. "It's just . . . It's been a nutty few days, and I'm not really acting like myself."

"Olivia, you deserve to be happy. You don't have to apologize for getting what you want."

I'm not sure I know what I want, Olivia thought. But those weren't words she could say aloud, not after everything she'd put Zack through. "I guess I'll see you over there," she said.

"See ya."

Olivia started the engine and pulled back onto the road. She spun around to wave at Zack, but he'd turned to stare at the ocean, a faraway look in his eyes she was sure he hadn't wanted her to see.

CHAPTER THIRTY

Marigold

As she made her way from the inn to her parents' cottage, Marigold thought about how many thousands of times she must've followed this route. Back when she was little, they'd walk into town after dinner for ice cream, and Marigold had been allowed to order whatever she wanted as a reward for completing the two-mile trip without complaining. She'd always get a triple scoop (with three different flavors, of course) in a cone, despite the fact that the top scoop would inevitably slide off onto the ground before they made it past the boardwalk. Olivia would roll her eyes while holding her demure cup of vanilla or butter pecan (even as a child, Olivia had had a horror of staining her clothes), and explain that the definition of insanity was "doing the same thing over and over and expecting different results."

Around thirteen or fourteen, Marigold would sneak out after everyone went to bed to meet friends in town, where they encountered little resistance to their quest to get drunk. The fancy hotel bar was staffed by college kids—generally older siblings of people they knew—and the owner of the dive bar happily turned a blind eye. They'd down too many rum and Cokes, then stumble back home through the woods, peeling off as they reached the paths to their own cottages. Marigold's cottage was the farthest away, which meant finishing the walk alone, but she never minded. The world felt like a safe, welcoming place, even when it was spinning. The trees were her friends, her protectors.

But today, the journey felt different. The familiarity of the wooded path seemed more mocking than comforting, the trees callously indifferent to Marigold's pain. How could everything look the same when the world was crashing down around her? She knew Olivia had been telling the truth; she'd seen it in her sister's eyes. Their mother was going to die, and Marigold had ruined the one thing that'd been keeping Lulu going, the event that'd allowed her to put on a brave face.

Marigold thought of all the ways she'd contributed to this mess: hiding her previous marriage from her family and Jonathan to protect her fragile ego, waiting too long to secure the marriage license, piling lie upon lie upon lie. But then again, hadn't she been right to try to sort it all out on her own? Who could she trust anymore? Not Olivia, who'd decided to keep Marigold in the dark, robbing her of the chance to deal with their mother's impending death on her own terms. Not Jonathan, who—the moment things turned rocky—fell into the arms of her best friend. And certainly not Natalie, whose betrayal felt like the most shocking letdown of all.

As she turned up the drive, Marigold wasn't sure what she wanted to find. Part of her hoped her parents had already left for the ceremony so she could delay this conversation until after the wedding, to let Lulu keep the mask on for just a bit longer. But Marigold also knew that there wouldn't *be* a wedding if she didn't let her mother help her sort through the mess she'd created.

Lulu was standing on the porch, staring out through the trees toward the ocean. She was dressed in the outfit she'd picked months ago—a long teal silk dress with a matching sequined bolero jacket, and a black cloche hat with teal feathers. As Marigold approached, her chest tightened, the muscles in her rib cage straining to protect a heart that felt dangerously fragile.

Although Marigold was certain she made no noise as she approached, Lulu still turned to look at her, sensing her presence as always. She beamed when she caught sight of Marigold, then her face fell as she registered the pain in her younger daughter's face. *She knows*, Marigold realized.

Lulu came down the front steps and pulled Marigold into a tight hug before stepping back to survey her with a sad smile. "Olivia told you?"

Marigold nodded, afraid to open her mouth lest a sob escape.

"I'm so sorry. You should know, everyone was against this plan—Olivia, Bill. But I was selfish and stubborn and got my way. I just wanted you to have a perfect weekend; I couldn't bear the thought of ruining your wedding."

Trembling slightly, Marigold made her way up to the porch and sank into an Adirondack chair. "And now I've ruined *your* perfect weekend," she said, no longer able to hold back tears.

"Don't be silly." Lulu sat next to Marigold and placed her thin hand on her knee. "You could never ruin anything."

Marigold let out a sound that was half laugh, half sob. "Wanna bet?" In one breathless rush, she told her mother everything: about the marriage license and her secret marriage to Hugo, her trip to Canada and her lies to Jonathan, and what she saw when she finally made it back.

"Oh my god, Marigold, sweetheart." Lulu closed her eyes, looking pained. "I'm so sorry you had to go through all this."

"It was all my fault. I deserved it."

"Absolutely not. You made some poor decisions, but you did it all for the right reasons. I know you were just trying to protect us . . . to protect me." Lulu shook her head. "If anyone's to blame, it's me. I encouraged you to have this big wedding instead of eloping. I was the one who placed all this pressure on you. This was all my doing."

"What?" Marigold wiped her eyes with the back of her hand. "Stop it. You deserved to have something to look forward to."

"That's just it—I never wanted it to be about me. I thought you and Olivia and Bill deserved one final, special family memory. I became so fixated on that, I stopped thinking about what you all actually wanted."

"I just wanted to make you happy," Marigold said softly. "I wanted you to have something special."

"That's the one good thing about dying," Lulu said with a smile. "*Everything* feels special. Every morning when I wake up, I feel overwhelmed by gratitude, knowing that I have one more day to spend with all of you. I don't need a big party. Every day feels like a party."

"I guess that's good, because it seems like the wedding is probably off."

"Have you spoken to Jonathan yet?"

"Yeah, we're meeting up to talk after this. But I don't really know what I want to say." Nausea twisted her stomach as she recalled the image of him kissing Natalie. "I'm not sure if I can forgive him. And I'm not sure he can forgive me. Doesn't seem like the best way to start a marriage, does it?"

"I don't think there's any way of knowing until you speak to him. Your heart will know what it wants when you see him."

"My heart hasn't been speaking that clearly lately."

"What do you mean?"

"I guess . . . I don't know, I've spent my whole life following my heart, and look where it's gotten me. With Jonathan, it was different. I was trying to let my brain make the decision for once, and it seemed like a good one."

"Do you love him?"

"Yes! But I also knew he'd be good for me, you know? He'd take care of me, like you said. And choosing him would show the rest of you how much I'd grown up, that I was finally capable of making smart choices."

The screen door creaked, and Marigold glanced up to see Bill, looking tired but incredibly handsome in his tux. "There you are!" He swept her into a hug, then stepped back to survey her. "What's wrong? Do I need to beat anyone up?"

"I'm fine. Just . . . figuring out some last-minute details."

Bill hesitated. He was rarely able to accept that there might be a problem he couldn't solve, especially when Marigold was visibly upset. But then he caught Lulu's eye and nodded.

"I'll head over to the yacht club and let everyone know that you're here," he said. "Take all the time you need. Just call when you're ready, and I'll send someone over with a cart." He kissed Marigold on the head, then got into their own golf cart and drove off a bit more slowly than usual, as if waiting to see if they needed anything else. Or perhaps because he was in no hurry to face the man he presumed was the source of Marigold's distress.

"If you hadn't seen Jonathan kissing Natalie, how do you think you'd be feeling right now?" Lulu asked as Bill rounded the turn into the woods.

Marigold closed her eyes and tried to shut out all the other noise. She thought about how desperate she'd been to make it back to the island in time, how terrified she'd been of Jonathan discovering the truth, of causing him so much pain. "I really don't know. But I guess it's time to go find out."

CHAPTER THIRTY-ONE

Olivia

After watching Zack disappear around the bend, taking the trail that cut across the island to the yacht club, Olivia had continued her search for Marigold, picking Natalie up along the way. Olivia wasn't quite ready to forgive her sister's duplicitous maid of honor, but they'd deal with that later, after they found the missing bride.

But without the ability to go off-roading, there'd been no way to follow Marigold into the woods. After a fruitless search of the shoreline, they'd decided that Olivia would drive Natalie (and Marigold's wedding dress) to the yacht club just in case . . . well, just in case someone pulled off a miracle. And then Olivia would drive to the cottage to continue the search for Marigold herself.

"Are you sure you have enough battery to get home?" Natalie asked, surveying the golf cart's power meter warily as she slid out of the passenger seat, clutching the dress.

"Yes, it'll be fine. There's always a buffer," Olivia said. "Now go look for Marigold inside and report back."

Olivia clutched her phone for the entire fifteen-minute drive back to the cottage, sighing when Natalie texted, still no sign of her. *I have to talk to her*, Olivia thought, glancing up at the sky as if looking for something to pray to. She had to apologize for what she'd said about Lulu, for stamping on Marigold's already-bruised heart on what was turning out to be the worst day of her sister's life.

As Olivia approached the cottage's gravel driveway, the cart sputtered to a stop in the middle of the road. "Goddammit." Olivia hit the steering wheel, then climbed out and began to jog up the driveway. She'd deal with it later. Right now, all that mattered was finding her sister. But as she scoured the cottage, calling Marigold's name, she was met only by silence. Marigold wasn't there, nor were Lulu or Bill. She trudged back out onto the front porch and leaned against the doorframe. She was out of options. With a sigh, she pulled out her phone and called her mother.

"Hey . . . I'm looking for Marigold."

"She's with us," Lulu said in a tone Olivia couldn't fully read. She sounded tired but not particularly tense. Had Marigold confronted her about stopping treatment? Was Lulu angry that Olivia had broken her promise not to say anything? And what had Marigold told her about her fight with Jonathan? "We're on our way to the yacht club."

"Okay . . ." Olivia said slowly. "Should I . . . meet you there?" It was the closest she could come to asking, *Is the wedding still on?*

Lulu paused. "Yes, but there's no need to rush. Marigold has a few things she needs to take care of."

"Is she okay?"

Another pause. "Yes, I think so."

"Are *you* okay?"

Lulu's voice softened. "Of course. It's just a party, Livvy. Everything's fine. We'll see you in a bit."

"Okay. I'll start walking. The cart is out of charge, and I—" The sound of crunching gravel caught her attention, and she looked up to see a man in tuxedo pants and a white dress shirt pushing a golf cart up the driveway, the back of his shirt drenched in sweat. It was Zack, looking more ridiculous and undignified than should even be possible in a (rented) Armani suit, but weirdly also sexy as hell. She couldn't imagine Andrew pushing a golf cart like that in the midsummer sun, let alone in his wedding finery. And suddenly, she realized she didn't want to imagine Andrew doing anything anymore. This was what Paula was talking about when she said, "That's the kind of love you want, sweetheart. That's all that really matters."

This was the type of person she was talking about. A man who sent his friend's future mother-in-law care packages in the hospital. Who acted with dignity and kindness even after being rejected by the woman he'd been crushing on.

"I gotta go. I'll see you in a bit." Olivia hung up, descended the front steps, and began to cross the lawn. "What are you doing?" she called.

"It was just sitting in the middle of the road. What if someone needed to get by?" Zack said, panting slightly as he pushed the cart up the final rise before letting it come to a stop by the charger next to the cottage.

"Ninety percent of the island is at the yacht club, waiting to see if this wedding actually happens. Trust me, no one's walking away from the scandal of the century." Olivia watched him produce a handkerchief from his pocket to wipe his forehead, then continued, "Have the guests figured out anything's wrong?"

"I'm not sure. But Carol is freaking out. Jonathan called me and asked me to swing by the cottage for some of Lulu's Xanax. I passed the golf cart on my way over and figured I shouldn't just leave it."

"That was very thoughtful of you. Though probably not worth ruining your shirt for."

Zack shrugged. "Any item of clothing that can't withstand a little sweat isn't worth holding on to."

"What's that? A quote from Chairman Mao?"

To her relief, he laughed. "How long will the cart take to charge?"

"About fifteen minutes, and we'll have enough power to get to the club. Why don't you head inside and get some water? I'll grab the pills."

Olivia headed upstairs to her mother's bathroom, found the Xanax, then made her way down to the kitchen. It was the only room in the cottage that looked entirely the same as it had in Olivia's childhood. Lulu couldn't bear to remove the faded yellow wallpaper with its little white flowers, or replace the deep, old-fashioned sink, or purge any of the knickknacks on the counters and windowsills: the weird milk jug that held decades-old dried baby's breath, the yellow-and-white antique cookie jar that never seemed quite clean enough to store actual cookies, the random soap dishes and vases that had been in the same spots for so long, they seemed more like barnacles on a ship than items that could be easily moved around.

Zack stood at the sink, gulping down a glass of water. He

swallowed, refilled the glass, then kept drinking. "Sit down a sec." Olivia took his arm and started to guide him over to the long wooden table that bore the scars of countless art projects and baking attempts gone wrong.

Zack hesitated. "I should get going. I don't want to leave Jonathan alone for too long."

"It'll take you longer to walk there than it will to wait for the cart to charge."

Zack followed her to the table, and they both took a seat on the vinyl chairs, the only items of furniture Lulu had taken from their pre-Bill apartment. "Pretty nutty day, huh?" Zack said, taking another, slower sip.

"Did you know there was something going on between Jonathan and Natalie?" Olivia asked.

"Jonathan swore nothing had happened before."

"And you believe him."

"Yeah, I do."

"I don't know what outcome I'm even hoping for at this point." Olivia certainly didn't relish the thought of her family facing two hundred bewildered guests, but that was a minor inconvenience, all things considered. "Going through with the wedding doesn't feel like the right move, does it?"

"No, it doesn't. They're both great people, but something about their relationship never felt organic to me. What about you?"

Olivia paused, considering this. "I don't think I gave it enough thought, to be honest. I was so relieved Marigold had found this amazing guy to take care of her, I didn't stop to think about whether she seemed happy." She gave Zack what she hoped was a meaningful look. "We're not always good at figuring out what we really want."

He raised his chin to meet her eye. "It's never been a problem for me."

Olivia felt herself blush. "I guess I'm not as evolved. Or self-aware. Whatever, who cares. All that matters is that I was a huge idiot. I've had a crush on Andrew for so long, it became a kind of habit. And it kept me from recognizing who I had *real* feelings for."

"That Dylan guy, right? The guy from the bonfire?"

His delivery was so deadpan, it took her a beat to realize he was joking. "Nailed it. How could you tell?"

"Oh, the loathing in your eyes was a clear giveaway."

"Loathing?"

"Yeah, the more you act like you despise someone, the more you secretly want to sleep with them. At least, that's what I think . . . or what I hope."

It's not too late, Olivia thought. *I haven't ruined everything.*

"I'm sorry I acted like last night was a mistake. I was confused and embarrassed and . . . I panicked. I never should've sent that email."

"Yeah . . ." Zack rubbed the back of his neck. "That was a pretty rough thing to wake up to. But I figured you just didn't want to ruin your chances with Andrew."

"I wasn't thinking about him at all," Olivia admitted. "I think I was worried about messing things up with you."

"Oh yeah? What things?" Zack cocked his head expectantly.

"Come on, are you really going to make me say it?"

"Say what?" Zack said, biting back a smile.

"Oh my god! I like you, okay? I really, really like you. I made a huge mistake. I don't care about Andrew at all and I'm sorry for dicking you around. It was unfair and unkind, and there's no reason you should forgive me, but I'm hoping it's not too late to . . ." She trailed off and looked away, too embarrassed by her undignified speech to gauge his reaction.

She braced for him to respond with a joke, or worse, to sigh and explain that she'd missed her chance. But he said nothing. Instead, he leaned forward, cupped the side of her face, and drew her toward him until their lips touched. Olivia had never felt herself respond to a kiss like this before. In an instant, every remaining ounce of tension in her body disappeared as a tingling warmth spread through her. Zack wrapped his arm around her, pulling her closer, kissing her more deeply.

Olivia shuddered and, overwhelmed by the intensity of her sudden need for him, leaned back with a laugh. "I guess I'll take that as a yes, then?"

CHAPTER THIRTY-TWO

Marigold

Marigold told Jonathan she'd meet him at the yacht club, but by the time she arrived, it was already a quarter to five. Guests were gathered on the lawn, dashing in and out of the club to use the bathroom and escape the heat. It was the worst place in the entire universe to have an emergency discussion about the state of their relationship.

There weren't many places to remain out of sight on this side of the island, which was swept mostly bare by the fierce ocean winds. There were only a few houses spread far apart, separated by expanses of sandy rock and scrub. But there was one place where the guests surely wouldn't venture, so Marigold texted Jonathan to meet her there.

When she descended the weathered wooden stairs built into the bluff, she spotted a man in a tuxedo sitting on a step facing the ocean, a bottle of whiskey on the ground next to him. Before she could call his name, he glanced over his shoulder, then rose to his feet to face her. She wasn't sure what tipped Jonathan off to her presence; he surely hadn't heard her quiet footsteps over the crash of the waves on the rocks below.

Marigold scanned his face for some sign of how he felt, but his eyes betrayed nothing.

"I'm so sorry," Jonathan said as she approached him. "That was . . . I have no idea what I was thinking. I was upset and confused, but there's no excuse for . . ." He sighed and let out a bitter laugh. "I can't believe I'd ever do something that shitty."

"I'm sorry too. It was ridiculous that I never told you that I was married before, and even crazier that I lied about what was going on the last few days."

"Yeah, but you did that to protect me, even if was a misguided attempt. What I did . . . that was pure selfishness."

She lowered herself onto the step, reached up for Jonathan's hand, and pulled him toward her. For a moment, she felt him resist, then he sat down next to her, close but not quite touching. The two inches between their bodies felt as vast as the slate-gray ocean stretching out below them. "I wasn't just trying to protect you," Marigold said. "I was also trying to protect myself. I was scared that you'd change your mind about marrying me if you knew I was the type of person who'd elope with a stranger after two weeks."

Part of Marigold hoped he'd contradict her, but instead he waited a long moment and said, "Yeah, that was a lot to process." He must've sensed that his words had stung, because he took Marigold's hand and squeezed. "Sorry, it was just too much to take in on my wedding day."

She squeezed back. "Tell me the truth," she said, meaning it. "If I'd told you earlier, before we got engaged, would it have changed how you felt?"

He fell quiet as he considered this. That was something she'd always appreciated about Jonathan, how he wasn't afraid to think before he spoke. "It's hard to say. I wouldn't have minded that you'd been married before—that's not a big deal. But, yeah, knowing that you'd eloped with someone you barely knew . . . I think it would've made me question if you'd given *us* enough thought."

"Even though we dated for two years before we got engaged?"

"I'm not saying it's rational. It's mostly because of my own insecurities—I always thought, always worried, that I'd tricked you into being with me. That at any moment, you'd come to your senses and realize you'd made some terrible mistake."

"What are you talking about? How could you have *tricked* me?"

"It was always just hard to believe that you'd choose me."

"Jonathan," she said, full of sudden tenderness for him. "What are you talking about? You're kind, brilliant, and handsome. You're the catch of the century. I never felt good enough for you!"

He laughed and there was less bitterness in it this time. "Well, this is a sticky wicket, isn't it?"

She smiled and nudged him the ribs. "Okay, never mind, I can't marry you now. That just gave me the ick."

His turned to her, his expression grave again. "Seriously, though. What do you want to do about . . ." He gestured toward the yacht club. "All this?"

Marigold took a deep breath. "I can't do it, I'm sorry. I can't marry you."

"I understand." His voice was full of sadness and regret, but there wasn't any perceptible pain. *He doesn't want to get married, either*, Marigold realized. *He just wanted to give me the chance to call it off first.* A gentleman until the very end. "I think . . . I think that's the right choice."

Marigold exhaled, feeling suddenly lighter than she had in days. "So what do we do now?"

"I guess we go up there and tell everyone." He picked up the bottle of whiskey, took a sip, then passed it to her with a smile.

She accepted it with a laugh and followed suit. "I might need a bit more of this first. Tess is gonna go nuclear."

"Whatever, she'll still get paid. No biggie."

He took the whiskey bottle back from her and took another sip. "So, ready to face the music?"

Marigold turned toward the yacht club, listened for a moment, then laughed. "I can't believe there's literal music to face. How long do you think they've been playing for?"

"Guess we'll find out when we get the bill."

Marigold shuddered. "Oh god, all that money . . ."

"Good thing your stepfather is a literal billionaire."

"Um, he's literally not. And I thought you hated when people misuse *literally*."

"I literally hate it."

Marigold rolled her eyes. "You and Natalie really are meant for each other. Or is it *one another*? I don't know, and I don't care."

"Come on," Jonathan said, wincing. "I told you, that was a mistake. I was out of my mind, and I—"

"It doesn't matter," Marigold said, surprised to realize she meant it. "And speaking of which, there's something I need to tell you. You know all those cards I gave you? I had some help writing them . . ."

Jonathan stared at her before understanding dawned on his face. "It was her the whole time, wasn't it?"

Marigold nodded.

"Okay, wow . . ." Jonathan said. "Okay."

They both rose somewhat shakily to their feet, drained from the conversation and slightly off-kilter from the whiskey. Jonathan pulled her into a tight hug. "I'll always care about you," he whispered. "Nothing will ever change that."

Marigold found herself blinking back tears as she pulled away. "Same."

They made their way slowly up the stairs. "Should we go now?" Jonathan asked.

"Just give me a few minutes. I have some more apologizing to do." First Natalie, and then . . . well . . .

It was probably too late to change things, but she had to try. She'd already ruined her chances with the most objectively perfect man on the planet.

She couldn't also lose the man who was perfect for her.

CHAPTER THIRTY-THREE

Natalie

Natalie stared longingly at the bar that'd been set up on the yacht club lawn. Her need for a strong vodka soda was a physical ache. She wanted to feel the alcohol scorch her throat and scour her insides, burning away the sludgy shame that'd been thickening for the past hour. But how could she possibly walk by so many people? Surely they'd notice the scarlet *A* Natalie could feel blazing against her chest. No, forget Hawthorne. She had nothing in common with poor, wronged Hester Prynne. Natalie's crime was closer to that in Poe's most famous tale, and it was just a matter of time before her guilty heart began to bellow, *I kissed Jonathan! The maid of honor hooked up with the groom on his wedding day! I'm the most treacherous, backstabbing bitch of all time!*

Oh, fuck it, Natalie thought glumly. They were all going to find out at some point. There was no way the wedding would happen now, and it wouldn't take long for the guests to discover why. If Marigold didn't tell people about the kiss, then Olivia would, and honestly, Natalie didn't blame them. With a sigh, she began to trudge across the lawn toward the bar. A uneasy tension had begun to spread through the crowd. None of the guests had set eyes on Marigold, and no one would confirm whether she'd made it back from New York. Bill, Lulu, Jonathan, Zack, and Olivia had all vanished, adding to the air of confusion and suspicion. Jonathan's parents had grown overwhelmed trying to field questions and were hiding in some remote corner of the yacht club. Natalie was vaguely aware of people trying to talk to her—she could see their mouths moving—but she couldn't hear anything over the shrill wail of her own thoughts.

You kissed your best friend's fiancé. On her wedding day.

And it was a great kiss.

You're the shittiest maid of honor in human history.

And you want to do it again.

She ordered her drink, downed it in three gulps, considered ordering another, then decided on water instead. It was going to be a long night no matter what; she needed to pace herself.

The vodka had its intended effect. A pleasant warmth spread through her body, and for one brief moment, she felt like she could breathe again. And then she remembered the look on Marigold's face, and the stinging accusations she'd made:

You loved being super-helpful Natalie. It was, like, your whole personality.

You let your fear of failure convince you that you're not good enough for anything, so there's no point in trying.

How much of that was true? Had all this happened because of Natalie's cowardice? If she'd just told Jonathan how she felt during college, or at the reunion, or at literally any moment before he and Marigold had gotten engaged, she wouldn't have ruined her best friend's wedding. But why hadn't she ever said anything? Because she hadn't wanted to look foolish? Or make anyone uncomfortable? Was this what happened when you had a pathological fear of conflict? You suppressed your own feelings, kept them in the dark until they turned putrid and toxic. Until they couldn't be contained any longer and the whole mess exploded, scalding anyone in the blast zone.

"Natalie?" She turned to see a pretty middle-aged woman in a plunging navy silk gown. Natalie didn't recognize her face, but the tightness of her skin and the plumpness of her lips marked her as a New York guest rather than a Maine one.

Natalie forced a smile and prepared to tell one more lie about where Marigold was and when the wedding would start. "Yes?"

"I know this is weird, but my neighbor's on the phone and she wants to talk to you?"

"Your neighbor?" Natalie repeated. Had word of her treachery already spread so far that strangers wanted to scream at her? She imagined trying to walk down the street in New York while people lined the sidewalks shouting, *Shame! Shame!*

"Jen Friedlander? You tutor her daughter, Esme? She knew I was at the same wedding as you, and she said you aren't returning her messages." The woman shrugged sheepishly and held up her phone. "She said you wouldn't mind talking to her for five minutes."

"Mrs. Friedlander called you. And asked you to find me. At the wedding," Natalie said, struggling to properly process this information. Her brain had reached its maximum storage capacity, like Marigold's perpetually full voicemail.

"Should I tell her you're busy?"

"Yes!" Natalie said shrilly. "Tell her I'm the maid of honor and we're about to . . ." She trailed off, then paused. "Actually, I'll talk to her."

"Are you sure?"

Natalie nodded, watched the woman unmute her phone, then took it from her. "This is Natalie!" she said in a voice that sound cheerfully deranged, even to her.

"Oh, good," Mrs. Friedlander said. "I told Laura you wouldn't mind talking for a minute. Listen, Esme had another idea for her essay, and I wanted her to talk to you first before she spent too much time on it."

"Right, of course. God forbid Esme waste an hour of her precious time."

"Exactly. So we decided that the whole volunteering-in-Mexico thing was overdone. These days, you need to focus on overcoming adversity. So Esme thought she'd write about the struggles of having ADHD."

"I didn't realize Esme had ADHD."

"She's being tested for it now, so she can get extra time on the SAT." There was a long pause. "Natalie, are you there?"

"Let me just get this straight," Natalie said tightly. "You're paying some quack doctor to diagnose her with a condition she probably doesn't have, to cheat on the SATs, and then you want her to write about *overcoming adversity*."

"Excuse me," Mrs. Friedlander snipped. "The doctor thinks she *does* have ADHD. It's hard to diagnose in girls."

"No," Natalie said.

"It's a very common phenomenon. You should do your own research."

"I mean, *no*, I won't do it."

"You think it's a bad idea? Fine, that's fine. You come up with something else, then. Whatever. Esme won't mind."

"No, I'm done. Find someone else."

"Excuse me?"

"You're the most entitled person I've ever met, which is *really* saying something given my line of work, and your vapid daughter doesn't deserve to go to college, let alone one of the places you're probably bribing at the moment."

"What the hell?" Mrs. Friedlander spat. "Do you know who you're talking to? I'll make sure you never tutor in this town again!"

"And I'll contact the admissions offices at all Esme's top choices to explain that I wrote all her essays for her. I'm so glad you called, Mrs. Friedlander. It was great catching up. Take care, now."

Natalie handed the phone back to the stunned guest. A few other people were also staring, but, buoyed by the high of telling the truth for the first time in her life, she found that she didn't care. That is, until she spotted Tess darting through the crowd, muttering manically into her headset. She'd already called six times to ask for an ETA on Marigold, and each time Natalie had said, "She's on her way!" but she wasn't sure she could keep up the ruse much longer.

When Tess's back was turned, Natalie slipped into the yacht club and headed to the wood-paneled office that'd been designated as Marigold's dressing room for that day—the one place Natalie was certain she wouldn't run into either Jonathan or Marigold. But just as Natalie began to pace around the room to decide on her next move, the door opened and Marigold stepped in. Her hair was slightly disheveled, yet other than that, there was no sign that she'd gone from an international flight to vaulting over fences and dashing into the woods. She wasn't wearing her wedding dress, nor were her hair and makeup done. But that didn't mean anything. It'd take her five minutes to transform from a weary international traveler into a radiant bride—if that's what she still wanted—as long as no one looked too closely at the exhaustion in her eyes. Natalie felt a surge of tender affection for her friend. Marigold hadn't done anything to deserve this, let alone on her *wedding* day: walking in on her fiancé kissing her best friend, learning that her mom was dying.

"Hey, I was looking for you." Marigold's voice was tired but calm.

"I'm really sorry," Natalie said. She meant it—she felt more guilt and shame than she'd ever experienced in her life. Yet at the same time, she would've been hard-pressed to explain exactly what she was apologizing for. Was it for kissing Jonathan? Or for the betrayal that had started years earlier? The moment Natalie had first started betraying herself, sabotaging her own chance of happiness along with everyone else's.

"I'm sorry too."

"What do *you* have to apologize for?"

"For all the nasty things I said back at the inn."

Natalie turned away, suddenly unable to meet Marigold's eyes. "I deserved them."

"No, you didn't. Jonathan and I were never right for each other. Deep down, we both knew it." A smile crept into Marigold's voice, giving Natalie the courage to look back up. "But you and I were made for each other. Our bond is stronger."

Natalie opened her mouth to laugh and was surprised when a sob escaped instead. Marigold closed the space between them and pulled her into a hug. "Are you really forgiving me?" Natalie asked after regaining enough composure to speak.

"Yeah. Do you forgive *me*? I mean, the way I've always taken you for granted. Maybe even taken advantage of you. You're right—I did always assume you'd be there to clean up my messes, and I didn't really stop to wonder what messes of your own you might be hiding. It was just easier for me to believe you had everything under control all the time."

Natalie shook her head. "I wanted you to see me that way. I wanted *everyone* to see me that way. What you said was right: it was easier to blame you than accept that I've been holding myself back, making excuses instead of going after what I want."

"You're not the only one." Marigold sank into an armchair and waited for Natalie to sit on the plaid couch next to it. "I spent the last four years convincing myself that he and I were right for each other. I was so desperate to be the type of person he'd fall in love with."

"So, what?" Natalie asked. "Marrying Jonathan was some kind of rebrand?"

Marigold leaned back against the chair. "Yeah, I guess. But it wasn't just about the optics. I really believed he'd make me a better person. That he'd turn me into someone who deserved a kind, responsible man who cured kids with cancer."

"But you love him," Natalie said quietly.

"I do . . . but I also love the *idea* of someone like him loving me. It's different with you."

"Is it?" She thought for a moment. "I fell in love with him when he was just a goofy college kid with a terrible haircut who made me laugh."

"And that's why you belong together."

Natalie turned to Marigold, startled. “Oh, come on.”

“No, I mean it,” she said firmly. “You and I have both wasted enough time worrying about what other people think. We both deserve to be happy. And I’m going to make sure it’s not too late, for either of us.”

CHAPTER THIRTY-FOUR

Olivia

"You drive," Olivia said as she unplugged the golf cart from the charger.

"Wow." Zack raised his eyebrows. "You really are a changed woman. What happened to the control freak whose domineering ways proved so irresistible to me?"

"I'm still a control freak. I just need to draft something on my phone."

"You can't be serious." Zack looked truly aghast, no hint of teasing in his face. "You're working. Now."

"No." Olivia slid into the passenger seat. "I need to draft my apology to Marigold."

Kissing Zack in the kitchen had been a top-notch distraction, but eventually, the seriousness of the situation had sunk in. She had to find her sister and apologize for ruining her wedding day. Or perhaps, more accurately, for making her already-ruined wedding day even worse. And she'd have a better chance of making things right if she sorted out her thoughts properly ahead of time.

"You're . . . emailing her?" he asked. She'd briefed him on the situation while they'd waited for the golf cart to charge.

"I'm writing some notes! Is that so terrible?"

Zack lowered himself into the driver's seat. "No, I guess not. But this seems like a situation where you really just need to speak from the heart."

"No one's first drafts are ever that good, especially non-sentient organs."

Zack turned the ignition, twisted to look behind him, and began to back down the driveway.

"You can turn around on the grass, if it's easier." Zack completed a deft reverse K-turn and steered the cart onto the narrow, tree-lined dirt path that led to the main road. "Stay to the left here; there's a ditch that's hard to see . . . oh, and watch out for those big roots up ahead."

"I thought you were going to write," Zack said dryly.

"I am!" But as she stared at the Notes app on her phone, she found herself drawing a blank. Her brain couldn't focus—an unusual sensation for her. The events of the past few days had thrown her entirely off-kilter; humans weren't designed to experience so many highs and lows in such quick succession.

"You know, organs may not be sentient, but apparently they can carry memories. I just read this incredible article about heart transplant patients who can recall information from their donors' lives, things they never would've known otherwise."

"Send it to me. I'll read it later."

"I will. I'd be curious to get your thoughts on it."

"Why?" She glanced up from her phone. "I'm not a scientist."

"I like the way your brain works."

"Turn left up there," Olivia said, then looked back down at her phone so Zack wouldn't see her enormous grin.

"Permission to take one hand off the wheel?"

"Um, sure . . . why?"

Without saying anything, Zack took Olivia's hand and squeezed.

They spent the rest of the drive in silence while Olivia wrote out a text with her free hand, letting Andrew know that she had to cancel their date.

To Olivia's surprise, Marigold was, according to Natalie, in her makeshift dressing room. Olivia hurried through the crowd on the yacht club lawn, avoiding the eye of everyone who tried to flag her down, ostensibly to ask if the ceremony was finally about to start.

"Olivia!" Liesl managed to grab her arm. "What's going on? The strangest rumors are flying around."

Olivia shook her off, then glared as Liesl fell into step next to her. "Rumors I'm sure you had *nothing* to do with."

"I'm just concerned about my oldest friend, okay? Where *is* she? Literally no one has seen her in two days."

"She's here."

"She is? Where?"

"Getting ready. But she wants privacy, okay? Just . . . tell everyone we'll start soon."

Liesl tried to follow her into the club, but Olivia blocked her way. "Sorry, family only beyond this point," she said sweetly, then slammed the door.

Olivia found Marigold and Natalie sitting in the office, looking surprisingly relaxed. "I'll let you two talk," Natalie said as she got to her feet. "I'm going to get some air. I'll be back in a bit."

"Go out the back, through the kitchen," Olivia advised. "It's a madhouse in front."

When Natalie left, Olivia took her empty seat. For a moment, they sat in silence—the only somewhat uneasy silence of sisters who had endless experience fighting, icing each other out, and then making up. Though never had Olivia felt like she'd been so clearly in the wrong.

"I'm sorry I made this terrible day even worse," Olivia said finally.

To her relief, Marigold laughed. "Worst. Wedding. Eveeeeer," she said, elongating the vowel with exaggerated vocal fry in a pitch-perfect imitation of Kara, the NYU student who'd occasionally nannied for them when they were younger. They hadn't seen her in almost twenty years, but still found themselves lapsing into Kara-speak when they were alone.

"Like, literally." Olivia smiled briefly, then turned serious again. "I'm really sorry, Mare. I can't believe I did that."

"It's okay. Mom explained that you were against it from the beginning."

"Still . . ." Olivia trailed off. "So what are you going to do now?"

"You mean, am I still getting married?"

"Yeah, I guess."

Marigold shook her head. "I talked to Jonathan. We both agreed it's over."

"Okay. Oh, wow." It was one thing to sense this coming; it was quite another to hear the words come out of her sister's mouth. "Are you okay? I mean, all things considered."

Marigold paused, considering this. "Yeah, I am. It's going to be a shit show telling everyone, but it's the right thing to do."

"God, he's such an idiot."

"Jonathan? No, he isn't. I mean, yeah, it was shitty of him to kiss Natalie. But that's not why we called off the wedding."

"Then why?"

Marigold's expression turned vague and distant, as if her mind were suddenly miles away.

Olivia sat up. "Oh my god! You're still in love with . . . that guy. In Canada."

"Hugo."

"His name is *Hugo*?" Olivia held up her hands in response to Marigold's glare. "Sorry, sorry. A fine name. But why did you lie about going up there? I could've helped you!"

"I guess I was just sick of the whole 'oh, Marigold's such a hot mess' narrative. I was tired of you getting to be the grown-up while I was the irresponsible screwup."

Olivia leaned back in her armchair. "I'm sorry I made you feel that way. It's not fair, and it's not true. I'm sorry."

Marigold looked sheepish. "I mean, it's a *little* true."

"Maybe. But I think I might've forced you into that role. It made me feel good to think of myself as the problem solver. I liked being needed—I didn't always want to let you grow up." Olivia paused as a painful thought pushed its way out of her mind. "And . . . I think that's why I agreed not to tell you that Mom was stopping treatment. I wanted to protect you. And I wanted to protect myself. If you didn't know, then I could pretend that everything was fine, at least some of the time." Olivia caught sight of Marigold's duffel bag. Her passport was sticking out of the side pocket. "So . . . are you going somewhere?"

Marigold followed her gaze. "I don't know, maybe. Hugo's heading out on some weeklong camping trip, and I want to catch him before he goes off the grid."

"So *call* him."

"I *have* called him. Multiple times. His phone is off. And besides, you know how terrible the reception is at the yacht club."

"Why can't you just wait for him to get back? Do you think he's gonna run off with a moose or something?"

"Really? That's the best you can do? A moose joke?"

"Sorry, you're right. Anti-Canadian bigotry is an insidious form of prejudice and deserves to be called out."

"I can't wait for you to meet him," Marigold said in a voice Olivia had never heard her sister use in relation to a boy—dreamy and affectionate, almost wistful. A voice that came out when Marigold was describing a particularly beautiful designer gown, or some hidden beach she'd stumbled across on one of her adventures in Greece or Thailand.

"Oh my god," Olivia said. "You really are in love."

Normally, Marigold would respond to an accusation like this with glibness, a shrug or an eye roll or some question about why people were so obsessed with the idea of love. But this time, Marigold met Olivia's eye and smiled. "Yeah, I guess I am."

There was a knock at the door, and then Lulu slipped inside, coming over to perch on the ottoman next to Olivia's chair. "You two okay?"

Marigold and Olivia exchanged looks, then both laughed. "Yeah, I think so," Marigold said.

Lulu turned to Olivia. "I'm so sorry for putting you in that terrible position. I never should've asked you to keep my treatment plans a secret like that. Do you forgive me?"

Olivia reached out to squeeze her mom's arm. "Yes, of course."

Lulu placed her hand on Olivia's and smiled, then glanced over to catch Marigold's eye. "Love has made your sister go soft. She never would've let me off the hook this easily before."

"Wait, *love*?" Marigold looked from Lulu to Olivia, startled. "What are you talking about?"

"You and Zack got back together, didn't you?" Lulu asked Olivia. "I saw you holding hands when you drove up, but maybe I shouldn't have made any assumptions."

"*Back* together?" Marigold jumped to her feet. "What's going on? What'd I miss? You and Zack?!"

"Why don't you try calling Hugo one more time," Olivia said, blushing. "Then I'll tell you the whole story."

CHAPTER THIRTY-FIVE

Natalie

Outside on the lawn, chaos was brewing. Some guests were already in their seats by the bluff, roasting in the late-afternoon heat. Most were still under the tent by the bar, making uneasy small talk as rumors thickened the heavy, moist air.

Yet Natalie felt lighter than she had all weekend. Lighter than she'd felt in years, if she were being completely honest. The mass of guilt, resentment, and shame—a weight she'd grown so accustomed to, she'd almost stopped noticing it—had vanished after her chat with Marigold, and she had no desire to face the sweaty, confused wedding guests, who'd surely demand updates. Nor did she relish the thought of rejoining the other bridesmaids, who were either relishing the drama (Liesl and Bri) or sending a flurry of answered texts to Marigold (Hannah and Richie.)

Marigold had gone off to find Jonathan so they could break the news to everyone. But until then, Natalie felt it was prudent to stay out of sight. There was a tiny coffee shop attached to the yacht club, whose infrequent, inconsistent operating hours had become a long-standing joke. It was only open from May to September, staffed by members' young adult children, who would often disappear on rainy days because business was slow, and on sunny days, when they decided they'd rather go sailing with their friends.

Craving caffeine and solitude above all else at the moment, Natalie made her way toward the coffee shop, where, while she couldn't count on the former, the always-empty annex would certainly provide the latter.

To her surprise, the tiny café was open, despite the fact that there were no other patrons in sight. Someone had probably volunteered for a shift in order to be around for the wedding festivities. "Hello," Natalie said as she approached the counter, where a girl of about eighteen or nineteen was staring at a phone.

The girl jumped, startled by the novelty of a customer. "Hi."

Natalie waited a polite moment, then said, "Can I order something?"

The girl stared at her as if still uncomprehending. "Sure," she said finally.

"Um . . . okay." Natalie scanned the coffee-making apparatus behind the counter, trying to gauge what kind of order would have the best chance at success. The filter coffeepot seemed to be empty, and the shiny espresso machine looked so new and unused, it could easily be for show. "Can I have a cappuccino, please?"

Yes, I'm ordering a cappuccino in the afternoon, deal with it, she thought, imagining Bill's look of horror.

"A cappuccino?"

"Or regular coffee. Or iced coffee. Whatever you have is fine."

"I can do a cappuccino," the girl said nervously. It sounded like she was speaking more to herself than to Natalie, like a kid psyching themselves up to jump off the diving board for the first time. She turned to face the machine, then paused.

"Seriously, anything is fine," Natalie said.

"Okay . . . how about an iced tea?" the girl asked hopefully.

"Sounds great."

After a long moment, the girl bent down to examine the contents of a small fridge below the counter, then stood up again. "I don't think we have any iced tea."

"Soda? Juice? I really don't care,"

"Is it true that Richie Rhodes is a bridesmaid?"

Natalie hesitated, torn between lying and prompting a slew of teen wedding crashers. "I'm not sure. Maybe? You know, I'll just take a bottle of water."

The girl nodded, grabbed a bottle out of the cooler, and handed it to Natalie. "That'll be twelve dollars."

"*What?* Are you sure?"

"I'll get it." Jonathan appeared at her side and waved his phone over the Apple Pay scanner. He took the water and handed it to Natalie with a smile.

"Thanks. I'll pay you back. Probably in installments. Do you charge interest?" She took the water from him, then paused. "What are you doing here? Shouldn't you be dealing with . . ." She gestured toward the front lawn. "All that?"

"I needed to talk to you first."

Natalie felt her stomach sink. Had he tracked her down to confront her? To blame her for ruining things with Marigold? What if she'd just *imagined* that he'd initiated the kiss? Perhaps she'd actually, like, lunged at him or something. "How'd you know I was here?"

"It's five fifteen. You always need caffeine at five fifteen."

"How do you know that?"

"See, this is why I could never read you. Why I convinced myself that . . ." Jonathan glanced over at the counter; the girl had already disappeared, most likely to go look for Richie. After confirming they were alone, he continued. "Was Marigold telling the truth? When she told me that you have feelings for me?"

Muscle memory compelled her heart to curl in on itself like a baby hedgehog, guided by instinct and experience to protect itself by any means necessary. If she told him the truth—if she forced her heart to unfurl—what would stop him from crushing it? He was probably just preparing to let her down gently, to explain that the timing wasn't right. Or worse, that he cared for her deeply . . . as a friend.

"Natalie?" Jonathan said. "Did you hear me?"

She lifted her chin to meet his eyes. "I don't just have feelings for you. I've been in love with you since college."

Jonathan turned away and ran his fingers through his hair, as if struggling to process what she'd just said. "Wow . . ." he muttered, beginning to pace. "I can't believe . . . I didn't . . . I'd totally given up on you because I assumed you only wanted to be friends."

"Sorry," Natalie said quickly. "I know my timing isn't ideal, seeing as you broke off your engagement less than an hour ago."

"Yeah, kind of . . . I mean, no. I asked you directly. Marigold wanted me to know. I just can't believe . . ." He paused and looked up. "That thing you said in your toast, about how falling in love is like finding someone tuned to your exact frequency. Marigold wrote that in a card to me once, and I thought it was so beautiful."

So that's why he'd given her such a funny look after her

speech. "Yeah, um, I might've helped Marigold with that from time to time."

"I know. She just told me. And you know what I thought when I read that line all those years ago? I thought: *That's how I feel around Natalie.*"

Natalie began to tremble, her body ill-equipped to handle so many strong emotions all at once. Elation and terror, joy and shame. "I really screwed things up, didn't I?"

"We both did. We *all* did."

"So . . ." Natalie took a deep breath and forced herself to voice the scariest question of all. "Do you think it's too late?"

After what felt like an excruciatingly long moment, he turned to her, face softening. "No, I don't think so."

Something rigid inside Natalie snapped, and she almost keeled over with relief.

He stepped forward just in time, and Natalie sank against him, still trembling. "I'm going to need some time to process everything," Jonathan said. "I woke up today truly believing I was going to marry Marigold, and even though I know we made the right decision, it's still a lot to wrap my head around."

"I know, I get it."

"But then, once this is really all over, I think you and I should spend some time together. Figure things out."

Natalie leaned against him, feeling the strength of his body bolster her, soothing her frayed nerves. The shaking stopped. "Yeah, that sounds good."

"What I mean is . . . will you give me the chance for a do-over?"

Natalie tilted her head to see him smiling down at her, flooding her chest with warmth. "I'd like that."

CHAPTER THIRTY-SIX

Marigold

"What's going on?" Carol asked as Marigold and Jonathan ushered their families and the bridal party out of the yacht club and onto the front lawn. "Marigold, where's your dress?"

"We're going to make an announcement," Jonathan said. He and Marigold hung back in the doorway so they wouldn't be spotted by the guests, though if she rose onto her toes, she could just glimpse the assembled crowd. "Zack, can you let the senator know there's been a change of plans?"

Zack saluted, and Marigold instinctively glanced at Olivia, curious to see how her sister would respond to the cheesy gesture, but she didn't stop beaming as Zack headed down the lawn toward the officiant.

Carol grabbed Jonathan's arm. "*What* change of plans?"

"Just . . . everyone please take your seats," Jonathan said calmly.

When no one moved, Richie said, "All right, everyone, let's

go . . . Move it." It was the first time most of them had heard her speak in real life, and, either surprised by her outburst or cowed by her commanding tone, the others began to follow her.

Lulu smiled at Jonathan, then whispered to Marigold, "I'm so proud of you."

"I haven't done anything yet!"

"Doesn't matter. I'm always proud of you." She took Bill's waiting elbow and joined the procession.

As the wedding party headed down the lawn, Marigold saw the guests' heads begin to turn their way. Jonathan took her hand. "Ready?"

Marigold nodded, and they made their way down the grassy slope. "Want me to do the talking?" he asked quietly. "You can even wait inside, if you want."

Marigold considered the implication of this hugely generous offer—not having to see the shock on the guests' faces. Or worse, the excitement at getting front-row seats to such a juicy scandal. The faux concern from Liesl and Bri as they tried to conceal their secret glee. Hannah's last-ditch attempt to "talk sense" into her. But caring too much about what other people thought had gotten her into this mess. It's what made her leave Hugo. What kept her obsessed with proving herself to Jonathan and his family.

"Thank you. But I want everyone to see us together. We need to make it clear that this a mutual decision, one that I'm taking responsibility for."

The string quartet couldn't drown out the agitated murmurs of the crowd as Marigold and Jonathan approached, or the gasps that rose up as everyone turned toward them. Her childhood friends and all their parents. Cousins, aunts, and uncles. Family friends. College friends. People she'd met through work.

Jonathan's colleagues. Most of Sandpiper Island. Hadn't she had nightmares like this growing up? Wasn't this just as terrifying as standing up to give a book report at school only to discover that you were naked? Wasn't wearing dirty jeans next to her tuxedoed ex-fiancé, in front of two hundred people in evening wear, pretty much the same thing?

"Dearly beloved," the senator began. "Please rise." Marigold shot him a confused look and he cleared his throat. "Sorry, please remain seated. The couple would like to make an announcement." He extended his microphone toward them, unsure who to hand it to. Marigold took it. "Um, hi everyone," she said. "Sorry to keep you waiting. And thank you so much for coming this weekend. I know Sandpiper Island isn't an easy place to get to, and it's meant the world to me, Jonathan, and to our families that you're here. We feel so, so loved."

It was true, she realized. This wasn't what she'd planned, or what her family had hoped for. But none of that could change the magic of sharing her favorite place in the world with people who'd played an important role in her life. And it certainly couldn't take away from what it'd given Lulu, who was sitting in the first row, eyes shining.

"You're doing great," Jonathan whispered, squeezing her hand.

She took a deep breath. "After a lot of soul-searching, we've come to a decision—one that's going to come as a surprise to a lot of you, but one that feels right to us . . ."

Marigold stumbled up the lawn in a daze, feeling almost drunk with relief. In the aftermath of the announcement, everything seemed funny to her: the way Hannah had burst into tears; the fact that Patty had broken the stunned silence by shouting, "Holy fucking shit"; how Bri had gasped and then audibly asked Liesl, "Wait, does this mean that Jonathan's single now?"

Marigold could hear the officiant asking the crowd to remain in their seats, explaining that the ceremony would continue in a moment. She grinned, thinking about what Bill had whispered to her when she'd finished her speech. She needed to make this fast so she didn't miss anything.

She ducked around the side of the yacht club and held her phone in the air, searching for the elusive spot where she'd get full reception. She was about to make the most important phone call of her life.

She took a step forward, then froze as four bars finally appeared on her screen. Without shifting her weight an inch, she pressed "Hugo" and held her breath as it rang.

"Hey." Hugo's voice sounded slightly distant, and there was more noise in the background than Marigold had expected. "Mare? You okay?"

"I'm fine. Are . . . are you okay?"

"Yeah, I'm . . ." He trailed off, then started again. "Did you make it back in time?"

Even over the phone, a thousand miles away, Marigold could sense the enormous effort it took for Hugo to ask the question, how hard he was fighting to keep his voice steady as he waited to find out if the woman he loved was about to marry another man. Or if indeed she'd already done so.

"Yeah, I made it back, but . . ." She could almost hear him holding his breath on the other end. "We called it off. Jonathan and I aren't getting married."

There was a long silence. Marigold lowered her phone to

check if the call had been disconnected. It hadn't. "Hugo? Are you still there?"

"Yeah." His voice was shaky. "I'm here."

"I couldn't do it. I don't love him. Not in the way I love you." Her heart was beating so hard, it felt like her blood was pushing the words out of her before her brain had time to make sense of what she was saying. And yet she knew they were truer than anything she'd said before. "I was an idiot to run away that time. I felt . . . well, it was so intense, and I was so happy, I assumed it had to be all wrong. Because I'd never wanted anything good for me that badly. Which is messed up to say, I know. But I'm not going to make that mistake again, and I'm ready to give this a real shot. I mean, if you'll let me." She took a deep breath. "I love you."

She heard a muffled noise that sounded sort of like a laugh, but she wasn't sure. Then Hugo cleared his throat. "I love you, too, Mare. Yes, let's give this a go."

"Really?" Marigold spun in a circle, too full of fizzy happiness to stand still a moment longer.

"Really."

"Okay, okay. I know you have that camping trip, but maybe I can fly up when you're back? Or maybe even head up a little early and wait for you? Do you need someone to watch Humphrey? Because I could—"

He cut her off. "I'm not going on the trip."

"Oh, I didn't expect you to cancel. Have your friends already left? I mean, it's fine if—"

"Yeah, they left."

"Can't you catch up with them?"

"That'd be tough because I'm in Maine."

Marigold froze. "Maine?"

"I got on the next flight to Portland after yours. I figured . . . well, I don't really know what I figured. But I wanted to be nearby if . . ."

"If I called off the wedding?"

"Yeah, I guess. I'm sorry. It sounds really weird saying it aloud."

Marigold laughed with a combination of joy and relief. "Weird and wonderful. Where are you?"

"I just got off the Sandpiper Island ferry."

Her heart soared. "Wait for me in the harbor. I'll meet you in an hour or so."

She wasn't sure where they'd go from there, but it didn't matter. They'd figure it out. Maybe New York for a few days, where Marigold could introduce Hugo to the city properly. Or some cabin upstate where they could get their bearings without the pressure of being around family and friends.

"I'll see you soon, then." She could hear the grin in his voice.

"See you soon."

Hugo's on his way, Marigold thought gleefully. She bounced in place a few times, then began to jog back up the hill. She didn't want to miss what was coming next.

Epilogue

In the end, it didn't matter that the altar didn't perfectly frame the sunset, or that the string quartet had been playing Pachelbel's Canon for half an hour by the time the wedding party walked down the aisle. Nor did it matter that no one was in a white dress.

Clutching Olivia's and Marigold's arms, Lulu looked as radiant as any bride, her smile as wide as the ocean as she made her way down the aisle. She stopped a few times to squeeze the outstretched hands of friends and family, or to say a special hello to anyone she hadn't yet seen. A number of people wiped away tears, while a few watched bewildered, still uncomprehending. ("Does *she* get the present we bought?" one woman whispered to her husband.)

From his spot next to the altar, Bill watched his wife glide toward him, and for the first time in many months, he thought about how lucky he was. How lucky they all were.

When Olivia, Marigold, and Lulu reached the altar, Olivia stepped aside to let Bill take Lulu's arm. She then moved to take her seat, but Bill motioned for her to stay. Olivia stepped away to take her seat, but Bill motioned for her to stay. "I'm not just renewing my vow to your mother, I'm renewing it to all of you." And so, the three of them stood there, under the warm glow of the setting sun, while the officiant led Bill and Lulu through a vow renewal ceremony. He hadn't had much time to prepare, and grew flustered while trying to adapt the line "till death do you part."

A few guests exchanged horrified looks, but Lulu merely smiled and said to Bill, "I'm not letting you off that easy," and relieved laughter bubbled up from the audience.

"No," Bill said, stroking Lulu's cheek. "Nothing can part us. I'm yours in this life and the next."

Olivia, who hadn't cried in public since flubbing the third-grade spelling bee, felt tears running down her face. A moment later, someone seated in the front row reached out and tucked something soft into her hand. She looked down to see a handkerchief. "Thank you," she whispered to Zack, then dabbed her eyes.

The officiant sped up, clearly eager to finish before he made another faux pas. "By the power vested in me by the state of Maine, I now pronounce you husband and wife . . . still . . . again." Bill's wide smile almost matched Lulu's as he bent down to kiss her, and the crowd erupted into cheers. In the middle row, Jonathan and Natalie sat side by side, not touching, but each very aware of the proximity of their hands.

And from the back, a man who'd slipped into an empty seat at the last minute met Marigold's eye. He'd sneak off when the ceremony concluded. In the end, she'd decided she wanted him there for her parents' vow renewal, providing her with silent support as they watched the final chapter of an epic love story, knowing that the second chapter of theirs was just beginning.

Acknowledgments

This book represents the fulfillment of many writerly dreams, and I'm grateful to everyone who guided and encouraged me. Thank you to the brilliant people at Alloy: Les Morgenstein, Josh Bank, Romy Golan and editors extraordinaire Lanie Davis, who's been cheering me on from day one, and Joelle Hobeika, who gave me the biggest break of my life and taught me how to write a novel; and especially Viana Siniscalchi, for devoting countless hours and considerable brain power to untangling the kinks in this story.

I'm incredibly lucky to work with such a talented team at Atria, especially Emilia Rhodes, who championed *Save the Date* from the beginning, and whose legendary editorial acumen honed and elevated this book in countless ways. Thank you to Elizabeth Hitti, Jimmy Iacobelli, Elly Otharsson, Emma Navarro, Zakiya Jamal, and Megan Rudloff.

I can't properly thank my endlessly supportive friends here, but a number of them spent the past decade encouraging me to finally write the grown-up novel of my heart. You know who you are, and this book wouldn't exist without you. And special thanks to Dr. Matt Kerr, my advisor on all things Canadian.

Thank you to my family, particularly my father, Sam Henry Kass, who made me fall in love with words, and my mother, Marcia Bloom, who taught me to see the world in a way that makes it worth writing about. I miss her every day.

And finally, thank you to Ben, who embodies the most attractive qualities of all the love interests in this book, and (almost) none of the irritating ones.

About the Author

Published previously under the name Kass Morgan, Mallory Kass is *The New York Times* bestselling author of numerous young adult novels, including the series The 100, which has been translated into over twenty languages and was adapted into a critically acclaimed hit television series that ran on the CW for seven seasons and was a Global Top 10 series on Netflix. She is also coauthor of The Ravens series with *New York Times* bestselling author Danielle Paige, which has been translated into fifteen languages. An executive editor at Scholastic, she lives in Brooklyn with her husband and son.

ATRIA BOOKS, an imprint of Simon & Schuster, fosters an open environment where ideas flourish, bestselling authors soar to new heights, and tomorrow's finest voices are discovered and nurtured. Since its launch in 2002, Atria has published hundreds of bestsellers and extraordinary books, which would not have been possible without the invaluable support and expertise of its team and publishing partners. Thank you to the Atria Books colleagues who collaborated on *Save the Date*, as well as to the hundreds of professionals in the Simon & Schuster advertising, audio, communications, design, ebook, finance, human resources, legal, marketing, operations, production, sales, supply chain, subsidiary rights, and warehouse departments who help Atria bring great books to light.

Editorial
Emilia Rhodes
Elizabeth Hitti

Jacket Design
James Iacobelli
Elly Otharsson

Marketing
Aleaha Reneé
Heaven Jenkins

Managing Editorial
Paige Lytle
Shelby Pumphrey
Sofia Echeverry
Abby Borchers

Production
Vanessa Silverio
Stacey Sakal
Jill Putorti

Publicity
Megan Rudloff

Publishing Office
Dana Trocker
Suzanne Donahue
Abby Velasco

Subsidiary Rights
Nicole Bond
Sara Bowne
Rebecca Justiniano
Germanie Louis